Tangled Threads by Carol Cox
Ruth Hunnicut is excited about taking the train to Windmere Falls, Colorado, on the lookout for train robbers—until she and her crime-fighting partner become their victims. In town, Ruth sets up a dressmaker's shop as her "cover," and two of her first customers are a handsome mine owner and the telegrapher's wife. Will Ruth's drive to find the thieves cause her to hurt her new friends?

Rescuing Sydney by Lisa Harris
Heading to Colorado in pursuit of train robbers, Sydney de Clermont is robbed and falls off the train and back into the life of her brother's old friend, John Langston. Her quest for clues to the robbery leaves her holding a payroll bag and gets them both a trip to jail for questioning. Can she keep her cover and protect her heart at the same time?

Skirted Clues by DiAnn Mills
Moment Alexander is tired of doing clerical work in the Chicago office and jumps at the chance to be an agent on the train robbery case. She must conquer her fear of horses when she is assigned work that requires her to ride out and investigate a ranch—and her first suspect is feisty rancher Brady Miller. Will she lose her focus when her heart refutes the clues?

Victorious by Kathleen Y'Barbo
Lady Victoria Barrett-Ames is a transplanted Englishwoman on a mission. Despite what the other agents think, Victoria is convinced the real mastermind behind the Windmere Falls, Colorado, train heists has yet to be caught. Gus Drummond, her boss, has the means and motive—but he seems to suspect *her!* Somewhere between fact-finding and crime solving, the pair discovers the impossible—love.

TO CATCH A THIEF

*Female Pinkerton Agents
Nab Their Men in
Four Interwoven Novellas*

CAROL COX
LISA HARRIS
DIANN MILLS
KATHLEEN Y'BARBO

BARBOUR
PUBLISHING

Tangled Threads © 2003 by Carol Cox
Rescuing Sydney © 2003 by Lisa Harris
Skirted Clues © 2003 by DiAnn Mills
Victorious © 2003 by Kathleen Y'Barbo

ISBN 1-58660-972-6

Cover image © Corbis

Illustrations by Mari Goering

All Scripture quotations, unless otherwise noted, are taken from the King James Version of the Bible.

Published by Barbour Publishing, Inc., P.O. Box 719, Uhrichsville, Ohio 44683, www.barbourbooks.com

Our mission is to publish and distribute inspirational products offering exceptional value and biblical encouragement to the masses.

Member of the
Evangelical Christian
Publishers Association

Printed in the United States of America.
5 4 3 2 1

To Catch a Thief

Prologue

1890—Chicago

Moment Alexander rose from the wooden chair in such a huff that she nearly bumped over her Remington Type Writer. She hated the contraption, which remarkably resembled a sewing machine with a foot pedal and a flower design on the side. Her two-finger approach to using the machine, often referred to as the biblical method—"Seek and ye shall find"—had put her in a most disagreeable temperament.

"I'd like sugar in my coffee," Harry Fletcher said from the other room.

"I don't care if you are my boss," she mumbled. "I was not hired to wait on you and your male cohorts but to be an investigator for the Pinkerton Detective Agency."

"Hush," Victoria Barrett-Ames whispered, her British accent sounding more musical than scolding. "Or he'll have you serving him with a spoon—and the rest of us with you."

Moment narrowed her gaze. Victoria had been reared in an exclusive English home and could be quite bossy. This time

Moment could not help but voice her frustrations.

"All they do is boast about their grand cases and order us to serve them and type their illegible paperwork." Moment glanced at the other two women working behind her, Sydney de Clermont and Ruth Hunnicut. "We were hired to be detectives, ladies, and the second we forget it, we give concession to their male dominance."

"Moment," Ruth whispered, "remember, we can't join the police department, and this is our only opportunity to do investigative work. I really don't like upsetting Mr. Fletcher; sometimes he frightens me with his booming voice."

"You have no backbone, Ruth," Moment said, instantly regretting her words. "Oh, I'm sorry."

"I'll go get them their coffee." Sydney laughed. "I can have it done while the rest of you are discussing it."

"Moment!" Mr. Fletcher thundered. "That's four coffees, two black, one with cream, and mine with sugar and cream."

"He sounds dreadfully upset," Ruth said, squirming in her chair.

"All right, Mr. Fletcher, I'm coming." Moment threw an exasperated look at her friends. "One day soon I'm going to demand a case for us. We can do things and go places where men could never step. Just you wait, our intellect and gender will serve us forthrightly."

A short while later, Moment carried a small tray with the four cups of coffee into a spacious office where the detectives often met. The aroma of the coffee smelled heavenly, and she decided to pour a cup of her own the instant Mr. Fletcher dismissed her. She ignored the other three detectives with him, her fury ready to unleash on all of them.

"How are you today, Miss Alexander?" one of the men asked, puffing away on a foul-smelling cigar. "We've been discussing you, haven't we, Harry?"

Mr. Fletcher nodded and tipped back in his chair, toying with his handlebar mustache. "Indeed." He gave her a long look followed by a slow smile. "Would you like a case of your own?"

Moment felt her heart beat furiously against her chest. "I'd welcome an opportunity to use my skills," she said.

Mr. Fletcher pointed to several pieces of paper before him. "One of our detectives in Windmere Falls, Colorado, is having problems involving a series of train robberies. He's asked for backup—"

"I'd love to," she said. "How soon can I leave?"

Mr. Fletcher chuckled. "Wonderful, you accept the case?"

"Absolutely, Sir."

He leaned forward and smiled at the men seated around him. One man coughed. Another snickered. She didn't care; let them make fun of her enthusiasm. "In four days I'd like for you to leave west by rail. The agent's name out there is Gus Drummond, and he will fill you in on the train robberies."

It's as though God has heard the desires of my heart. "Thank you, Sir. I will not let you down."

"I'm sure you will be all Gus needs to solve these crimes." He nodded at her in his typical dismissal gesture. "Would you mind sending in the other women? They will also be going."

Tangled Threads

by Carol Cox

Chapter 1

The narrow passenger car swayed, and Ruth Hunnicut braced for yet another jolt. Fortifying herself with the thought that journey's end lay only a short distance ahead, she gritted her teeth and wished for the thousandth time that the owners of the Denver & Rio Grande Railroad had seen fit to spend a bit more money on thicker padding for their seat cushions. The opportunity to prove her merit as a Pinkerton operative would be worth even greater discomfort than this, but it would be nice if she arrived at her destination in one piece.

She turned her attention to the grandeur of the Colorado scenery sweeping past the window. Such towering mountains and awe-inspiring vistas didn't exist anywhere near Chicago. Nor had she ever seen vast stands of pine, spruce, and aspen like the ones that covered the slope before her.

"Ah-choo!" Sydney de Clermont dabbed at her nose with a snowy handkerchief.

"God bless you." Ruth tried to conceal her grin. Beside her sat one person who didn't share her appreciation for the stunning scenery. Poor Sydney had been sneezing ever since they entered the forested region. Despite the incessant sniffling, Ruth felt grateful they had been paired together. At least with Sydney as a partner, she wouldn't be subjected to the constant expressions of concern for her spiritual welfare, as she would have been with Victoria Barrett-Ames or Moment Alexander. She felt a rising sense of excitement and wished she could hurry the train to its destination through sheer force of will.

Instead of cooperating with her desire for haste, the train began to slow down. Ruth pressed her face against the window and peered out. Just ahead, a bridge spanned a narrow canyon.

"Don't anybody move!"

Ruth's gaze jerked back to the railcar's interior, where three men crowded through the doorway. Each wore a mask that covered the lower half of his face, and each brandished a pistol. Ruth pressed her lips together to control their trembling. *What irony! We come out to capture the robbers and wind up being their next victims.*

"Put your valuables in these bags, and be quick about it," the tallest man rasped. He focused a threatening gaze on the passengers while his companions moved along the aisle collecting watches, jewelry, and money. "And don't do anything stupid." He waved the barrel of his revolver toward a man who had half-risen from his seat. The would-be hero settled back and regarded the leader with a baleful glare.

Beside Ruth, Sydney stifled another sneeze and let out a strangled moan. Ruth risked a sideways glance and repressed a cry of her own when she saw her friend's pallor.

One of the bandits paused in the aisle next to Sydney and held out a coarse gunnysack. "Put your valuables in here, and be quick about it."

Ruth fumbled with the clasp of her mother-of-pearl brooch and dropped it in the bag.

"Anything else?"

She and Sydney shook their heads in unison, and he moved on to the seat behind them. The leader followed the other two outlaws down the aisle, walking backward so he could keep his gun leveled on the passengers in the front of the car. Ruth closed her eyes. If she believed in prayer, this would have been a good time to put it to use. Failing that, she drew in one ragged breath after another, trying to stave off the light-headed feeling that threatened to overcome her.

Beside her, Sydney stirred and rose from her seat. Ruth watched her friend make her way to the rear of the car, toward the door through which the robbers had just exited.

"Where on earth are you going?" Ruth called.

"I need to get some air." Sydney's faint reply floated back to her.

"At a time like this?" Ruth sprang to her feet and hurried after Sydney as best she could, trying to adjust her gait to the car's rocking motion. She saw Sydney open the door and step out onto the platform. At the same moment, the train gave a lurch that sent Ruth sprawling across a seat in an undignified heap.

"Can I help you, Miss?" A face sporting a gap-toothed grin appeared above the seat back.

"Thank you, but I think I can manage." Ruth scrambled

to her feet and tugged her skirt into place, furious at the thought of so many male gazes witnessing her graceless fall. "I need to get to my friend." She pushed her way past the man and then froze in place.

The rear door of the car hung wide open, but Sydney had disappeared.

"Sydney?" Ruth continued until she stood in the doorway, unwilling to believe the sight that met her eyes. *"Sydney!"*

"You'd better come back inside, Miss. We're picking up speed, and it'll be hard to keep your footing out here."

Ruth spun around and came face-to-face with the portly conductor. "You have to stop the train! My friend is gone!"

"Can't do it," he told her. "That bunch got away with more than just personal valuables; they made off with the payroll we were carrying. Our first priority is to get to Windmere Falls to report the theft." He reached out to draw her inside.

Ruth jerked her arm away. "What about your passengers? Forget about the payroll; my friend needs help."

"Don't worry. We'll notify the sheriff as soon as we reach town. He'll bring a search party out after her and have her back in no time, you'll see. Besides," he added, "the way that gentleman admirer of hers jumped off the train right after she did, I'd say your friend already has all the help she needs."

Ruth stared. "What admirer? What are you talking about?"

One corner of the conductor's mouth crooked up in a sly grin that set Ruth's teeth on edge. "Why, that big fellow who couldn't keep his eyes off her. He couldn't have been more than a second behind her." He eased Ruth back into the car and closed the door with a firm snap. "Settle down, folks, settle down. We'll have the law out after that bunch as soon as we get to town. Only a little longer now."

Ruth managed to get back to her seat before her legs gave out. What on earth should she do now? She had braced herself for many possible scenarios during this investigation, but she'd never envisioned anything like this.

Had Sydney fallen from the train or leaped off in pursuit of the fleeing robbers? Knowing the answer wouldn't bring Sydney back, but it would at least tell Ruth whether to be furious at Sydney for her foolhardiness or worried sick about her welfare. She decided to opt for being angry; worry would take too much energy right now, and she didn't have any to waste on fruitless speculation.

The thought of Sydney's so-called admirer flitted through Ruth's mind. She hadn't noticed anyone paying either of them special attention and couldn't imagine who he might have been. One of the gang, perhaps? Worry reared its head again. She almost hoped the conductor had made up the whole story.

What on earth should she do? At this juncture, she would have welcomed even Moment's or Victoria's company. The other two women, though, had left for Windmere Falls a week earlier and were presumably already established in the jobs the Denver office had arranged for them at the Windmere Falls Mercantile. She would have to find a way to alert them once she arrived.

Ruth weighed the wisdom of seeking them out immediately and enlisting their help in finding Sydney. But there could be no advantage in revealing their connection before they even started their investigation. No, she would have to keep to herself and proceed according to the plan.

She settled back in her seat and prepared to endure the train's jostling as best she could. She had only a short time to rethink her strategy. Never before had she felt so alone.

Ruth left the train as soon as the conductor had the step in place, avoiding his outstretched hand with a sniff of disdain. She gave orders for both her bags and Sydney's to be taken to the hotel and then surveyed the street before her.

She longed to confer with Moment and Victoria but didn't dare risk it. Lifting her chin, she set off along the boardwalk toward the restaurant down the block.

Ruth pulled her shawl more tightly around her shoulders and tried to ignore the shiver that ran along her arms. The calendar might indicate summer, but the Colorado mountains hadn't seen fit to acknowledge that fact. How would Sydney fare alone in the wilderness? *If she is alone.* Thoughts of the florid conductor and his taunting smile flitted across her mind. Alone or at the mercy of a complete stranger, which would be worse?

Ruth's steps slowed when she neared the restaurant. She cast a doubtful glance at the three men lounging along the boardwalk. Dressed in rough Western garb, not one of them fit her idea of a trustworthy Pinkerton agent. Still, one of them had to be Gus Drummond, the man they had been directed to contact upon their arrival. The two closest to Ruth eyed her with appreciative glances.

Harry Fletcher's instructions rang in her memory. "He said he would be waiting outside the restaurant when the train pulls in. He's a tall, broad fellow with red hair; you shouldn't have any trouble recognizing him. You'll have to find a way to engage him in conversation without arousing suspicion."

And just how did Mr. Fletcher expect her to go about that? Maybe she could pretend to ask directions. But which one should she ask? The man farthest from her removed his hat and ran his fingers through his thick russet hair. Ruth smiled and picked her way past the other two. With a surge of relief, she planted herself in front of her contact. "Mr. Drummond?"

Cool blue eyes gazed down at her from a considerable height. "Ma'am?"

"I'm Ruth Hunnicut."

Drummond stared at her with an expression of mild puzzlement. "I'm pleased to make your acquaintance. Is there something I can do for you?"

Relief turned to frustration. She appreciated the fact he didn't want to publicize their relationship, but surely he could unbend a little to make this a bit easier. "Ruth Hunnicut," she repeated. "From Chicago."

Drummond gave a polite nod and waited.

"I just arrived," Ruth added through clenched teeth. "*On the train.*" Mr. Fletcher hadn't mentioned a tendency toward simplemindedness.

Drummond clenched his hat in his fists and took a step backward. "I hope you had a pleasant trip."

Ruth reached out and seized his sleeve. "Don't you understand? Harold Fletcher sent me."

19

"Fletcher?" The beginnings of comprehension and a look of horror registered on his face.

Ruth tightened her hold on his sleeve. "Do you need to sit down, Mr. Drummond? You look like you're about to topple over."

The tall man snatched his arm from her grasp and squared his shoulders. He directed a malevolent glare at her, then cast a glance at a group of patrons emerging from the restaurant. "That's right, Ma'am," he said in a loud voice. "The hotel is just down the street." He took her elbow in a grip that made her wince. "Allow me to escort you."

Ruth had no choice but to try to keep up with his long-legged stride unless she wanted her arm wrenched from its socket.

Drummond stopped in a shadowed area between two buildings. His bulk loomed over her. "Do you mean—" he began. "Do you mean to tell me *you're* my contact?"

Ruth drew herself up to her full five-foot-three-inch height. "It's about time you understood. That's exactly what I've been trying to tell you for the past five minutes."

"I asked for competent help, and they sent me a woman?"

"Would you kindly refrain from bellowing and let me explain? I did not come out alone. My partner, Sydney, went out to our car's platform just after the robbers—"

"Robbers? They've hit the train again?"

"Listen, won't you? Sydney went out after them and either fell off or jumped, I'm not sure which. That fool of a conductor refused to stop the train to find out."

"You mean Sydney is still out there?"

"That's right. The railroad is probably notifying the sheriff about the robbery this very minute, but if the conductor's attitude is any indication, they'll be more interested in seeing the thieves apprehended than in Sydney's welfare. That's why I came directly to you. We need to plan our course of action."

She waited while Drummond stared into the distance. "I understand your concern for your partner," he said at last. "But I don't see any cause to be overly upset."

Ruth blinked. "And what exactly do you mean by 'overly upset'?"

Drummond favored her with a patronizing smile. "I'll grant you this is unfamiliar territory for you both, but the agency must have confidence in Sydney's abilities, and so should you. I'm sure he'll be able to take care of himself."

"He? He?" Ruth grabbed his jacket lapels and jerked his face down to her level. "*Listen to me*: Sydney is a woman!"

Drummond's eyes bulged, and his jaw sagged. "A woman?" At Ruth's nod, he spread his arms wide as if appealing to the heavens. "What was that idiot thinking of? He sent me two women?"

"Actually, there are four of us."

Chapter 2

Ruth descended the stairs to the hotel lobby.

"Room all right, Miss?" The string-bean clerk kept his eyes focused on the newspaper on the counter.

"It will do for now." It would have to. Back in Chicago, the thin, sagging mattress and spare furnishings wouldn't be deemed fit for the meanest of lodgings. At the moment, though, she had more important things on her mind.

She stepped outside and cast a worried glance at the massive peaks surrounding Windmere Falls like vigilant sentinels. *Sydney, where are you?* What dangers lurked in the shadow of those craggy slopes? Her stomach knotted at the thought.

Her footsteps echoed along the boardwalk. Locating the building the Denver office had rented in their names was the first item on the agenda she and Sydney had agreed on. A seamstress shop made an ideal cover for their move to Windmere Falls. Only now did Ruth realize how much she'd relied on Sydney's support in accomplishing these initial tasks.

She had neither Sydney nor her support; she did have a

job to do. Shoving her worries about her missing partner to the back of her mind, Ruth gathered her flagging spirits and set off along the main street.

She walked past the weathered storefronts, noting the barbershop, mercantile, and telegraph office. She passed the gunsmith's shop and the doctor's office, then crossed to the other side of the street. Up ahead, she spotted a window that bore no business name. No sign hung above the boardwalk. Ruth caught her breath and quickened her steps.

She peered through the dusty glass into a dim interior. Pulling her handkerchief from her sleeve, she used it to clean a spot wide enough to look through. A small pile of debris lay in the middle of the floor. Otherwise, the place was empty.

"Ain't nobody there."

Ruth whirled at the sound of the voice behind her. A gnomelike man no taller than she stared at her with benevolent interest.

"I beg your pardon?"

"I said there's nobody t' home there. Hasn't been for nigh on two months now. If you're lookin' for a shylock, Missy, you're plumb out of luck."

A broad smile stretched across Ruth's face. "You're saying that this establishment used to be an attorney's office?"

"Mm-hm. Up until he won a big pot playing poker. Pulled down his shingle and lit out that same night."

Ruth felt a tingle of excitement run up her arms. "Could you direct me to the bank, please?"

"Straight ahead, two doors down." The gnome nodded his head toward the east. "What do you mean to do?"

Ruth adjusted her straw boater and folded her handkerchief into her reticule. "I mean to take care of some paperwork and get a business started."

Half an hour later, she ended a most satisfactory interview with banker Will Bowen and set her steps toward the Windmere Falls Mercantile. A signed lease and the key to her new shop lay tucked safely inside her reticule.

Inside the mercantile, the mingled scent of pickles and horehound assailed her nostrils. A small knot of older men spun tales of long ago near the cracker barrel. A flash of motion on her right caught her attention.

Victoria Barrett-Ames reached up to put a tin of Royal baking powder on a shelf. When Ruth's gaze met hers, Victoria inclined her head. "Good afternoon." Her clipped British tone carried across the width of the store.

Relief flooded Ruth. She no longer had to carry the burden of Sydney's disappearance alone. With quick steps, she started toward the counter.

A slight jerk of Victoria's head brought Ruth to a halt. She stared at her fellow operative, mortified at how close she had come to forgetting their need for secrecy.

She cleared her throat. "Good afternoon. I'd like to look at your fabric and notions."

Victoria's face showed no sign of recognition. "We have a very nice selection. They're over in the far corner." She pointed with a graceful hand, the helpful store clerk to a T.

Ruth nodded and turned toward the back of the store. She caught a brief glimpse of a broad white shirt front in time to bring her hands up to cushion the collision.

"I'm terribly sorry!" She tipped her head back to make eye contact with the dark-haired man she had just rammed into.

Eyes the color of maple syrup gazed back at her. "No harm done."

Ruth realized her hands still pressed against the man's chest. She snatched them away and gripped them together in front of her. The stranger's eyes glinted with amusement. When he smiled, a deep crease formed in his left cheek, and his dark eyebrows tilted upward.

"I don't remember seeing you around town before," he said. "I'm Mark Chandler, owner of the Redemption Mine."

"I'm Ruth Hunnicut, newly arrived from Chicago." She extended her hand and looked down to see it dwarfed in Mark Chandler's rugged grip. The approval in his eyes warmed her from head to toe. Turning on her brightest smile, Ruth beamed up at him. "I do apologize for my clumsiness, Mr. Chandler, but I'm happy to make your acquaintance."

"Call me Mark. Things aren't nearly as formal out here." He settled back on his heels and regarded her thoughtfully. "This is quite a red-letter week for Windmere Falls, having a bevy of lovely ladies arriving all at once."

Ruth felt her cheeks flame and hoped he would continue to chalk their arrivals up to coincidence.

"The young lady over there behind the counter came to town with a friend only a few days ago." He nodded toward Victoria, who responded with a gracious smile. "The three of you will brighten our beautiful scenery even more."

Ruth bit her tongue to keep from correcting him. Without knowing how long it might take for Sydney to catch up to her, she saw no need to complicate the situation further. She caught Victoria's flicker of surprise when she said nothing but held her tongue. Explanations would have to wait.

"What brings you to Windmere Falls?"

"I've read so much about the West in the Chicago papers." She recited the story she and Sydney had worked out. "I could scarcely believe such thrilling stories could be true. I just had to come out to see for myself."

Even as she spoke, her mind whirled. How should she deal with Sydney's absence? If she said her friend had disappeared en route, he would certainly wonder why she wasn't camped out down at the sheriff's office demanding her recovery. But if she neglected to mention her business partner, how would she explain Sydney's arrival when she was found?

"A friend may be joining me soon," she improvised. "We'd planned to come out together, but her travel arrangements changed at the last minute."

"And where do you plan to go once she catches up with you?"

Ruth smiled. "We're going to open a seamstress shop right here in Windmere Falls. We have a wonderful location on Main Street. I've just been to see Mr. Bowen at the bank to sign the papers."

"Carl Thompson's old law office?" Mark broke into a broad smile. "That should work out well, and I'll know where to find you—if I need any sewing done, that is." He nodded to her, then to Victoria, and left.

Ruth busied herself inspecting notions and bolts of fabric. When the last of the cracker barrel contingent left, she carried a reel of ribbon to the front of the store and set it on the counter.

Victoria leaned across and grasped Ruth's forearm. "What's all this about your friend's change in travel plans? Where is Sydney?"

"I don't know." Emotion threatened to choke her, but she cleared her throat and went on to explain the details of Sydney's disappearance.

Victoria's expression mirrored her own anxiety. "Whatever shall we do?"

"I've already let Mr. Drummond know, and after I left him, I made sure the sheriff had been notified. Beyond that, I don't know what else we can do."

"Mr. Drummond has been here long enough to know the lay of the land. Surely he will make inquiries on his own."

"I hope so." Ruth heard the doubt in her voice and tried to project a more confident mien for Victoria's sake. "I'm sure he has it well in hand. Although I must say that initially he seemed far more concerned about being 'saddled with four females,' as he put it, than with Sydney's well-being." She felt immense gratification at Victoria's indignant sniff.

"In the meantime," she went on, "I can't see anything to do but carry on as we planned, unless we confess our roles as detectives right away and try to save Sydney."

Victoria pondered a moment, then shook her head. "Sydney wanted this chance as badly as we did. What if we revealed our mission now, only to have her turn up right away? She'd never forgive us."

"Then I'll keep after Mr. Drummond and the sheriff

for news, and we'll just hope for the best."

"As soon as I see Moment, I'll let her know we need to pray."

"That's a nice idea." Ruth steered the conversation to a more palatable topic. "What did you think of Mark Chandler?"

"Don't you mean, what did he think of you?" Mischief sparkled in Victoria's blue eyes.

Once again, Ruth felt blood rush to her cheeks. "A mine owner might be able to provide us with a lot of information about payrolls and shipments."

Victoria nodded and covered Ruth's hand with her own. "All joking aside, I do believe we should cultivate his acquaintance. And since he seems to have been quite bowled over by you, you're the obvious choice to pursue that particular lead." One corner of her mouth quirked upward.

A stream of customers entered, and Victoria stepped into the storeroom to call Moment to the front to help. Ruth moved back and waited until Moment got an opportunity to approach her without arousing suspicion.

"I understand you're interested in this ribbon?" Moment held up the reel of ribbon and joined Ruth. Leaning close, she whispered, "Victoria told me everything. How dreadful for Sydney!"

Ruth kept her voice at a normal volume. "That's right. I'm opening a dress shop, and I need to place a fairly sizeable order. Could you assist me?"

Moment picked up a pad of paper and a pencil and followed Ruth to the far corner of the store, safe from the ears of the two matrons who had engaged Victoria in a discussion about the merits of Lydia Pinkham's Vegetable Compound.

"I truly do need these things," Ruth said, handing Moment her list.

Moment gave the paper a cursory glance and tucked it in her apron pocket. "We have all these items. I'll send them over later today." Lowering her voice, she said, "What impression did you form of Mr. Drummond?"

Arrogant, biased, and insufferable. "Call it woman's intuition, but he struck me as being less concerned about Sydney than the fact that he's had four women foisted upon him." She suppressed a smile at Moment's look of outrage. "My feelings exactly. I am determined to show him his preconceived notions about women and their abilities are totally, incontrovertibly wrong."

Chapter 3

Ruth dropped her scrub brush into the nearby pail and rose to her feet, uttering a low groan when the muscles in her back protested. Soap, water, and plenty of elbow grease had removed the layers of dirt and cobwebs and transformed the formerly dingy shop. Sunlight streamed in through the now-glistening front window, illuminating every corner of her new domain.

Her new, empty domain. Somehow when she and Sydney made their plans, the thought of having to furnish a storefront in addition to stocking it hadn't occurred to either of them. How on earth did she expect to open a legitimate-looking business if she didn't even have a chair to sit on?

The door swung open behind her, and she turned to see a skinny youth, his arms piled high with bolts of cloth.

"Here's the goods you ordered from the mercantile, Miss. Where shall I put 'em?" His incredulous gaze swept the room and returned to meet Ruth's.

"Oh, dear. I was just wondering that myself."

He nodded toward a door in the rear wall. "Mr. Thompson

left in a hurry. I bet some of his things are still back there."

In her exhausted state, Ruth had noticed the door but hadn't thought about what might lie behind it. She hurried to pull it open and crowed with delight when she discovered a room containing a jumble of shelves and tables. "Wait a moment while I scrub one of these," she said.

The youth shifted from one foot to the other while she cleaned two months' worth of grime from the table and tugged it into the outer room.

"Just stack it all on there," she told him. "I'll sort through it once I have everything else in place."

He unloaded his burden with a sigh of relief and hurried out. Ruth set about dragging the rest of the furniture to the front of the shop. To her delight, the treasure trove yielded two chairs. She and Sydney would at least have someplace to sit while they waited for business. Behind a set of shelves and yet another layer of dust, she discovered a second door. This one opened onto a narrow staircase that led to a room upstairs. Ruth sighed and sagged against the doorframe. That solved the problem of finding living quarters. She would retrieve their things from the hotel as soon as she finished cleaning.

While she scrubbed, she went over the scene on the train again. Try as she might, she couldn't remember anything that could have caused Sydney to leap off like that. She pushed damp strands of hair off her cheek with her forearm and glanced out the window, noting the sun's low position with alarm. The thought of Sydney spending the night in those cold mountains was too dreadful to be borne.

By the time Ruth had found a lamp to light the shop, fetched a clean bucket of water, and used it to sluice the dirt from her face and arms, the sun had set. Pools of light spilled from the buildings lining the boardwalk and splashed into the dusty street beyond. Windmere Falls appeared safe enough, even after dark. She removed her filthy apron and pinned her hair firmly in place. Like it or not, Gus Drummond was about to receive another visit.

To her surprise, she found her quarry lounging in a dimly lit spot between the bank and the newspaper office. He glanced up when she approached, then looked past her, giving no sign of recognition until Ruth came to a stop directly in front of him. He took a step backward, two deep lines appearing between his eyebrows.

"What do you think you're doing?"

"I might ask you the same thing. Why are you loitering here instead of looking for Sydney?"

"Didn't have to." Drummond rolled a toothpick from one corner of his mouth to the other. "The sheriff and his men set out looking for the payroll *and* your friend hours ago. Everything's under control."

"That's all you've done? Mr. Drummond, it seems to me you're taking entirely too cavalier an attitude to all this."

Drummond clamped his teeth together, severing the toothpick. He spat out the remains and looked at Ruth with distaste. "The whole point of getting new faces out here was so you wouldn't be recognized as Pinkerton men. . .women. You've already been seen talking to me once today. If you keep this up, it might lead to exactly the kind of suspicion I wanted to avoid. From here on out, keep your distance unless we have a legitimate reason to converse. Good evening, Miss Hunnicut."

Ruth watched him saunter off. So this was the way Pinkerton men behaved. The one person she should have been able to count on had proven undependable. She set off in the direction of the sheriff's office. If she had to take matters into her own hands, so be it.

A couple emerged from the building ahead and angled toward the hotel across the street. In the gloom, Ruth couldn't make out details of their appearance, but she noted the way the man bent solicitously over his companion. Ruth started to walk past, focused on outlining her demands for the sheriff to step up his efforts.

"Ah-choo!"

Ruth shot a startled look in the couple's direction. "Sydney?" They disappeared into the hotel. Ruth hurried across the street and followed them into the lobby.

"Sydney, it *is* you!" She crossed the distance between them with quick steps and wrapped her friend in a tight embrace. "I'm so relieved. I was just on my way to see the sheriff and ask him whether I needed to organize a search myself."

Sydney cleared her throat and glanced at the man beside her, his dapper bearing a stark contrast to her own bedraggled appearance. "May I present Deputy Charles Bennett? He kindly offered to escort me to the hotel. Deputy Bennett, this is my friend, Ruth Hunnicut."

Sydney's companion swept his hat off and bowed. "I'm

pleased to meet you, Miss Hunnicut. I know this must have been a trying time for you."

"More than you can imagine." Relief swept over Ruth. "Sydney, I've been worried sick. What on earth happened to you?"

Sydney wrapped her arms around herself and lowered her gaze to a point near Ruth's feet. "I don't want to talk about it," she whispered.

Tentacles of dread twined through Ruth. "The conductor said someone jumped off after you. Did he follow you? Hurt you in any way?"

"Don't ask me about it, Ruth. Please."

"And she still won't say a word about it?" Moment stared at Ruth, her eyes wide pools of concern.

Ruth shook her head and gripped the edge of the mercantile counter. "I feared the worst at first, then assumed she felt reluctant to speak in front of the deputy. Once we reached our hotel room, I expected she would open up, but she simply will not discuss it. I'd intended to move our things over to the shop, but she fell asleep the moment she lay down on the bed, and she hasn't woken yet. I haven't had the heart to disturb her."

Two women entered, walked over to the counter, and looked at Moment expectantly. Ruth forced herself back into her assumed role. "Yes, I need some black paint," she said. "And a paintbrush and some pasteboard, if you have it. I'm going to try my hand at sign painting."

"Right away." Moment rummaged on the shelf behind

her, then deposited a brush and a small can of paint on the counter. She disappeared into the back room and emerged holding a piece of pasteboard. "Will this do?"

"Thank you. That will do nicely." Ruth paid for her purchases and left.

Back outside, she stood ready to step off the boardwalk and cross the dusty street when the sign for the telegraph office next door caught her attention. She hefted her parcel higher in her arms and went inside.

The hollow-cheeked man behind the counter looked up when she came through the door. With a smile of welcome, he shoved back his chair and got to his feet. "Welcome to Windmere Falls. Emmett Duncan at your service. How can I help you?"

Ruth blinked at the effusive welcome, then allowed herself to bask in the man's open admiration. Gus Drummond could take lessons in deportment from Mr. Duncan, even if the man's skinny face and sharp nose reminded her of the turkeys her uncle raised.

The telegrapher swiped his hand across his balding pate and swallowed. His bobbing Adam's apple made his resemblance to a turkey even more pronounced.

Ruth shifted her load to one arm and dabbed at her mouth with her free hand to hide her smile. Recovering, she introduced herself. "I'd like to send a telegram."

"Certainly, certainly." Mr. Duncan picked up a form and held his pen at the ready.

Ruth thought for a moment. "I need to let my uncle know I've arrived safely—and ask about my aunt," she improvised. "She's been in poor health for some time now." If their investigation necessitated a number of telegrams to and from the home office, it would be well to establish a reason for the flurry of communication from the outset.

"That's too bad," Mr. Duncan said. Then he brightened. "I suppose that means you'll need to check on her frequently. It'll be nice to see a pretty face around here."

From the light of anticipation that sparked in his eyes, Ruth felt sure her visits would be accepted without question. Using the code she'd worked out with Mr. Fletcher before leaving Chicago, she dictated a brief message.

With that accomplished, Ruth returned to the shop. She wondered briefly whether she should have mentioned Sydney's disappearance but shrugged the thought away. Sydney could fill Mr. Fletcher in herself, assuming she ever decided to discuss the matter with anyone. Once again, irritation with Sydney's strange reticence flooded her. Ruth pushed her annoyance aside. The task ahead would require all her energy.

Back inside the shop, she set the pasteboard on one of the tables and began penciling in the letters with care. If they wanted their shop to be accepted as a legitimate business venture, it had to look like one. Her brow furrowed, partly in concentration over her task, partly due to her confusion over Sydney.

How could she depart in such a dramatic manner and expect to keep the particulars to herself? In her need to share the news with Moment as quickly as possible, Ruth had left out the details of her attempt to extract the facts from Sydney.

Concern turned to fear, then irritation, as Sydney steadfastly refused to impart even the smallest crumb of information about her disappearance.

"I'm not asking out of idle curiosity." She'd lost count of how many times she had repeated the phrase. "You must realize how desperately worried I've been. All of us have. If you've been harmed in any way. . ."

Sydney's response never altered: "I told you, I don't want to talk about it."

Ruth dipped her brush in the black paint and wiped the excess off on the side of the can. She focused on making her strokes even, controlling the movements of her hands while her thoughts ran unchecked. What could have caused Sydney to behave in such a way? No amount of cajoling, pleading, or outright demands for a full account had swayed her in the least.

You have a job to do. She would keep that thought uppermost. Sydney was a grown woman with a mind of her own. Ruth would have to accept her desire for privacy, stop worrying over something she could do nothing about, and focus on the task that brought them all to Windmere Falls in the first place.

She brushed on the final stroke and stepped back to admire her handiwork. *R & S Fashions.* The words marched across the pasteboard in bold block letters. Underneath, in finer script, she had painted: *For ladies and gentlemen of discriminating taste.* Not a fancy bit of work, but good enough to serve its purpose. She replaced the lid on the can. Once the paint dried, she would set the sign in place in the front window. At least it would look like they were serious about making a go of things.

"Good morning. Are you open for business yet?"

The deep voice startled Ruth from her thoughts. She turned to see Mark Chandler framed in the doorway.

Chapter 4

"I didn't mean to frighten you." Mark sauntered toward her, a crooked grin pulling at the corners of his mouth. "Would you like me to come back another time?"

"Not at all." Remembering Moment and Victoria's admonition to extract all the information she could, she favored him with her brightest smile. "As a matter of fact, you're our first customer."

"Our?"

"The traveling companion I mentioned yesterday. She managed to get here after all. We'll be running the shop together. Now what can I do for you?" she asked, hoping to stave off further questions.

Mark held up a tattered scrap of fabric. "I'd like a new shirt to replace this one. It's never been the same since that black bear tried to eat my laundry."

"I see." Ruth smoothed the frayed strips of fabric out on her worktable and shook her head. "There's barely enough left to give me an idea of the size, let alone tell what the original looked like."

"It wasn't all that different from the one I'm wearing. Maybe you could get some idea from it."

"Of course." Ruth picked up a measuring tape and a pad of paper and stood before him, realizing she had just encountered a problem they hadn't foreseen. When she and Sydney discussed the shop, she'd always pictured herself measuring other women. Not men. And certainly not a man as attractive as this one. She held the tape six inches in front of one of his shoulders and stretched it toward the other. No, that wouldn't do. She peered up at the numbers and caught sight of those maple syrup eyes instead.

She cleared her throat and moved around behind him. That was better. Now she could actually touch his shoulder with the tapeline and stretch it across his back without being distracted by his smile. She jotted the numbers down on her pad, then had him hold his arms out and checked the length of his sleeves.

Now for the back length. She positioned the end of the tape at the nape of his neck, let the free end fall toward his tapered waist, and then noted the measurement.

And now his waist. How was she going to accomplish that? When sewing for her mother or sisters or friends back home, Ruth would have stretched the tape around them without a moment's thought. Just the idea of wrapping her arms around Mark Chandler made her weak in the knees. The tape dangled from her hand while she gnawed her lower lip.

"Everything all right?" A trace of amusement laced his voice.

Ruth bristled. She was a professional seamstress, at least

in theory. Moreover, she was a duly appointed Pinkerton agent. Time to get over her squeamishness and attend to the business at hand. Drawing a deep breath, she stretched her arms around his waist and tried to pass the measuring tape from one hand to the other.

"Need any help?"

With her ear pressed against his back, Ruth couldn't miss the laughter rumbling in his chest. She bit back her irritation and tried to inject a cool tone of competence into her voice. "No, thank you. I'm almost—"

The bell over the front door jingled.

"Ruth! What on earth?"

Ruth jerked upright. The measuring tape fluttered to the floor. She turned to find Sydney standing in the doorway with one hand pressed against her lips.

With her dignity in as many shreds as Mark's ruined shirt, Ruth tried for a diversion. "Good morning, Sleepyhead. I wondered if you were planning to wake up anytime soon."

Sydney blinked and fixed Ruth with an accusing gaze. "You were just—"

"Taking the measurements of our first customer." Ruth emphasized the last word, then turned to Mark with a bright smile. "This is Sydney de Clermont, the other half of R & S Fashions."

"I'm pleased to meet you."

"And this is Mark Chandler," Ruth continued. "The owner of the Redemption Mine. He needs a new shirt and was kind enough to bring his business to us."

Sydney brightened and looked at him with interest. A good night's sleep had brought the color back to her cheeks. Dressed in a crisp white blouse and green skirt, with her red curls neatly combed, she looked like her old, charming self. "You own a mine?"

Ruth felt a tug of resentment. She had cultivated Mark Chandler's acquaintance. He wouldn't have come to the shop this morning if not for their meeting at the mercantile. That made him her lead, not Sydney's. If Miss de Clermont chose to vanish and leave the work of setting up the shop to Ruth and then reappear without so much as a word of explanation, she could find her own clues.

"Why don't you see if you think we'll need anything more for our living quarters?" Ruth suggested. "Upstairs," she added, when Sydney showed no sign of moving along. Sydney finally took the hint and exited through the rear door after another long glance at Mark.

"Did you get all the measurements you needed?"

"What? Oh, yes." Ruth jerked back around at the sound of his voice. "Yes, indeed. I'm sure I have enough." She knew exactly how far her arms had to stretch to reach around him. Surely she could make an accurate enough estimate from that. It would have to do, in any case. She had no intention of putting herself in that vulnerable position again.

Mark seemed to understand their session was over. He shifted his weight and glanced at the door. If she didn't get her wits together and ask him some questions before he left, she would miss a golden opportunity.

Unable to meet the amusement in his eyes, she forced a

smile and focused her gaze on the cleft in his chin. "How long have you lived in Windmere Falls?"

"Three years." Now that she had opened up a line of conversation, the man seemed in no hurry to take his leave. He rested one arm on the worktable and leaned toward her. "It had the likeliest prospects of any place I'd seen, so I decided to stay."

"And you enjoy the work involved in a mining operation?" What a stupid question. But what on earth should she ask? What query would elicit the information she needed to help ferret out the robbers? Interrogation proved much harder during an actual investigation than it seemed back home under Mr. Fletcher's tutelage.

Mark didn't seem put off by her query. "I do, for the most part. A lot of it is just plain hard work, but I've always enjoyed physical labor. Now that I have a full crew to help, it's taken a lot of the load off me. As long as I'm able to meet the payroll and keep them on," he added bleakly.

"Is it difficult to meet the payroll?" He couldn't have given her a better opening. Perhaps interrogation wasn't so difficult after all.

The light in his eyes dimmed. "It can be. You met one of the reasons on your trip here."

"The robbers?" Ruth felt proud of her artless tone and hoped the face she showed him appeared equally innocent.

He nodded, his face twisting into a glower at odds with his customary cheerful expression. "Part of the money they stole was supposed to pay my crew. That's the second time it's happened to me, and there have been other robberies, besides. I talked to my men yesterday evening. They've agreed to stick it out until I can scrape another payroll together. But some of them have families to feed. They can't keep doing this indefinitely, and I can't keep asking them to. The first robbery was bad enough. This one really set me back. If they hit the train again when it's carrying my payroll. . .well, I won't be in the mining business much longer if that happens."

The resignation in his tone tore at Ruth's heart. Up to this moment, solving the robberies had been an exciting battle of wits. Even after encountering the outlaws herself, she still thought of the stolen goods as "the loot," something separated from the lives of those around her. Mark Chandler's plight brought home the sharp awareness that money wasn't the only issue. Its loss affected people like the ever-widening ripples in a pool. First him, then his miners, then their families—how many others after that? And Mark hadn't been the only victim.

"That's terrible. And you say other mines have lost money, as well?"

"The Tough Nut, the Glory Hole, the Mary Ann. They've all taken losses."

Ruth kept her gaze on him while making mental notes of these additional leads. "How do you think the robbers know when to strike?"

"That's a good question." His face darkened, and he spoke with a vehemence that startled her. "They have to be getting inside information, but from whom? And if it's from someone local, that means it's someone I know and probably trust."

"Maybe I could help you find out who's responsible."

The words tumbled out before she thought. But on further reflection, why not? What better way to delve into the case than to act as an innocent bystander fascinated by this bit of local crime?

Mark's grin returned. "I'm sure I'd find your views on the matter fascinating." Their gazes locked, and his smile faded. Ruth found it difficult to breathe.

Drawing in a gulp of air, she smoothed her moist palms against her blue merino skirt. "Do you know what fabric you'd like the shirt made from? Let me show you what we have in stock." She led him to the display table and indicated the bolts of cloth with a sweep of her arm. She hoped he would take his time perusing the offerings. It would give her a moment to catch her breath. Someone back home had told her the air in Windmere Falls would be thinner because of Colorado's higher altitude. That must be the reason she found breathing so difficult now.

Chapter 5

R uth gave the broom a final push and watched the dust billow off into the street. Trying to keep their section of the boardwalk clean had turned into a never-ending struggle, but the time spent sweeping meant time outdoors where she could unobtrusively observe the comings and goings around town.

Not that it had done her any good so far. She set the broom down with a thump and leaned against a lamppost with her arms crossed, unmoved by the glorious Colorado sunrise. For all the progress the fearless female Pinkertons had made to date, they might as well have stayed in Chicago.

The door of the mercantile swung open, and Victoria appeared. She smiled and waved when she caught sight of Ruth. "Do you have a moment before you open your shop?" she called. "I need to speak to you about that order of ribbon." She made her way across the street. Pulling a pad of paper from her pocket, she flipped through the pages as though searching for information.

Ruth had to smile at her friend's subterfuge. Victoria

performed her role to perfection. And business at the mercantile seemed to be booming, judging by the steady stream of customers she watched go in and out during the course of a day. R & S Fashions had garnered its share of patrons, as well. If only their detective work could thrive like this!

"Are you as frustrated as I am?" Ruth asked, bending her head to look over the sheet of paper Victoria held out to her. "We don't seem to be making any progress at all. If we hadn't seen the robbers with our own eyes, I'd wonder if they even existed."

"I heartily agree. Judging from what we have seen so far, Windmere Falls hardly seems to be the hotbed of crime we were led to believe." The crisp morning air brought a touch of color to Victoria's fair complexion. Even this early in the day, she looked like a fashion plate in her pale lavender dress and hat with its jaunty feather swaying in the breeze.

"Do you have any idea what we should do next? Between being confounded by the robberies and worried about Sydney, I'm at my wits' end. It almost seems wrong to draw payment for our detective work if we can't do better than this."

"Take heart, Ruth. We know we are on the side of right, and we have a secret weapon: prayer. In the end, we shall prevail." Victoria tilted her head to one side. "Speaking of prayer, would you and Sydney care to accompany Moment and me to the prayer service tomorrow evening? According to the Epistle of James, the effective, fervent prayer of a righteous man avails much. I believe we can take it that the petitions of four righteous women will have an equal effect."

Righteous women? Did Victoria honestly include her and

Sydney in that category? Ruth had made her distaste for attending church clear from the beginning. She opened her mouth to decline, but Victoria's hopeful gaze shifted its focus and settled on something behind her. Something distasteful, from the way her lips compressed into a line of disapproval.

Relieved at her deliverance, Ruth turned to see Gus Drummond approaching.

"Good day, ladies." He tipped his Stetson, then glanced around the empty street and lowered his voice. "Any progress yet?"

"We were just discussing the case," Ruth told him.

"Yes, and saying we felt quite assured of eventually catching the thieves," Victoria added.

Drummond snorted. "Meaning that you haven't any more idea who's responsible for the robberies now than the day you stepped off the train. Right, Miss Vicky?"

"Lady Victoria to you, Mr. Drummond."

Ruth's glance darted back and forth between the two. If Drummond didn't recognize the danger represented by the fiery glint in Victoria's eyes, he had only himself to blame when he suffered the consequences. And suffer he would, judging by the flush of purple that suffused Victoria's face. A delicate shade of purple, though. One that complemented the nosegay of artificial violets on her hat.

Drummond, either unaware or unconcerned by his imminent peril, drew the corners of his mouth down into a frown. "Every time I see one of you, I am reminded that the Chicago office never learned the meaning of fair play."

Ruth blinked. "And what is that supposed to mean?"

The broad-shouldered man leaned back on his heels and fixed them with a look of disgust. "It took some doing, but Fletcher finally owned up to the real reason he sent the four of you out here. It seems he never forgot the time I bested him at that turkey shoot the last time we were together. You, dear ladies, are his underhanded way of taking it out on me." He turned on his heel and crossed the street, heading for the restaurant.

Victoria's delicate countenance darkened to an even deeper shade. Ruth could feel the blood rush to her own face. The women exchanged incredulous glances.

"Am I to understand that Mr. Fletcher considers us to be some sort of revenge?" Victoria demanded.

Ruth stared after the retreating figure. "It certainly sounded that way." Drummond had never attempted to hide his disdain for women operatives, but to know that Harold Fletcher shared that contempt. . .

At least I can make a living as a seamstress.

No. She swallowed hard, forcing back the bile of disillusionment. Whether Gus Drummond and Harold Fletcher liked it or not, she was a Pinkerton, and Pinkertons didn't give up. "You're quite right, Victoria. Things may look dismal now, but somehow we *will* prevail."

The anger blazing in Victoria's eyes and her answering nod were agreement enough. She stalked off toward the mercantile, and Ruth went back inside the shop. Even through her disappointment, a sense of smugness vied for attention. For all her talk of prayer, Victoria felt just as angry as she did. It only went to prove what Ruth had long believed: Once you scratched the surface of these church people, they acted just like everyone else. Sometimes worse.

What they needed now wasn't prayer but action. "Sydney!" she called up the stairs. "You'll need to watch the shop for awhile. I'm going out."

The door to the Redemption Mine's office stood open. Ruth rearranged the bow at the neck of her blouse, patted her ash blond curls into place, and stepped through the doorway.

"I hope I'm not bothering you."

Mark Chandler looked up, his startled frown smoothing into a smile of welcome. "Not at all. Please come in."

"I've come to help," Ruth announced without preamble. "If we're going to solve this problem, it's high time we put our heads together."

"Problem?" His warm gaze bored into hers. Apparently she still hadn't become accustomed to the high altitude. The thin air seemed to be causing her shortness of breath again.

"The robberies. From what I've gathered around town, no one has any clue as to the identities of the thieves or whoever is supplying them with information. I thought if we discussed it—"

It didn't last long, that quick twitch of his lips, but long enough for Ruth to catch it. Just what was it about women using their minds that men found so amusing? First Gus Drummond, then Mr. Fletcher, and now Mark Chandler. She leveled a stern gaze at him and continued.

"I thought if we discussed the robberies, it might prove

enlightening to both of us. Perhaps talking about it will bring to mind some connection you haven't made before."

"I appreciate your interest." Mark Chandler paused, seeming to choose his words with care. "But I don't know that talking about it will help solve anything. What I'd like to see is some action from the law. Our esteemed sheriff doesn't seem to be able to do more than send out calls for help from other quarters. As for that so-called Pinkerton agent, I haven't seen him do anything to justify the agency's reputation. The fellow spends most of his time lounging around town instead of getting down to business."

Ruth's stomach clenched like a vise. She mustn't make a misstep now. "If they aren't doing anything, then it's high time you put your own mind to the task. Do you have any theories, any suspicions?"

"Nothing of any value. All I know is that every time the train has been robbed, there's been a good reason for it. My payroll or someone else's, a shipment of bullion. To my way of thinking, they must be getting advance notice of what's being shipped and when. But that's as far as I've gotten. The information is getting to them somehow, but from where, I don't know." His chin jutted forward, and the veins in his neck knotted. "Believe me, if I had a definite suspect, I'd go after him myself, whether the law decided to lend a hand or not."

Ruth reflected on his comments and nodded. "Inside information can only come from a limited number of people. Why don't we make up a list of who that might be and see if any names seem worthy of investigation?" She eyed a loose sheet of paper on Mr. Chandler's desk. Her fingers itched to pick up a pen and start writing down possible leads, but she restrained herself. She had to keep up the pretext of being nothing more than a helpful bystander. "Who would be aware of what the train was carrying on any given day?"

He drummed lightly on the desk with his fingertips. "To tell you the truth, I've already drawn up a couple of lists."

Ruth bit her lip to restrain her cry of excitement. "Why don't we look at them? Together we may see something you've missed before."

He hesitated, then reached toward the lower right-hand desk drawer. "Just because a name is on here doesn't mean I consider that person under suspicion," he cautioned. "All I've done is list everyone I could think of who had some knowledge of the times I had payroll coming in or planned to ship ore out."

"I understand. It will just provide a starting place." Ruth could barely contain her excitement as she watched him slide the drawer open and shuffle through the papers inside.

"Here, I think these are the—"

A wiry man tapped on the open office door and leaned inside. "Mark, you're supposed to be meeting with that banker right now."

Mark slammed the drawer shut with one hand and yanked out his pocket watch with the other. "I completely forgot the time, Ed. Tell him I'll be right there." He turned to Ruth. "We'll have to look at this another time, I'm afraid."

"But—" He couldn't leave now, not when that list was almost within her grasp. "Surely this is more important."

Mark slipped his jacket on and ushered her toward the door. "We'll see if we can discuss the possibilities some other time. You may be able to take time from your work to play detective, but I have a mine to run."

If only she could tell him this was her work! Unbidden tears of frustration sprang to her eyes, and she dashed them away with the back of her hand.

"Hold on. I didn't mean to upset you." He stopped in midstride and eyed her with a look of consternation. "How about if we meet at the prayer service tomorrow evening and talk things over afterward? A healthy dose of prayer may be just what we need to see our way clearly on this."

"I'm afraid I won't be going to the prayer service. Sydney and I have other plans." Maybe nothing more than darning stockings or tacking a new bit of ribbon on her collar, but he didn't need to know that. She tried to ignore his look of surprise.

"All right, then. We'll make it another time." With a quick smile, he turned and hurried away.

Ruth stared after him, a feeling of dismay seeping through her. Not another one! She already heard more than enough about the need for church attendance from Moment and Victoria.

Tears stung her eyes once more. Up to this point, she had felt so sure that Mark Chandler was someone to be trusted. Always before, she had been able to rely on her intuition. Had it let her down for the first time?

Mark winced when he heard the sound of voices raised in

song wafting from the open church door into the summer evening. His lack of vocal ability didn't bother him; being late did. Up until recent days, punctuality had been his trademark. But up until now, he hadn't known Miss Ruth Hunnicut. Her presence seemed to have a strange affect on his ability to concentrate.

He removed his hat and slipped into the small sanctuary. Spying an empty seat near the back, he made his way toward it. From across the aisle, the two ladies from the mercantile nodded a greeting. Mark nodded back. Funny how he found it hard to remember their names, seeing that they had been in town longer than Ruth Hunnicut. All four newcomers were attractive young women, but only Ruth captured his interest and his thoughts.

He wondered yet again why she had looked so flustered when he mentioned getting together after church. Come to think of it, though, neither Ruth nor her fellow seamstress had darkened the church doors since their arrival in Windmere Falls. The realization left him oddly unsettled.

John Langston, filling in for Pastor Griffin, started naming off the prayer requests for the week. Mark allowed his mind to wander. What would Ruth be doing at this moment? Surely not sewing. It might be her livelihood, but it was not important enough to miss church for. He straightened the cuff on his new shirt. He recognized quality workmanship when he saw it, and hers ranked with the best.

Mark suppressed a smile, remembering the way he'd barged into her shop. He had to admit his story of needing another shirt sounded pretty thin, but he had to have some excuse to see her again and couldn't think of anything better on the spur of the moment.

And no wonder. Acting on a whim like that ran completely counter to his detail-oriented way of living. On a typical day, he had his schedule drawn out in such detail that his men could set their watches by his comings and goings. But not since Miss Ruth Hunnicut arrived in town. More than once, he'd been so caught up in daydreams of her bright smile and winsome personality that he found himself hurrying to get to appointments on time—and failing to do so as often as not.

Speaking of daydreams, Mark realized he had succumbed to yet another one. He forced his attention back to the front of the church, where John Langston asked for special prayer for Pastor Griffin's recovery from his hunting accident.

Mark glanced around, hoping no one had noticed his lapse in attention. Would Ruth Hunnicut continue to turn his way of doing things upside down? And would he care if she did? He grinned and then composed his face into a sober expression as the congregation bowed their heads to pray.

After the final amen, he stood in line to shake hands with John Langston, then stepped outside and breathed deeply of the clear mountain air. How he loved this place! His thoughts turned unwillingly to the recent robberies. If they continued, would they put him out of business? Could he find a way to stay on in Windmere Falls if that happened? Aside from his current problems, he had a good life here. All he needed was someone to share it with. Ruth Hunnicut's image popped into his mind. What would it be like to look at that face for the rest of his days? He pictured the two of them discussing the day's events over dinner, spending their evenings reading by the fire, walking into church side by side. His happy thoughts ground to a halt when he tried to imagine them worshiping together.

Just where did she stand spiritually? The more he wondered, the more he realized how little he knew about her. He could remedy that only by spending more time with her. Mark grinned at the prospect. Not an unpleasant task at all.

Chapter 6

"Why me?" Ruth pulled a half dozen pins from between her lips and stabbed them into the dressmaking form in front of her.

Sydney set her parcel down on the cutting table and began sorting through the bright reels of ribbon she had just brought from the mercantile. "I discussed it with Moment and Victoria while I picked up our order. None of us is happy about having to tell Mr. Fletcher we haven't made a lick of progress, but it has to be done. And since you've already established a reason for sending messages back to Chicago, you're the logical choice."

Ruth groaned. Much as she wanted to, she couldn't fault their logic. Checking on her sick aunt had been part of her cover; therefore sending Mr. Fletcher news of their failure would be her responsibility, no matter how distasteful the task. She squared her shoulders and marched across the street before she could change her mind.

Emmett Duncan looked up when she entered and sprang to his feet with a welcoming smile. "As I live and breathe, if it isn't Miss Hunnicut! I've been watching you coming and going past the window and had about given up on ever seeing you in here again."

Ruth forced a smile. A telegrapher was privy to a wealth of information about community members. She couldn't afford to alienate this potential source of knowledge. "I hadn't realized you felt so neglected, Mr. Duncan. But I'm here now, and I need to send another telegram."

"Not bad news, I hope." He reached for the pad of forms and leaned across the counter, his face only inches from hers.

She restrained herself from backing away by a mighty effort. "Just checking on my aunt." Behind her, the door swung open. Ruth turned to see a pale, washed-out woman enter and hover near the back wall. Good. A third party ought to put a quick end to the telegrapher's unwanted advances.

She glanced back at Emmett Duncan and blinked. In contrast to his eager expression a few moments before, the lines around his eyes had deepened, and his mouth looked like he'd just bitten into something sour. "My telegram," she reminded him.

"Of course." He jotted down the message she dictated, casting irritated glances at the other woman all the while.

"Emmett?" The newcomer's voice was as thin and colorless as the rest of her.

"Not now. Haven't I told you not to disturb me when I'm working?" He collected Ruth's money, his glance skittering away before he made eye contact. "Thank you, Miss Hunnicut. I'll get word to you right away if there's a reply."

Bemused by the abrupt change, Ruth pushed the door

open and stepped out into the bright sunshine of a cloudless summer day. She turned to make a quick detour to the mercantile and collided with the pale woman.

"I'm so sorry. I didn't see you come out."

"That's all right." The woman gave her a shy smile. "I'm used to people not noticing me."

Ruth couldn't think of an appropriate response. "Did you finish your business so quickly?"

The smile disappeared, to be replaced by drawn lips and downcast eyes. "Emmett's right. I should have waited until he got home."

"Home?"

"Where are my manners?" Her pale blue eyes clouded. "My name is Alice Duncan. Emmett is my husband."

Emmett Duncan had a wife? Ruth's distaste for the man increased tenfold.

The desire to confront the scrawny telegrapher and tell him exactly what she thought of him warred with compassion for Mrs. Duncan's obvious need for friendly attention. Compassion won out.

"I'm Ruth Hunnicut. My friend and I own R & S Fashions, right across the street. Would you like to come over for a cup of tea?"

The woman hesitated, an expression of longing playing across her face. "I shouldn't. I need to get back home to my daughter. A neighbor is watching her for me."

"Surely she won't mind if you're out a little longer."

"Well, maybe for just a few minutes." She stepped off the boardwalk and accompanied Ruth toward the shop, casting a furtive glance back over her shoulder. The gesture raised Ruth's ire further. What kind of man must Emmett Duncan be that his own wife was afraid of him?

Sydney looked up from the sewing machine at the sound of the jingling bell and gave Ruth a puzzled frown. Ruth couldn't blame her for her confusion. In her drab, threadbare dress, Mrs. Duncan hardly looked like a potential customer.

"This is Alice Duncan," Ruth said. "I've just met her at the telegraph office where her husband works and invited her for tea so we could all get better acquainted."

To her relief, Sydney rose to the occasion with alacrity. "What a splendid idea! A spot of tea is exactly what I need right now. Let me just finish this seam." She snipped off the last threads from the dress she'd been making for Mrs. Porter and laid the folds of calico on the cutting table. "Help me get the tea things, will you, Ruth?"

In the back room, she closed the door and whispered, "What's going on?"

Ruth hurried to explain the circumstances of their meeting and felt gratified when Sydney's indignation matched her own. "If you could keep her occupied for a few moments, I'd love to slip back over there and give Mr. Roving Eye a piece of my mind."

"I'll be happy to," Sydney said. "I forgot to pick up another packet of pins at the mercantile. You can use that as an excuse for leaving."

They carried the tea tray into the shop to find Alice Duncan stroking Mrs. Porter's unfinished dress, a wistful expression on her face. "You have such lovely things in here.

I never even noticed a new business had opened, but then, I don't get much time just to look around town."

Ruth filled the teapot and set it on their little stove. "Do you live some distance away?"

"No, we're right in town. Emily, our daughter, is crippled and requires a lot of care."

"What a shame!" Sydney exclaimed.

"Seven years old and she can't even cross the room by herself."

Seeing the pain that shadowed the woman's eyes, Ruth made up her mind. "If you don't mind helping Sydney set things up, I need to run a quick errand. I'll be back before the tea is ready."

"I don't mind a bit. I'll just sit here and admire all this beautiful fabric."

Ruth dashed across the street and purchased the pins in record time. Hoping Sydney would keep Alice's attention directed away from the window, she strode next door to the telegraph office, intent on putting Emmett Duncan in his place. She had just begun to turn the door handle when she heard voices from inside.

That wouldn't do at all. She didn't want an audience for her confrontation. Letting the handle slip back into place, she decided to wait a moment and see if whoever was inside would emerge before she needed to get back to the impromptu tea party.

"I just got word." The deep male voice filtered through the loose-fitting door. "The old trapper's cabin next Thursday at nine."

"So soon?" Duncan's reedy whine couldn't be mistaken. "I do have responsibilities at home, you know."

"Yeah, we know how much time you spend at home. Thursday at nine. You be there, understand?"

Ruth tapped her foot and waited for the visitor to come out, but the door didn't open. She concluded the caller had gone out a back way. She reached for the handle again but then changed her mind. What she wanted to say to Emmett Duncan would take more time than she could spare at the moment. Right now, she needed to get back to the shop.

"Amazing," Ruth said later when she and Sydney were closing up the shop for the evening. "Alice is a sweet, intelligent person, but you'd never guess it from the way her husband speaks to her."

Sydney swept up loose threads from the area around the sewing machine and clucked her tongue. "I simply don't understand it. Granted, she isn't the most outgoing person I've ever seen, but with a little attention to the colors she chooses and the way she styles her hair, she wouldn't look nearly so mousy. Even so, that's no excuse for her husband to give her the kind of treatment you described."

"My feelings exactly. It's a shame she couldn't stay longer. Still, maybe even the short time we spent together will give her spirits a lift."

"I hope so." Sydney tossed her mane of coppery curls with vigor.

Ruth smiled. It was a relief to see her friend shed the cloak of gloom that had enveloped her ever since her arrival in Windmere Falls. She'd tried hard to abide by Sydney's wishes and not press for answers about her disappearance. Still, there were times she'd dearly love to shake Sydney until her teeth rattled and make her account for every harrowing moment Ruth had spent worrying about her safety.

Sydney's stubborn refusal to open up proved every bit as baffling as the mystery they'd been sent to solve, but Ruth had no recourse but to wait it out and give Sydney time to work through things on her own. In a way, it was a relief. She didn't need more than one puzzle to solve at a time.

Chapter 7

*B*ong. *Bong. Bong.* The church bell's clear notes echoed through the streets of Windmere Falls, calling the faithful to worship. Ruth tucked a stray curl behind her ear and reached for her reticule. Its sky blue color coordinated well with her paisley shawl. The perfect accessory for the well-dressed lady. No one would guess it hid a .32 Harrington & Richardson break-top revolver in its depths. Hardly the perfect lady's accessory, but imminently suitable for a well-trained Pinkerton operative.

Downstairs, Sydney sat sipping a second cup of tea. She blinked when Ruth descended the stairs and headed for the front door. "You're going to church?"

"No, just out." She wondered whether she should tell Sydney about her errand, then decided to hold her tongue. Sydney had been keeping secrets of her own. Now it was her turn.

She slipped out the door and stood blinking in the bright light of a perfect summer morning. On a day like this, it would be hard to believe evils like train robbers and heartless husbands could exist.

She crossed the street and hurried west along the boardwalk. When she drew even with the doctor's office, she slowed her steps. In a moment, the church building came into view. Ruth stopped and drew nearer to the wooden building fronts.

From her vantage point, she peeped past the corner of Doc Wingert's office in time to see Moment and Victoria speaking to a nice-looking young man in the church doorway.

Probably the preacher. If he was anything like the Reverend Norton Sanders back home, he stood to make a pretty penny out of the trusting souls in Windmere Falls before moving on to greener pastures. Watching Sanders's systematic fleecing of his flock and the elders' refusal to address the issue had soured her on church forever. Maybe when they had cracked the case of the elusive train robbers, she would turn her attention to the tall young clergyman. It couldn't hurt to keep an eye on him during her stay. No telling what kind of hanky-panky a little attention might avert.

Ruth watched a last few churchgoers approach. Banker Will Bowen pulled up in his buggy just ahead of Doc Wingert. Mabel Hawkins, the town gossip, came bustling along just as the bell tolled a final reminder that the service was about to start.

A lone figure angled toward the church. Ruth recognized Mark Chandler's measured gait. She pressed back against the storefront's rough wood and then relaxed when she realized the morning sun would be in his eyes, preventing him from seeing her.

Mark hurried up the church steps and exchanged a few words with the preacher. Ruth watched with narrowed eyes. She would definitely have to keep an eye on this one. Mark had already suffered enough loss. In her experience, men of the cloth had a keen interest in getting their hands on all the money they could.

The church doors swung shut and silence reigned on the streets of Windmere Falls. Satisfied that everyone she planned to check out that morning was safely ensconced inside the church building, Ruth made her way from building to building, checking for anything out of the ordinary: freshly turned earth, notes or scraps of paper in out-of-the-way places, horses she hadn't seen around town before. A survey of the livery revealed no unfamiliar mounts. Her hike up to the mine offices proved fruitless. Her only moment of excitement came when she discovered a patch of newly dug ground behind the boardinghouse. After scrabbling through the loose soil with her hands, she replanted the seed potatoes she had dug up.

What now? Disappointment rose up in her throat like bile. Ruth forced the bitterness back down and tried to focus her thoughts. What had she actually seen during the robbery? She cast her mind back to the day of her arrival, trying to remember every detail.

Rough voices. Masked men. Their slow procession through the jolting passenger car. Sydney walking back down the aisle, almost on the heels of the outlaws. Following her, falling, realizing Sydney had disappeared. Shock and fear numbing her mind, obliterating any details that might have given her some clue to the robbers' identities. Were they short, tall, stocky, thin? Had their voices sounded young or old?

Ruth kneaded her forehead with her fingertips, trying to recall some scrap of memory that would unlock the puzzle. She had always fancied herself a keen observer of human behavior, but she had to admit she didn't notice much during that stressful time.

And for once, intuition didn't seem to be helping her at all. Maybe Mr. Chandler had the right idea, with his charts and tables. Ruth retraced her steps and headed back to the shop. At the moment, the only inspiration to cross her mind involved a change of clothes and a pan of steaming hot water in which to soak her aching feet.

"Did you have a nice time?" Sydney's look spoke of consuming curiosity, but to her credit, she didn't press for details.

"Very. It's a lovely day." Ruth made a show of checking her fresh attire in the looking glass, trying not to let Sydney see her disappointment. After all, nothing had changed, but she had counted so much on finding some clue. This morning's failure had put her back where she started.

Sydney peered out the window at the azure sky. "It does look inviting. It almost makes me want to take a turn around town."

Sydney wanted to leave her self-imposed role as a hermit and venture outside?

Sparing only a fleeting thought for her tender feet, Ruth pulled her hat off the shelf. "Let's go for a walk."

"Now? But you just got in."

"So I'll go back out again. It's a beautiful day; we might as well enjoy it to the full. Come on."

To her gratification, Sydney barely hesitated before setting aside her copy of *Godey's Lady's Book* and getting to her feet. "All right, then. Lead on."

They started toward the east end of town, with Sydney chattering away as though she didn't have a care. Buoyed by Sydney's gaiety, Ruth threw back her head and laughed as they rounded a corner—and careened into someone.

Before her, Victoria bore a dazed expression, the plume on her hat knocked askew by the impact.

"Are the two of you all right?" Moment asked.

"Yes, you both took quite a wallop," a baritone voice added.

Ruth noticed their companion for the first time and recognized the pastor she had seen at the church earlier.

"What a happy coincidence!" Moment said. "We've been telling Pastor Langston about the two of you. Ruth, this is John Langston, who's filling in during Pastor Griffin's convalescence."

Turning on her heel and striding away seemed the most desirable course of action, but Ruth stiffened her spine and extended her hand. If she planned to investigate the man after finishing her work on the train robberies, it would be better to stay on good terms with him so he wouldn't suspect her interest later.

"How do you do?" She forced herself to look directly at him. Instead of meeting her gaze, the good reverend stared over her shoulder, a bewildered expression on his face.

Of course. Sydney. She'd better remember her manners. "Allow me to introduce my friend, Sydney de Clermont." Ruth turned to present Sydney, but no one stood on the boardwalk behind her.

"I'm. . .sorry," she stammered, feeling as dumbfounded as John Langston looked. Really, this tendency of Sydney's to disappear was getting out of control.

"Apparently your friend had other things to do." His voice held a note of wry amusement. "She darted off between those buildings." He pointed in the direction of the boardinghouse.

"Oh. Yes, she did mention a pressing engagement."

"What a shame," Victoria said. "We were just discussing the recent rash of robberies and the way the villains manage to disappear afterward."

"Pastor Langston mentioned Poe's story 'The Purloined Letter,' where an object remained hidden, even though it was out in plain sight," Moment said. "Do you suppose it's possible the culprits are people we see every day?"

"Actually, one of my parishioners came up with the idea," Mr. Langston said. "He wondered whether it might even be one of the mine owners using his status as a so-called victim to cover his activities."

Not Mark Chandler. Ruth wouldn't even entertain such a notion. On the other hand, how much did she really know about him? Her intuition told her he could be trusted. But did she have proof of anything regarding Mark, other than the feelings that erupted whenever he came near her? And he did seem to be thick with the pastor. . . .

She turned back to John Langston. He flushed when she

caught him staring. "Pardon me," he said, "but you look familiar. Have we met before?"

Ruth choked back a tart reply. She had heard lines like that all too often from Chicago's would-be suitors. Apparently even men of God weren't immune from such typical male subterfuge.

"Excuse me," she said. "I must catch up with my friend. It was nice to meet you."

"What a shame you have to run off so quickly. I would have enjoyed conversing with you at greater length. Perhaps our paths will cross again someday."

"I'm sure they will." Ruth walked away, trying not to notice the disappointment on Moment's and Victoria's faces. She turned in the direction Mr. Langston had indicated.

Where had Sydney taken herself off to this time? Despite her aggravation, Ruth admired the way her friend had avoided meeting the preacher. Sydney had no more use for men of the cloth than she did. Ruth made a mental note to follow Sydney's example and be quicker on her feet the next time she saw the Reverend Langston coming.

She sank onto a bench outside the hotel and mulled over his statement. Could Mark be involved in the criminal ring, feigning the outrage he showed to the world? Her heart cried out no, but her sense of duty prodded her onward. She must investigate all leads to the best of her ability, even if the subject of her investigation happened to be Mark Chandler.

❧

"Blessed are they which do hunger and thirst after righteousness: for they shall be filled." Mark pondered the words on the page before him, then closed his Bible and checked his pocket watch. *Time to head over to the mine.* He stood and reached for his coat. Some of his men saw no sense in taking time to read the Bible, but they didn't understand how much his relationship with the Lord mattered to him. Work duties were important. No one believed that more than Mark. But he would never be able to make it through the day without a regular dose of God's Word.

Especially when disaster might be looming.

When he thought about those lowdown bandits, he had to struggle to hold onto the peace he'd gained from the Scriptures. Every fiber of his being wanted to cry out against the injustice of someone's greed being able to set back the hard work he'd put in over the last few years.

As always, a smile lit his face when he came into sight of the mine entrance. He had carved the Redemption out of the bedrock with his own two hands. The sight of it never failed to fill him with an overwhelming sense of accomplishment. He didn't want to consider the possibility that all his effort might have been for nothing.

A speck of color between a timber and the rock it supported caught his attention. A tiny blue wildflower had managed to cling to life in a crevice of stone. Mark started to pluck it, then stayed his hand. They were two of a kind, he and the small wild bloom. Tearing it away from its roots would undermine the flower in the same way losing the Redemption would effect him.

The little blossom stirred in the morning breeze. Something about its ability to maintain that delicate beauty in a harsh environment reminded him of Ruth Hunnicut. The very thought of her brought another smile to his lips, lightening his mood like the sun breaking through after a mountain thunderstorm. Like the flower, she had the tenacity to bloom and flourish in a rugged land. Coming out West on her own, drawn only by the lure of stories she'd heard, took a special kind of courage. No wonder he enjoyed spending time with her so much.

And she wanted to help catch the train robbers. Mark chuckled at the idea. He found her enthusiasm for trying to solve the crimes endearing, if preposterous. Still, that strength of character drew him to her. If only he had a better idea of her standing with God.

Chapter 8

Ruth worked her way along the garments laid out on the table in the back room, readying the latest finished projects for delivery. First was a checked gingham housedress, altered to fit Mrs. Cummings's expanding figure. According to Mrs. Cummings, her clothing had shown a mysterious tendency to shrink of late. Ha! Ruth had seen her tucking into a hefty meal at the restaurant only last week. If she ate that way all the time, Mrs. Cummings alone would keep her and Sydney in business.

Next came a shirt Gus Drummond had brought in for mending as a ruse to give them an opportunity to talk about the case without raising suspicion. Ruth only wished that they actually had something to discuss.

The third item was a velvet jacket with leg-o'-mutton sleeves for Octavia Nelson, who had set her heart and a good portion of her husband's income on keeping up with Eastern fashions. If theirs had been a legitimate business, Ruth would have been overjoyed at the steady flow of customers that streamed through their door since she first set the sign for

R & S Fashions in the shop window. She sometimes had to remind herself that making and mending garments for the citizenry of Windmere Falls served only as a cover for their real job.

An empty spool rolled to the floor near her feet. Ruth gave it a kick that sent it spinning into the corner. Considering how little progress they'd made on the case so far, the seamstress shop might just as well be their true occupation. It was a good thing the mercantile had been doing a booming business too. If the current state of affairs didn't change, all four of them might need a source of income when the Pinkerton Agency gave them the boot.

She snatched up the schedule of upcoming jobs and scanned the list. More mending, alterations, and a fitting at three o'clock. Enough work to keep their sewing machine humming.

Ruth aimed another kick at the empty spool. Sydney could handle the fitting. If she didn't get out and find some way to break this case open, she would only confirm the opinions the Pinkerton men held of women's abilities. She glanced out the small window and noted the sun's position. If she took care of the deliveries now, she'd have the afternoon free for investigating. She gave the finished garments one final inspection.

The bell over the shop door jingled. Maybe Mrs. Cummings had come by to pick up her dress. If Ruth didn't have to make the trip out to her home, it would give her more time to pursue the case. She pushed open the door to the front room with a rising sense of hope and halted in midstep.

Not Alice Duncan. Not now. She needed to be outdoors getting down to business, not entertaining the telegrapher's neglected wife.

"Good morning." Ruth tried to inject a note of welcome into her voice, hoping she sounded more charitable than she felt.

"Hello." The woman reached out timidly to touch a length of watered silk. A dreamy expression lit her face, giving her pale complexion a hint of color. "This is lovely. It must make up beautifully."

"It does." Ruth forced a smile and nodded as though she had nothing better to do. Alice sighed and stroked the material with the tip of her finger. "I love coming in here. You have such pretty cloth. It makes me feel better just to come in and look around and spend time talking to you."

Ruth tried to squelch the prickle of conscience that shot through her. Had she ever seen Alice Duncan looking even remotely happy before? And her visits to the shop truly didn't last for more than a few minutes. Surely she couldn't begrudge the downtrodden woman that modicum of comfort.

"Would you like a cup of tea?"

Alice perched on the edge of a chair and shook her head. "I really shouldn't stay long. I spent more time at the mercantile than I'd planned, and I need to get back to Emily."

Remorse smote Ruth yet again. In addition to the burden of being married to Emmett Duncan, she had her sickly daughter to care for. The woman needed a friend, and Ruth had been elected. Pinkerton or no Pinkerton, she couldn't find it in her heart to brush Alice's need for companionship aside.

"How is Emily?"

Alice's gentle smile slipped. "Her legs hurt her last night. I was up with her for hours. She's sleeping now," she hastened to add. "I wouldn't have left her if she still needed me."

"I know you wouldn't. I'm sure she's just fine in your neighbor's care." *I'm also sure your loving husband didn't lift a finger to help.* "It's nice of your neighbor to lend a hand so you can get out. You need a break once in awhile."

"It does help my outlook to be able to have a few moments to myself. And Emmett. . .well, Emmett's so busy with his job that he's too tired to spell me when he gets home. His job carries a lot of responsibility, you know. People depend on him."

"Mmm." Ruth considered it wiser to keep her opinion of Alice's husband and his roving eye to herself. "That must make it difficult for you."

"I wouldn't admit it to anyone else, but it does wear on me sometimes. Emmett feels such a responsibility to the people here. Why, sometimes he's called out late at night to send an urgent message. Last Tuesday, for instance, the station manager heard about a damaged bridge on the line west of here. Emmett not only went out after dark to send word to the repair crew, he waited at the office for hours to be there when the reply from the repair crew came in."

"Really?" A faint ripple of interest stirred in the back of Ruth's mind. So Emmett Duncan was gone from home at odd hours? She cast her thoughts back to the night in question. She had stayed up putting in a hem until quite late. Surely she would have noticed a light burning at the telegraph office at that time.

Had there been one? No. That didn't necessarily mean anything, but her training had taught her to look for things that didn't fit.

With a rising sense of excitement, she asked, "Does this happen a lot?"

"Not all the time. It seems to run in spurts. He'll have a spate of off-hour calls, then he'll turn into a regular homebody again." Alice rose to her feet. "Dear me, I didn't mean to take up your whole morning. Thank you for lending a listening ear. It means more to me than you know."

"Wait!" She couldn't let her leave now, not when she'd just imparted such potentially important information. As much as she'd regretted Alice's appearance earlier, Ruth was now frantic to find a way to keep her there. But how? She threw a wild glance around the shop. *Think. Think. Think!* Her gaze lit on the fabric table.

"You've been through so much, what with Emily's condition and all the time your husband has to spend away from home. You need something to give your spirits a lift. How about a new dress?"

Alice's lips formed a small O. "A new dress? For me?" Her gaze lingered wistfully on a bolt of deep rose calico. She reached out as if to touch it, then drew back and clasped her hands together. "Oh, I couldn't. But thank you for thinking of me. It was a lovely idea."

"And we're going to go ahead with it." Motivated by a

sudden longing to bring some happiness into Alice Duncan's life as well as the desire to learn more, Ruth felt more determined than ever to put her plan into action. She held up her hand when Alice seemed about to protest. "And don't think you'll have to pay for it. This is a gift from me to you."

Alice opened her mouth as if to speak, but no sound came out. Tears pooled along her lower lids, and she chased them away with her fingertips.

"Let's get started right now, before you have to get back to Emily." Ruth steered her toward the fitting area, snatching up her measuring tape on the way.

She stretched the tape from Alice's shoulder to her wrist. "It must be difficult to spend your evenings alone. Does it happen often?" she asked again. The twinge of guilt at using Alice's desire for friendship to further her own ends caused her a momentary pang. Moment or Victoria would probably have a Scripture verse at the ready to rebuke her duplicity.

"Sometimes it seems he's hardly ever home," Alice confided. "And his late hours aren't all related to business. I learned recently that he spends a lot of time over in the saloon. Not drinking," she hastened to add. "At least, not much. He says he's found he has a real knack for playing cards, and lately he's been on a real winning streak."

Ruth made encouraging noises and took more measurements, hoping the flow of information would continue.

"It isn't like he's just out to gamble." Alice lifted her chin. "He's doing it for Emily and me." She caught a glimpse of

Ruth's skeptical expression in the looking glass and turned to face her.

"It's true. I—I have to admit I didn't see it that way at first. I felt like Emmett should be spending more time with us, and I'm afraid I spoke to him rather sharply about it."

Ruth ducked her head to conceal her amazement. She couldn't imagine Alice raising her voice to anyone, least of all her husband.

"And he explained it all to me. Doc Wingert says there's a specialist in Denver who could help Emily, but she'll need an operation, an expensive one. We could never scrape together enough to pay for it from what he makes at the telegraph office, and it's been eating me alive, knowing we couldn't give our little girl the chance to get better. I'd been feeling like Emmett was ignoring us just when we needed him most, but it turns out that all the time I'd been fussing about him being gone, he was winning at the poker table, getting money to help our Emily. Isn't that wonderful?"

Ruth murmured agreement and made a show of jotting down Alice's waist measurement, her mind whirling with questions. Emmett had recently come into money. Had he actually won it gambling? The odd hours, the sudden income—all these things could add up to something of interest to the Pinkertons.

Or had she reached yet another dead end?

"There, that'll do it." She made a final notation on her sheet of paper and smiled at Alice. "What about a shirtwaist dress made of this wool serge? You'll be the envy of all the ladies of Windmere Falls."

Alice blushed. "I'll be thrilled just to have something new to wear. Ruth, I know how much work is involved. You said not to pay for it, and I can't right now, since I'm saving every penny for Emily's medical expenses. But I have to do something." She looked around the shop and spied a blouse Sydney had cut out that morning. "What about this? I could take it home and work on it. It wouldn't be much, but it would be something. Would you let me do it? Please?"

Why not? The blouse was a simple one, not demanding a great deal of skill. More importantly, it would bring Alice back to the shop again in case Ruth had further questions.

"All right." She wrapped the pieces of fabric and a spool of thread into a neat parcel and placed it in the woman's outstretched hands. "We'll call it even then."

Ruth drummed her fingers against the doorframe as she followed Alice Duncan's progress down the street and tried to make sense of what she had just learned. Emmett left home at odd hours. Because he truly wanted to obtain funds to help his crippled daughter? Because he didn't want to spend time with a wife he scorned? Or because he was part of the gang of robbers she'd been sent to find?

Moment, Victoria, and Sydney sat huddled in the storeroom of the mercantile, where Ruth had called an emergency meeting after putting a "Closed" sign in the window of R & S Fashions and hustling Sydney across the street.

"What do you think?" she asked after summing up her conversation with Alice.

"It isn't much to go on, is it?" Sydney looked unconvinced.

"I know. There isn't one specific thing I can put my finger on, but it feels right." She held up her fingers one by one as she listed significant points. "Emmett Duncan came into a substantial sum of money, supposedly through his newly acquired skill at the gaming table. But he lied to his wife about being at the telegraph office last Tuesday night. I know that for a fact. And he—well, I'm not sure he takes his marriage vows seriously." She recounted the obvious interest he had shown in her, even with his wife present.

"To me, it all adds up. If he casts a roving eye at other women and lies to his wife about his whereabouts, why couldn't he lie about where the money came from? And if it's from a source he has to lie about, why couldn't it be that the money came from his share of the proceeds from the robberies?"

She sat back, pleased with the way she'd outlined her position.

Moment and Victoria exchanged glances and nodded in unison. "It makes perfect sense," Moment said.

Ruth's confidence soared. "You think so?"

"Of course. Which verse am I thinking of, Victoria?"

"Luke 16:10," the Englishwoman replied without hesitation. " 'He that is faithful in that which is least is faithful also in much.' Not to imply, of course, that honesty with his wife is of little importance."

Moment picked up the thread of thought. "Mr. Duncan has no compunctions about misleading his wife, which indicates a basic lack of integrity. It wouldn't be much of a stretch for him to go from that to getting involved in criminal activity."

Ruth fought down the urge to scream. She had reached her conclusion through sound reasoning, not biblical analogies. Was there nothing these two wouldn't tie in to Scripture? "So you think it's worth pursuing?"

"Absolutely." Moment beamed. "It looks like you've come up with the first solid lead in this case."

Victoria nodded agreement. "Remember, the Lord will bring to light the things of darkness. We came here to seek the truth, and He promised that the truth will make you free."

Chapter 9

Victoria's comment haunted Ruth all the while she worked on Alice's dress. Did she really want to learn the truth? The more she toyed with the possibility of Emmett Duncan as a suspect, the more plausible his involvement in the robberies seemed. The idea of bringing him up short had great appeal, but what would that do to his wife? Justice would be served, but Alice would be put in the untenable position of having a frail child to care for and no means of support.

The subject of her thoughts walked through the door at that moment. Ruth fixed a welcoming smile on her lips. "Just in time!" She snipped off the last thread and held the dress up.

Alice's eyes widened when she saw the finished garment. "It's gorgeous." She traced her finger along the soft gathers. "I've never worn something so lovely in my life."

"Then it's high time you did. Take this into the back room and try it on."

It seemed only a few moments before she came back into

the shop and stood for Ruth's inspection. Ruth took a second look at her new friend. Today her face glowed with excitement, and instead of hanging in wispy strands at the sides of her face, her hair was neatly crimped in soft waves.

Alice stood before the looking glass and stared in childlike wonder. The graceful lines of the pleated skirt added to her youthful appearance. A wistful look crossed her face. "Maybe Emmett would stay home more if I took the time to look nicer for him. What do you think?"

Ruth held back the angry reply that sprang to her lips. If Emmett Duncan cared at all, he could have found ways to ease his wife's burden instead of adding to it. She settled for a question of her own: "Has he been spending his evenings away again?"

Alice nodded, and her lower lip trembled. "I'd planned to surprise him by making a special dinner and wearing this dress tonight. But he told me he'd already planned something for this evening."

A likely story. What would Emmett have planned for a quiet Thursday evening? The conversation she overheard at the telegraph office sprang unbidden to her mind. *Thursday at nine. The old trapper's cabin.* Ruth clapped her hand to her lips. Could this be the breakthrough she'd been looking for? If she could find a way to spy on the meeting, she might solve the case tonight.

"Ruth?" Alice held out a parcel. "Here's the blouse I took to finish. This won't nearly make up for what you've done on this dress, but take it with my heartfelt thanks."

Ruth pulled open the wrappings, hoping she wouldn't

have to redo too much of the work. Her jaw dropped when she beheld the creation nestled inside the brown paper. Instead of a simple blouse, Alice had transformed the pieces of handkerchief linen into a fashion piece. Even stitches marked each neat seam, and eyelet embroidery outlined the soft bow at the neck.

"Is it all right?" Her visitor's worried query snapped her to attention.

"All right? It's breathtaking. I had no idea you had this kind of talent."

A pink flush suffused Alice's cheeks. "My mother taught me. I haven't used those skills in a long time, what with having to care for Emily. I hope you like it."

"Consider this an even trade. You do some of the nicest work I've ever seen." She hugged her and sent her on her way, then sat down to ponder the implications of Emmett Duncan's plans for this evening. The meeting might be nothing more than a private poker game among friends. But her intuition told her it carried a heavier significance.

Could she stand the thought of ruining Alice Duncan's life if it did?

To ignore this lead meant throwing her own integrity to the winds and letting down the people who trusted her to do her job. It also meant watching Mark Chandler continue to be hurt by one robbery after another.

Assuming, of course, he wasn't involved in the holdups himself.

What would she do if Mr. Chandler, instead of Emmett Duncan, turned out to be the guilty party? There seemed to be no getting around it. Either way, someone she cared for would be hurt. *The truth shall make you free.* She didn't feel free; the responsibility of interfering in people's lives grew more complicated by the moment.

She considered going upstairs to talk over her dilemma with Sydney. But Sydney wouldn't have the answers. Ruth knew who did. Stepping into the back room and closing the door, she dropped to her knees.

"Lord, we haven't been on speaking terms for a long time now. And I know that's my fault, not Yours." Instead of the sense of rebuke she expected, a feeling of peace washed over her. A feeling of welcome. "I've let people and their failings come between us, and I need to make things right with You again. And then I'm going to need Your direction and Your courage. . . ."

❧

Moonlight cast a silver glow over Windmere Falls. A light breeze ruffled through the aspen leaves. Ruth crept along the alley that ran behind the seamstress shop and emerged at the west end of town. Melting into the shadow of a pine tree, she scanned the main street from end to end.

A few evening strollers sauntered along the boardwalk. No one looked her way. No one seemed to sense anything out of the ordinary.

Good. She had gotten away unnoticed. Pulling the hood of her dark blue cloak up over her head, she picked her way along the edge of the road that led out of town.

Extracting the location of the cabin from Gus Drummond had been like balancing on a tightrope of truth.

"And just what is your interest in that old place?" he demanded.

"Someone mentioned it the other day. I feel it's important to have a thorough understanding of this area. You never know when a small scrap of knowledge might prove important in an investigation." Drummond's skeptical expression told her she hadn't convinced him. She just hoped he wouldn't guess she planned to visit the cabin that very night.

Sydney had joined Victoria and Moment for an evening of discussion about the case, seeming to accept it without question when Ruth begged off at the last moment, pleading an upset stomach. That had been no exaggeration. The closer she came to her goal, the queasier she felt.

Thankfully, the moon shone brightly enough to light up the ribbon of road ahead. Without it, her progress would have been slowed to the point she would never reach the appointed meeting place in time. A loose rock rolled under her foot, and she stumbled. She paused, panting from exertion and nerves. Did all Pinkertons feel this anxious during the chase?

The breeze pushed a cloud across the moon. Ruth took a deep breath and pressed on, feeling her way step by step.

A meadow shone pale in the moonlight, and beyond it she saw a dark shape near the edge of the trees that must be the cabin. Now she welcomed the darkness as she flitted through the deepest shadows toward the lonely building.

The clouds parted as if on cue, and Ruth scrutinized the layout. Instead of being set back in the trees as she had first thought, the cabin stood a good ten yards away from the treeline. She wouldn't be able to approach it that way.

Three horses stood tethered to a hitching rail. How many men were coming to tonight's clandestine gathering? If only three, she might take a chance on crossing the open ground without being seen. If more arrived before she reached the cabin, she could wind up being exposed to view.

She would have to risk it; she saw no other way. Ruth eased through the meadow grass, step by cautious step.

She reached the cabin wall without incident and circled to the darkest side. Now what? Ruth realized she'd left a significant gap in her plans. Even if she hid long enough to identify those present as they left, it still proved nothing. She needed hard facts and needed them quickly.

There had to be a window. She peered around the nearest corner and saw a rectangle of light on the ground. Her heart leaped with excitement, then she realized the window was too high for her to see through.

Maybe she could overhear their conversation. Stepping from one tuft of grass to the next, she crept to a point below the windowsill and flattened herself against the rough logs.

Sure enough, voices drifted out into the night. Ruth rose up as high as she dared and closed her eyes, focusing all her attention on listening.

"All right, what's it about this time? I have a family waiting for me, you know."

Emmett Duncan! Ruth would recognize that thin, reedy tone anywhere.

"Right, Emmett. You're a real devoted family man." Two voices rumbled with laughter.

Ruth pressed her knuckles against her temples and tried to place the other voices. One sounded vaguely familiar—the one she'd heard telling Mr. Duncan about this meeting, perhaps.

"Let's get on with it. What's so important we had to come out at this time of night?"

"Two things," the second voice said. "First off, the Ghost says he heard more Pinkertons are expected out here. He wants us to be on the lookout."

Ruth stiffened. If the thought of detectives arriving caused the group to worry, something had to be amiss. She became so caught up in speculation she almost missed Emmett's reply.

"The Ghost," he scoffed. "Why would anyone want to go by a ridiculous name like that?"

"Be careful what you say," the third voice cautioned. "You never know where he is or when he may be listening."

"All because of that fool mask he wears," Emmett said. "And this scheme of his for dropping notes in a hollow tree to get word to us. I'm getting tired of not knowing who we're working for. If we have to take him on trust, he ought to show some faith in us. We're all in this together."

"Quit complaining," put in the second man. "We're making plenty from these jobs. I don't care who's running the show as long as I get my cut."

Ruth's heart hammered against her ribs. These had to be the robbers! Following her instincts had paid off. She could hardly wait to wipe the superior smile off Gus Drummond's face.

"There won't be any cut if we wind up in jail. The Ghost is serious about this Pinkerton business. He wants you to keep a close watch on any telegrams to or from Drummond."

Emmett Duncan snickered. "I sent telegrams for that Pink weeks ago, asking for reinforcements. You haven't noticed any new men around town, have you? He's worrying for nothing. If that's all this meeting is about, I'm heading home." A chair scraped on the wooden floor.

"There's more. The Ghost heard that one of the mines is supposed to be sending out a shipment of bullion soon."

The third man let out a low whistle. "That could be the big strike we've been looking for. Any idea which mine?"

"Probably the Redemption. Our friend Mr. Chandler has already provided us with a couple of good hauls. We may have him to thank for the biggest one yet." A round of guffaws met this statement.

Relief swept over Ruth like a tidal wave. Clearly, Mark had no involvement with the gang.

"But whichever mine is involved, we need to keep our eyes and ears open and be ready to make our move when the time comes. Emmett, the Ghost expects you to watch for any messages that will give us specifics on when that shipment is going out."

"Maybe." Footsteps echoed inside the cabin. Ruth ducked down low when they approached the window. "Seems to me I'm doing more than my share of the work here. It's only right that I get a bigger share."

"Why, you skinny little weasel! I ought to—"

"Hold on, both of you. Emmett, the rest of us take our

own risks. Like you said, we're all in this together."

"I'm taking more risk than any of you. You let Mr. High and Mighty Ghost know what I said, and be quick about it."

Be quick about it. Ruth's throat constricted as a series of pictures flashed through her mind. Three masked men bursting into the passenger car where she and Sydney sat. Pistols waved in their direction. A gunnysack thrust toward them and a voice saying, "Put your valuables in here, and be quick about it." The same voice she had just heard.

Emmett Duncan. She had him dead to rights.

Exultation turned to panic when she heard the scrape of boots on the floor and realized the meeting had broken up. Without hesitation, she stole back across the open ground. She took shelter behind a scrub oak and peered through the branches. If she could get a clear look at the other two men, she would be able to break the back of the gang this very night.

She bit back a cry of dismay when a cloud blocked the moon's light just as the three men emerged from the cabin. Ruth could hear the creak of saddle leather when they mounted their horses. Their dark forms passed within twenty yards of her, but darkness obscured any identifying features. She couldn't even tell what color the horses were.

So much for capturing the whole gang. Still, she had the goods on Emmett Duncan, and Mark's name had been cleared. That alone made her nighttime foray worthwhile. Once in custody, Emmett might well divulge the identities of his partners in crime.

"You're sure?"

"Absolutely." Ruth looked at her fellow detectives, pleased by their rapt attention. "I not only heard them talking about past robberies, but planning more. Emmett Duncan is one of them, without a doubt."

Victoria stood and wrapped her arms around Ruth's shoulders. "Congratulations. You're the first to catch your man. And you shall have the honor of notifying our esteemed colleague."

"Just as soon as I leave here. I wanted to let you three know first." She took her leave and strode along the boardwalk, wondering where she might find Gus Drummond. Her initial elation had ebbed. Why? As Victoria said, she had been the first to succeed. This moment should be one of the proudest of her life.

All she had to do was pass her information along to Drummond, thereby maintaining her cover. The arrest would be made, and she could rejoice in knowing she had proven her worth as a Pinkerton.

And Alice Duncan would be humiliated and left alone to fend for herself and her crippled child. All through the efforts of her good friend Ruth.

Her steps dragged to a halt, and she leaned against the corner of the restaurant. She had managed to clear Mark's name, but that came at the cost of betraying a friend's trust. She must be doing something wrong. Didn't people say life became simpler with God at its center?

The truth shall make you free. Victoria's words rang in her mind. Truth had exonerated Mr. Chandler, but that same truth meant prison for Emmett Duncan and a lifetime of poverty and shame for his wife.

"The other ladies said you had something to tell me."

Drummond's voice startled her from her reverie. Ruth turned with a sense of foreboding, knowing her decision had just been made. "I know who one of the robbers is."

Chapter 10

Mark left the sheriff's office with the first ray of optimism he'd felt in weeks. He spotted Ruth Hunnicut farther along the boardwalk and hurried to join her. "Great news!" he said. "They've captured one of the thieves."

She turned a somber gaze toward him. "I know."

"How about a little more excitement? Drummond finally came through. This may mean the whole gang will be behind bars before long."

"I'm sorry, Mark. I am happy for you. It's just that there's more to this than you realize."

She studied his face, then scanned the street and led him to a quiet spot. "No one must know what I'm about to tell you."

What dark secret could his lovely Ruth possibly have? Whatever it might be, he would listen and assure her of his support. Then perhaps she'd join him in celebrating.

She drew a deep breath. "Drummond didn't discover Emmett Duncan's guilt. I did."

"What?"

"Mark, I'm a Pinkerton agent."

Her grave expression spun out of focus for a moment. Surely he hadn't heard right. "Say that again. Slowly."

"I'm not really a seamstress. That only provided my cover. I came here for the express purpose of unmasking the robbers."

Ruth Hunnicut, a detective. A Pinkerton, no less. And only a few days before, he'd compared her to a fragile mountain flower. He threw back his head and laughed at the memory. Catching sight of her narrowed eyes, he controlled his mirth.

"I'm not ridiculing you, believe me. I'm laughing at myself and my stupid male pride. If you want the truth, I admire you immensely. You cracked the case when no one else could. But you don't seem very happy about it."

"It's Alice Duncan. What I've done has caused nothing but upheaval in her life, but she doesn't know that. Yet."

"You're going to tell her?"

"Not about being a Pinkerton, but I have to let her know I'm responsible for what's happened. I couldn't live with myself otherwise."

Mark touched her face with his fingertips. "I'll be praying for you." To his delight, she covered his hand with her own.

"I'd appreciate that." She looked down for a moment, then met his gaze. "I allowed some things to come between me and the Lord for awhile, but we're back on good terms again." Her smile sent a rush of joy through him that eclipsed his pleasure at the capture of one of the robbers.

"Ruth?" Sydney poked her head into their room. "Alice Duncan is downstairs asking for you."

The moment she'd dreaded had come. Ruth forced herself off the bed and descended the stairs.

Alice waited in the back room, her red-rimmed eyes telling Ruth all she needed to know about her friend's state of mind.

"You've heard about Emmett?" At Ruth's nod, she broke down and wept. "I should have known he didn't come by that money by any honest means. But I wanted to believe it for Emily's sake."

Ruth wrapped her arms around the distraught woman. She held her close, her guilt mounting with every ragged sob that tore from Alice's throat. Following their plan to maintain the lady Pinkertons' covers, Gus Drummond had made the arrest. It would be simple to let him take credit for Duncan's capture. It would be the easy thing. But it wouldn't be right.

"Sit down, Mrs. Duncan." She steered her to a chair and knelt beside her. "I have something to tell you."

"How did she take it?" Mark settled Ruth on the couch in his office and sat next to her.

Ruth fixed her gaze on her lap and twined a handkerchief between her fingers. "Better than I expected. She doesn't hate me, at least. I know I did the right thing, but she's going to have an unspeakably hard time of it, and it's all due to my meddling."

"Not meddling, duty." He lifted a tear from her cheek with the back of his finger. His touch sent a warm glow clear down to her toes. "You came out here to do a job, and you succeeded. Alice and Emily are Emmett's victims, not yours."

"That's kind, but I can't ignore the facts. Now she won't even have the money Emmett gave her for Emily. She's giving it back. Every penny. I just wish I could give her enough to get Emily the help she needs."

His arm slid behind her shoulders. "Why don't I take care of that?"

Ruth sat erect and swiveled to face him. "What do you mean?"

"Drummond recovered Emmett's share of the money. I got back enough to meet the next payroll. That means I won't have to use up all my savings, so I'll have some cash on hand. It might as well go toward helping Emily."

Gratitude welled up within her. "That's a wonderful plan. Maybe you'll get the rest of your money back soon."

"Not as long as Emmett refuses to name his accomplices." He scooted toward her, closing the gap between them. "Since the rest of the robbers are still at large, does that mean you'll stay on the case? Or will you be going back to Chicago right away?"

Ruth caught her breath and tried to focus on his words rather than his nearness. "When we first came here, my goal was to prove my ability to Mr. Fletcher, then go back and demand my fair share of cases. But now. . ."

His fingers teased at a ringlet over her left temple. "Now?"

She stared up at him, trying to concentrate. "Something changed inside me since the day I stepped off the train. When I thought about packing my bags and heading back East, I realized Chicago isn't home anymore. This is."

That maple syrup gaze bored into hers. "Then you'll be staying?"

"I thought I'd ask Alice to come work at the shop. She's a wonder with a needle, and we truly do need help to keep up with all the sewing. Besides, it will free Sydney to continue the investigation." She smiled. "I believe my days as a detective are over."

"It sounds to me as though you'll need a new career." His breath stirred a loose strand of hair at her temple. "What would you say to becoming the wife of a mine owner?"

Ruth studied the face of the man she loved. Placing her hand against his cheek, she traced the crease there with her thumb. "As long as he's the owner of the Redemption Mine, I think that's a fine idea."

CAROL COX

In addition to writing, Carol's time is devoted to keeping up with her college-age son's schedule, home schooling her young daughter, and serving as a church pianist, youth worker, and 4-H leader. The Arizona native loves any activity she can share with her family in addition to her own pursuits in crafts and local history. She also has had several novels and novellas published. Carol and her family make their home in northern Arizona.

Rescuing Sydney

by Lisa Harris

Dedication

To my husband, Scott, who has always believed in me.
My mom, sister, and three precious children,
who tirelessly cheer me on.
My wonderful crit buddies, who not only correct my work,
but encourage and motivate me on a daily basis.
And, most of all, to my heavenly Father,
who rescued me with His unconditional love.

*I sought the LORD, and he heard me,
and delivered me from all my fears.*
PSALM 34:4

Chapter 1

T he train thundered beneath John Langston as it rounded the bend, throwing him against the man next to him. His jaw muscles tensed at the reality that his grandfather's gold watch had vanished into the pockets of one of the masked bandits. He'd heard of the rash of train heists that had plagued the Denver & Rio Grande line, but he never dreamed he'd become one of their victims.

The train rocked to the left as it followed the curve of the tracks, hugging the steep mountain cliff. A smartly dressed woman stumbled down the aisle, brushing against his shoulder. His eyes narrowed, trying to place the ravishing redhead. *Sydney de Clermont?* His heart quickened at the recognition. Surely this wasn't André's younger sister?

He hesitated, contemplating the wisdom of leaving his seat while the train was being robbed. The woman stepped outside the car, and he made a hasty decision. Her face had been whiter than a fresh Colorado snowfall, and he'd never been one to ignore a woman in distress.

He picked up his canvas bag, rather than leave it next to

the man beside him, and hurried toward the back of the car. The train lurched. He grabbed one of the seats to catch his balance. Whatever he did, he needed to get Sydney back inside the train where she wasn't in danger of the robbers catching her—or of falling off. If memory served him correctly, Sydney had never been known for her grace.

He stepped into the bright sunlight. The train's brakes squealed. A woman screamed, and a streak of white flashed in front of him. His breath caught in his throat as she tumbled to the rocky ground below, rolling to a stop a few yards from the tracks.

John pulled his pack closer to his body and jumped off the train.

Sydney heard the whoops of men and the galloping of horses. In the Colorado sunshine, she caught a glimpse of the riders and their mounts flying into the distance, chasing the ghost of the departed train through the mountainous terrain.

She touched her ankle and winced at the sore spot, but the throb in her leg didn't stop her from slowly standing. She knew she'd wake up in the morning with a pack of bruises and sore muscles, but she shoved the pain aside, thankful nothing seemed broken. The train had been robbed, and there were far more pressing matters at hand.

Falling off the railroad car had not been her intention, but the graceless descent from the train might prove to be a stroke of luck. Her partner, Ruth Hunnicut, would no doubt be worried, but what better way to search for evidence than to pursue the robbers from the ground? Her job as a Pinkerton operative was to leave no stone unturned, or as Allan Pinkerton's own famous motto went, "We never sleep."

Capturing this notorious group of train robbers was the reason she'd taken the westbound from Chicago to Windmere Falls in the first place. Her own brother, killed a year ago during a train heist, had given her the determination to become one of "The Pinks." She'd pledged to bring criminals to justice. Finally, she'd been given her first assignment outside the dingy Chicago office.

"You're lucky I didn't break my neck coming after you."

Sydney whirled around. "John Langston?"

He smiled, boyish dimples appearing beneath pale gray eyes. "I thought you might need some help."

How could she begin to describe the mixture of feelings John's surprise appearance brought to the surface? He'd been her brother's best friend, a part of their family. Then he'd gone off to school two years ago, and she hadn't seen him since. Not even when André died.

Help was the last thing she wanted from John Langston. Besides, she had work to do. "Thank you, but I'm fine." She took an uneven step forward and stopped to check her left shoe, now missing a heel.

"Where are you headed?" John asked.

Sydney sneezed and shoved a stray curl under her feathered hat, which she'd retrieved from the ground. "Windmere Falls. All I have to do is follow the tracks. It can't be too far."

John chewed on a blade of grass and let out a low laugh. "You do realize, don't you, that you can't just follow the tracks to the next town? There's a bridge for the train up ahead."

Sydney eyed the rocky terrain and grabbed a handful of her skirt's soft material in each hand. "Then I'll go under it."

"The land's pretty rough, and we're both headed in the same direction." John patted his canvas bag. "Might as well go together."

Sydney knew her protests sounded ridiculous. Anger from the belief that he'd let her brother down clashed with lingering remnants of a schoolgirl infatuation. She pushed away the memories. Dozens of people on the train were depending on her to find whatever evidence she could. She couldn't afford to blow her first assignment.

"I'm sorry," she said, determined to curb her temper. "You just caught me off guard."

"Don't worry about it." John swung his bag higher on his shoulder. "Won't take more than a couple hours, I'm thinking. We should get into town before dark."

The surrounding aspens were beautiful, but the thought of being alone after dark sent shivers down her spine. Pinkerton detective or not, she wasn't prepared to fight a bear or whatever else might be hiding in this wild country.

"There is one other thing," John said. Sydney followed his glance to her black shoes, barely peeking out from under the hem of her skirt. He crouched down in front of her. "May I?"

John reached for her foot with the good shoe, forcing her to place a hand on each of his shoulders for balance. Before she could object, he'd snapped off the remaining heel.

"That should do it." He stood and took a step back.

"Now, we'd better get going. Once the sun drops behind the mountains, it's going to get downright chilly, and I'd like to be sitting in front of a hot meal by then."

Sydney opened her mouth in protest, then quickly shut it. Stranded in the Colorado wilderness with John Langston might prove to be as unsettling as riding a train during a robbery.

Chapter 2

John Langston had changed little since the last time Sydney saw him. He walked beside her, a lean, solid figure at home in this rough country. Dark hair curled slightly over his ears and under his collar. His strong hands, rough from working outside, the cleft chin, and those narrow brows were all familiar features to her. She'd known John for a dozen years—from a distance.

"Were you traveling alone?" she asked.

"Yes." A branch snapped under John's boots as he led the way down the narrow canyon, the trestle bridge looming above them.

Sydney spoke her concerns aloud. "I had a friend on board. I hope she's all right." There had been no gunshots, but that didn't take away the lingering apprehension for Ruth and the other passengers' lives.

"From what I saw, the men seemed more concerned about the amount of loot they could take than injuring anyone."

"There's been a rash of train heists lately." Sydney bit her lip. She didn't want to appear overly interested in the robberies, but maybe John had noticed something she'd missed. She chose her next words carefully. "I wonder if there's anything we saw that could help the sheriff catch the bandits."

"I can't say that I noticed anything outstanding about the men. Before I knew what happened, they'd taken my grandfather's gold watch and gone on to the next car."

"I'm sorry. It must have meant a lot to you."

"It did."

The men had hurried through the cars, grabbing jewelry and money from vulnerable passengers. There hadn't been enough time to study the robbers. Sydney categorized the facts she'd gathered during the robbery and sighed at the lack of information. Four men. Two were short and stocky, the other two, tall and lanky.

Nothing stood out. She had failed to detect a characteristic gait or distinct mannerism that might prove to be helpful in capturing the fugitives. Nothing had been out of the ordinary—likely the way the thieves planned it. Plain handkerchiefs masked the lower part of their faces. The brown pants and overcoats they wore could have been owned by half the men in the territory.

Sydney and John continued to walk, with only the sound of their footsteps and the occasional cry of a bird breaking the silence. She glanced at him and braved forward with a question—a difficult one at best.

"Why didn't you come to the funeral?"

He scrambled up a slight embankment and turned to help her before answering. "I received a telegram from your mother the day after Christmas."

"André died Christmas morning." Sydney's voice quivered at the memory of her brother.

"Did he suffer?" John stopped and looked at her, his mouth drawing into a tight line.

She shook her head. "He died instantly."

"My mother had a stroke five days before Christmas."

A tremor of guilt shot through Sydney's heart. "How is she?"

"She died a month later. That's why I never made it to the funeral. I took care of her those last few weeks. I sent your parents a letter, but they must not have received it."

The anger in Sydney's heart melted. All this time she'd been angry at John for not being there for her family, never knowing what he'd been going through.

"When I heard about André," John said, "well. . .I found the loss difficult to handle."

Sydney held up her hem a few inches and stepped over a fallen tree limb. She caught his tender expression. "I was furious with you for not coming, and I don't even know why. You were just someone else to be angry with besides God."

"God didn't kill your brother, Sydney."

"I know." She closed her eyes for a moment. She did know—somewhere deep inside—but the truth didn't always take away the pain. "André told me you were going to school to become a minister."

"I just finished last month. I've been asked to work in Windmere Falls. The pastor there was injured in a hunting accident and needs someone to help out temporarily."

Sydney forced a neutral expression. Before André died, she believed preaching God's Word and giving students an education were the two noblest professions on earth. One educated the mind and the other the heart. But now she wasn't sure. Where had God been on that fateful day when André took a bullet to his heart?

She didn't want John to know the extent of her anger toward God or the doubts that continually haunted her. He wouldn't understand how everything she believed in had been ripped out from under her when André died. Best she simply change the subject. "I'm sure you didn't intend on jumping off a train today."

John laughed. "Didn't you know? Ladies in distress are my specialty?"

"So you think I'm a lady in distress?" Sydney regretted the sudden iciness in her voice. She had fought for independence from her parents and didn't want to have to convince John she could take care of herself. She was a professional. A Pinkerton.

John must not have noticed the sting in her voice, or if he did, he chose to ignore it. "What about you? Why did you decide to come to Colorado?"

"I'm going to work in Windmere Falls as a seamstress. I've been traveling with a friend, Ruth Hunnicut. We're starting a business together." She didn't want to lie about her position as a Pinkerton agent, but she also couldn't give away her assignment. Even if he was an old family friend.

"What do your parents think of you living so far from home?"

Sydney swallowed hard at the mention of her parents. "They weren't thrilled with the idea, did everything they could to stop me from coming, but I'm twenty-one now. Old enough to decide what I want to do."

He smiled, and once again she remembered her schoolgirl infatuation. He looked just as handsome, just as charming with his rugged good looks as he had years ago. She stopped for a moment, pulling at her left shoe. Uncomfortable to begin with, they'd become even worse on the rocky terrain.

Standing straight, she tugged on her white shirtwaist, now a dingy gray, and shook her head. What had come over her? She'd been hired to do a job. Just because John Langston once held a corner of her heart didn't mean he had any claim on it today.

John looked back as Sydney struggled up the slight incline behind him. He had to give her credit. She hadn't complained about the heat, the bugs, or the rough terrain. Not once.

Seeing her again brought back memories of her family's home outside Chicago—familiar and inviting. Mr. and Mrs. de Clermont had always made him feel like part of the family. "How are your parents?"

"The past year's been difficult," she said, "but they're no strangers to hard times."

"I wish I could have been there."

John turned and caught the look of pain that flickered across her face. Reddish hair shimmered with golden glints, giving her an angelic look. Why had he never noticed her beauty? Had she changed that much in the past two years, or had he just been too busy to notice? Even with a smudged shirt and a few pine needles mingling with her curls, she looked striking.

He maneuvered through the trail of aspen a few steps ahead of her. In a few short months these trees would be draped in gold. Living in Chicago hadn't lessened his love for the mountains. He'd grown up less than a hundred miles from here and loved the outdoors—the smell of fish frying over an open fire, sweet wild berries eaten by the handfuls, a quick dip in a frigid stream.

Sydney, on the other hand, possessed all the characteristics of a city girl. Her clothes, smart and stylish, hadn't been fashioned for an excursion through the woods. He laughed to himself. From outward appearances, they were total opposites.

But there were other qualities that impressed him, including the strong faith in God that she possessed growing up. Was Sydney the answer to his prayers for a God-fearing wife? The unanticipated question startled him.

A piercing scream rang through the trees, interrupting his thoughts. His heart lurched within his chest. He dropped his bag and ran to Sydney.

Chapter 3

John heard the unmistakable clacking noise of a porcupine. "Sydney?"

She stood still, arms stiff against her sides, eyes riveted on the ground. "What was that?"

"A porcupine. Don't move. You've got some quills stuck in your dress." He examined the bottom of her skirt, where a dozen or so barbed quills had burrowed into the soft fabric. Fortunately, none had penetrated the skin. "I'm going to have to take them out."

"I've never seen such an animal," Sydney exclaimed in disgust.

After making sure he'd located all the quills, he sat her down on a rock and slowly began to pull them out, one by one. "It's a good thing these didn't go past the material. From what I hear, impalement from a porcupine quill is quite painful."

"Sounds horrible." She leaned over and examined one of the quills.

John tried to stop the laughter, but it erupted before he

could control himself. "Sydney, believe it or not, porcupines are very slow and docile animals. In fact, I'm surprised you saw one, let alone got close enough for this to happen. What did you do? Trip over the poor creature?"

He didn't miss the fire in her eyes as she glared at him. "I bent to fix my shoe."

Gently, he pulled out another quill. "Normally, they're tricky to spot. They usually stay hidden in the backwoods."

"I guess I'm bound to be forever in your debt."

He grinned at the tart tone of her voice and pulled out the last quill. "Worse things have happened, you know."

He chuckled to himself at her resolve for independence, and somehow he liked the idea of her being indebted to him.

❧

Sydney ignored her parched throat, determined to keep up with John. She was anxious to reach town, where she could receive firsthand news of the robbery. Maybe Ruth had noticed something in her absence.

John interrupted the comfortable silence that had fallen between them. "I thought you might want to freshen up. There's a stream ahead."

Sydney followed his gaze through the trees and saw a glimmer of water sparkling through the pines.

"I figure we can't be too far from town at this point," he said. "Another hour or so, and we should be sitting down for an overdue meal."

The thought of dinner made her mouth water. "Sounds wonderful to me."

She made her way through the underbrush toward the stream, thankful he'd been considerate enough to give her a few minutes of privacy. Water never tasted so good. She let the icy liquid fill her mouth, delighting in the coolness as it ran down her throat.

The beauty around her was a sharp contrast from Chicago's crowded streets and buildings. The clear stream trickled musically down its path, wandering over rocks and pebbles.

"The heavens declare the glory of God; and the firmament sheweth his handywork." The verse from Psalm 19, memorized in her childhood, came unexpectedly and unwanted.

Sydney forced a tight rein on her thoughts. She knew the day would come when she would have to confront her doubts in God and face the pain and bitterness she had allowed to seep into her heart.

But not today.

Besides, had she already forgotten her assignment? Here she was, following the probable trail the train robbers had taken toward Windmere Falls, and so far she hadn't found anything.

Determined to concentrate on the work at hand, she turned around. Her eyes scanned the area for anything out of place, some sign that the thieves might have passed this way. If they had stopped for a drink, this would be the most logical place. The sun shone through the trees, and something glimmered on the ground half a dozen steps to her right.

Sydney crossed the short distance and picked up a man's button. Rubbing the shiny silver piece between her fingers, she slowly continued to scan the vicinity. Ten steps away from the river produced something else. An empty payroll bag.

She played the plausible scenario over in her mind. One or more of the men comes for a drink. A loose button, gripping bare threads, falls to the ground. Sydney looked again at the unique button with its etched star pattern. She recalled the faint smell of alcohol as the four bandits passed through the train car. Dropping the payroll bag had been the mistake of an overconfident and possibly intoxicated man. Obtuse, but not the first time a criminal had left evidence near the scene of the crime.

She worked her way toward the stream. This time she found several sets of footprints on the ground besides her own. Mulling over the possible evidence, Sydney made her way back to where John waited for her. Maybe getting stranded in the woods would prove to be a stroke of luck after all.

"Sydney," John said.

She raised her brows in surprise at the sight of a man on horseback beside John.

"It seems your friend, Miss Hunnicut, helped organize a search party," John said. "This is Deputy Charles Bennett."

The deputy dismounted from his horse and stood before her, hands resting on his holster. "Glad to see you're all right, Ma'am. Your friend's a bit worried."

Sydney sneezed. "Thanks to Mr. Langston, I'm fine."

"I'd be happy to escort both of you back into town. It's not far, and I'm sure you're ready for a hot meal." The deputy's glance rested on the bag in Sydney's hands, and a puzzled look crossed his face. "A payroll bag?"

"I found it down by the stream." She saw suspicion flash in his eyes. *Surely he doesn't think we've been involved in the heist.*

"The train you were on was robbed, the payroll stolen." His glance shifted to John. "I'm sorry, but I'm going to have to place the two of you under arrest for suspected train robbery."

Chapter 4

Sydney paced the length of the room, wondering how long she and John would be forced to remain in the jail cell. Twilight began to melt into darkness, and her stomach reminded her that except for some of John's dried jerky, she hadn't eaten anything for several hours. Grasping one of the metal bars that secured the cell, she looked down the small hall toward the front office.

Besides the cell, the jail boasted nothing more than a desk, a couple of wooden chairs, and some wanted posters nailed to the wall. A stark contrast from the police headquarters in Chicago. Considering the fact that Gus Drummond had to send for reinforcements, Sydney wondered about the quality of Windmere Falls's law officers. The sheriff and his deputy had left over an hour ago to verify their stories—an inconvenience, to say the least.

She pushed back a strand of loose hair and tucked it under her hat. Hopefully, Ruth had been able to secure her bags and have them taken to the hotel. Right now, all she wanted was a long, hot bath and a clean set of clothes.

Reaching into her pocket, Sydney fingered the silver button, sighed with frustration, and started pacing again. The facts whirled through her tired mind like the wheels on a train.

She'd had no choice but to give up the payroll bag to the deputy, but at least this one piece of evidence had gone unobserved. Her thumb traced the distinct star embossed on the front. She had no reason to mistrust the sheriff and his deputy, but that didn't mean she was ready to relinquish her finding.

John sat in the corner on a wooden bench, his elbows resting against his thighs. She'd enjoyed their conversations on politics, the future of the railroad, and especially his take on the robberies.

His theory was that it was an inside job. Four years earlier, two brakemen masterminded a train robbery that yielded over $20,000 and left the express manager dead. It was a good conjecture she would be sure to discuss with Mr. Drummond.

"Sydney?"

Pulled out of her contemplation, she turned to face John. A smudge of dirt smeared across his cheek. She'd resisted the urge all afternoon to wipe it away. "I'm sorry. What?"

He stood and shoved his hands inside his pockets before leaning back against the cool brick wall that encased them on three sides. "I have a feeling they'll be coming to let us out any minute, and I wanted to ask you a question."

Sydney lowered her brow, curious at his apparent nervousness. "Of course. Anything."

"I'd like to call on you once we both get settled in." He

cleared his throat. "That is. . .if you don't mind."

John had always been one to come straight to the point, though his forwardness on this issue surprised her. "I'm not sure, I. . ." Her voice trailed off as she turned to the small barred window opening where a silvery moon shone into the cell.

John Langston wanted to court her?

Her eyes widened in surprise at the thought. Surely she was letting her imagination get the best of her. He had been close to her family for years and had been André's best friend growing up. It was only natural he'd want to check on her now and then.

No doubt, being far away from friends and family, he'd enjoy seeing someone from home. Maybe dinner at the hotel or a ride on a Sunday afternoon. It would be perfectly acceptable. After all, John had always seen her as André's little sister. Why should anything be different now—even though she was all grown up? Besides, despite her previous attraction to him, thoughts of romance would only get in the way of her investigation.

But as friends. . .

"Of course," she said. "There's no reason why two friends can't see each other now and then."

"Friends—"

Metal keys clanked against the lock of the jail cell. Sydney turned and frowned at the interruption. What had John planned to say? Thoughts of freedom quickly outweighed her disappointment.

"I apologize for the inconvenience." Sheriff Masters, a tall man with a weathered hat and silver badge, opened the cell door. Sydney stepped out ahead of John, thankful to be free.

"My deputy was just doing his job," Masters continued. "Can't be too careful these days with this gang of train robbers on the loose."

"And you think one of them is a woman?" Sydney feigned disgust, hoping to get more information out of the man.

"Not likely, but with no good descriptions from eye witnesses, we're bound by law to follow any leads, Ma'am."

"Of course."

Sydney and John followed him down the short hall and into the front office, where the sheriff set the key ring on a nail against the wall. He folded his arms across his broad chest. "Again, my apologies. Your stories checked out. You're both free to go."

"Ruth will be worried sick, I'm sure." Sydney managed to stifle a sneeze. "I think I'll go straight to the hotel and see if she's there."

Sydney turned as Deputy Bennett stepped into the office. "I'd be more than willing to escort you, Ma'am."

John watched the deputy who arrested them saunter into the room. He'd changed into a fashionable chesterfield overcoat and bowler hat and looked more like he was ready to go courting than chase down a pack of outlaws.

Sydney smiled at the man, her green eyes sparkling in the light of the kerosene lamp. "I would appreciate that, Deputy. I'm sure my friend must be beside herself with worry."

"It's the least I can do to make up for arresting you." Charles Bennett ignored John and took hold of Sydney's arm.

Several soft red curls framed her face. John noticed a

slight limp in her gait. Despite their afternoon hike, she still looked beautiful—and he obviously wasn't the only one to notice. Sydney told John good-bye, her dress swishing behind her as she headed out the door.

John grabbed his bag off the desk and turned to the sheriff. "If you can point me in the direction of the parsonage, I'd be obliged."

Sheriff Masters led him outside onto the boardwalk and pointed west of town, where the last shaft of sun had long since slipped behind the mountains. "The church is on the other end of Main Street. Hosea Griffin and his family live just beyond a half-mile or so. You can't miss it."

By the time John turned back to Sydney, she was crossing the street with the deputy. John tried never to make quick judgments of people's character, but something about Charles Bennett bothered him. He pushed away an unwelcome pang of jealousy as the deputy opened the door of the hotel for Sydney, his hand resting briefly against the small of her back.

He followed the boardwalk down the busy street, lit only by the smoky glow of gaslights and the full moon above. The silhouettes of the mountains loomed beyond, a distant shadow in the night.

Sydney had obviously been taken aback by his question in the jail cell. How could he have been so forward? Feelings of attraction had been heightened by the drama of the afternoon. She was right. It was much too soon to think of her as anything other than a friend. Still, Sydney de Clermont needed someone to watch over her in this town. That provided reason enough to call on her as soon as they both settled in.

Chapter 5

To weeks after her arrival in Windmere Falls, Sydney sat in the dress shop surrounded by articles of clothing waiting to be mended. She still didn't have any firm leads on the robbery. Thinking Mabel Hawkins, the town gossip, might be a good informant, she'd listened to rumors of banker Will Bowen's new stable boy, Deputy Bennett's interest in schoolteacher Rachel Parker, and Miss Hawkins's own account of the train robberies. After putting up with her ramblings for a good hour, she concluded that the source of the woman's information was merely her own vivid imagination.

Sydney set the cotton plaid dress down, pleased with her work. She was a good seamstress, but she longed to prove to the world she was just as good a detective.

The bell on the front door jingled, breaking the silence of the afternoon. Expecting Ruth, returning from her errand at the telegraph office, Sydney was surprised to see John enter the small establishment.

"You'd think that living in the same town, we'd see more

of each other." A broad grin covered his face.

She swallowed hard. Those piercing gray eyes of his were enough to make her forget her newly formed resolution. It wouldn't take much to fall for John, except she wasn't looking for a husband. And even if she were, she certainly wasn't material for a preacher's wife. She hadn't even told Ruth about John, despite her friend's barrage of questions. Sometimes the past simply needed to be forgotten. The best thing she could do was stay busy and focus on the real reason she came to Colorado.

"I'm just now feeling settled in." She stood and tapped her fingers against the wooden counter.

"The shop looks great." John took off his hat and glanced around at the tables and shelves that neatly displayed colorful bolts of fabric and notions. "You and Miss Hunnicut have done a nice job fixing it up."

"Thanks. Did you need something?" Sydney grimaced at the impression her words must have left. He'd come to see how she was doing, and she'd spoken to him as if he were one of her customers. "What I mean is, are you settled in as well?"

John leaned against the counter, rotating the brim of his hat with his left hand. "I certainly can't complain. The Griffin family has made me feel right at home. Every night it's fried chicken and mashed potatoes, or ham and gravy. Mrs. Griffin's a fine cook."

Sydney laughed, trying to ease the unspoken tension between them. "You could benefit from a bit of fattening up."

John patted his stomach. "Apparently Mrs. Griffin thinks the same thing."

He looked at her, his eyes full of concern. She knew what his next statement would be before he spoke it.

"I've missed seeing you at church." He held the hat still between his hands. "I preached my first sermon in town last Sunday. We had quite a crowd."

"That's wonderful." She'd tried to come up with an excuse days earlier, knowing she'd run into him and he'd ask her why she hadn't attended. Problem was, she didn't have an excuse—unless anger toward God counted, and she wasn't ready to confess that to the handsome preacher. "The dress shop has taken up so much of my time."

"Maybe next Sunday. Mrs. Griffin said I could invite a guest for Sunday dinner. You'd be more than welcome."

She wouldn't lie, but she couldn't make any promises. "We'll see."

"I think she said she's making cherry pie."

Sydney laughed. "Cherry has always been my favorite."

She looked at him, trying to convince herself that her heart wasn't racing faster than normal and her hands were clammy from the warm summer afternoon and not his lopsided smile. Why did he have to be here now, in this town? If only things had been different. If André hadn't died and she wasn't here on a case trying to prove herself. . .

"I guess you're working this afternoon?" John asked.

Sydney pointed to the pile of clothes to be mended. She needed to finish the standing collar on Rachel Parker's new day dress, alter the bodice of Hannah Ray's riding habit, and hem a pair of the sheriff's trousers. There was even an eggplant-colored skirt from Victoria Barrett-Ames, one of the other Pinkerton operatives working the case. It had been a subtle way to pass on a message from Gus Drummond.

"The pile never seems to end."

The door jingled a second time, and Deputy Bennett entered the room carrying several shirts, the second batch this week. Sydney sneezed twice, then forced a smile at the deputy, whose cologne assaulted her senses.

"Miss de Clermont," he said, placing the garments in front of her. "I find that I'm in need of your services once again."

The two men greeted each other guardedly, and John moved to leave. "I'll come by another time, Sydney. Take care."

She nodded her thanks and watched John leave the shop, his fleeting glance one of concern.

"More shirts, Deputy?"

"You did such a fine job the last time." Deputy Bennett folded his arms across his chest.

"It was hardly a show of my expertise. Two loose buttons and a frayed hem."

"Maybe I should commission a shirt, possibly two."

Sydney nodded and glanced at the door, wishing Ruth would return. "We have a nice selection of fabric if you're interested."

Despite the fact she found the deputy's forward manner offensive, she wouldn't miss this opportunity to find out more regarding the law office's take on the train robberies.

"I suppose you've been working hard, trying to track down suspects for the robbery case." She gave him her most innocent look, attempting to leave the impression that she was taken by his heroic efforts to save the townspeople from a vicious gang of thieves.

Bennett's chest rose and a smile crossed his face. "You know it's our first priority to ensure the safety of this town, especially the women."

Helpless women, no doubt. She inhaled another whiff of his strong cologne and continued. "Any leads? It's a shame there are men here who are destroying this town financially because of their greed."

"Four train robberies in four months, including the one you were on. You're right, it is a shame."

Sydney looked over the shirts he handed her to repair, pretending to examine them closely, while all the time taking careful note of any information he might have.

"We brought in Jeb Lawson for questioning the day after the last robbery, but it turned out he had a solid alibi. A shame, really. I'd hoped for a break in the case."

"Any idea if this is an inside job?"

The deputy shook his head. "You know what my opinion on all this is?" He rested his hands on the counter and leaned forward. "I've had my suspicions on Harold Butler for some time now."

Sydney raised her eyes, meeting his gaze. "I don't believe I've met him yet."

"He's a big talker. You know, the kind who always has a lot to say, but never really says anything at all."

Sydney smiled back at the deputy and said nothing. Yes, she knew the type.

"Last Friday night I caught him snooping around the

train station. Wasn't any reason for him to be down there so late. Weren't any trains due until morning. The next day, I saw him send a telegraph. Found out it was to Denver. Passing on information, I'd say."

"That's all very interesting, Deputy Bennett." Sydney brushed an imaginary piece of lint from one of the shirts. "When would you like these back?"

"First of next week will be fine." The deputy started for the door, then turned back to her. "I did have one other thing to ask you, Miss de Clermont. The hotel makes a downright fabulous chicken and dumplings, and I was wondering if you'd care to join me for dinner Sunday afternoon?"

"Thank you, but I won't be able to this time."

The thought tempted her, but only for the purpose of gathering information. Something told her if she accepted the deputy's invitation, he'd expect more than just coffee with his dessert.

Besides, if she were honest with herself, there was only one man with whom she wanted to eat Sunday dinner.

After leaving Sydney at the dress shop, John crossed the street and entered the Windmere Falls Mercantile. He studied the list Mrs. Griffin had given him, his real reason for coming into town, but his thoughts were far from fresh eggs and flour.

A pretty brunette looked up from behind the counter, her bright smile contagious. "Can I help you, Pastor Langston?"

"Miss Alexander, isn't it?"

She smiled and nodded her head. "You have a good memory, especially considering the fact you've met quite a number of people since your arrival."

He matched her smile. "A necessary skill for a minister, I'm learning. And for your offer to help. . ." John handed her the scrunched piece of paper and gave her a sheepish smile. "I'm sure you'd do a lot better getting what Mrs. Griffin requested than I would. If you don't mind."

"Of course not."

John let out a breath of relief. "I do need a new pair of gloves."

Miss Alexander nodded toward the back of the store. "You should be able to find what you need in the back corner."

John made his way past a neatly organized aisle of dry good items and stopped at a small display of ready-made shirts, boots, and gloves. Miss Alexander was an extremely attractive woman who seemed to have a strong relationship with the Lord. She attended church along with several other unattached young women who had made his acquaintance since his arrival. But none of them interested him enough to take a second look. Not like Sydney.

I never expected to feel this way about Sydney, Lord. Ever since he jumped off the train after her, he'd found himself fighting a strong attraction toward her. Before, she'd been André's little sister, but the couple of times he'd seen her lately only reinforced the reality that Sydney was all grown up.

As a man who felt called to serve God full-time, how could he be interested in a woman whose faith was obviously floundering? That, however, didn't stop the fact that she occupied the majority of his waking hours—and his dreams at night.

John decided on a pair of black gloves, forcing himself to push aside thoughts of the redheaded beauty. His time in Windmere Falls was temporary. In a couple of months, he'd be going back to Chicago—leaving Sydney behind.

He'd have to start praying hard for Sydney's spiritual situation and for a way to quiet the stirring of his heart.

Chapter 6

Sydney scanned the horizon as gray clouds emerged from behind the distant mountains. A sharp breeze tugged at her hair, and she could feel the moisture in the air. She hadn't counted on an afternoon storm, but there would be plenty of time to visit Mrs. Norton and get back to town before the rain began.

Today, in spite of the finished shirtwaist she carried in her leather pouch for Mrs. Norton, her plans had nothing to do with her undercover occupation and everything to do with detective work. The arrest of Emmett Duncan from Ruth's efforts had done little to solve the case, considering the fact there had been another train robbery yesterday afternoon. The payroll had been stolen again as well as many of the passengers' personal belongings.

Will Bowen, the banker, had even gathered a small group to go to the sheriff's office and voice their protests that something had to be done to stop the robberies. Little did the townspeople know, besides Mr. Drummond, that there were already four other Pinkerton agents just as anxious to catch the crooks.

Or should she say *three* other detectives working the case? Sydney didn't oppose Ruth's decision to marry Mark Chandler, but lately Ruth would much rather talk about wedding dress styles than leads on the case—and a lead was exactly what she had today.

Following John's theory that at least one person who worked on the train was a part of the robberies, she had done some investigating. One name stood out. Philip Norton had been working on the train as a brakeman each time it had been robbed. And, according to Mabel Hawkins, he was a troublemaker. This statement had been confirmed by Deputy Bennett, who arrested him once for intoxication.

Hopefully, John's hunch was right, and before long, they'd be able to close the case. Sydney kicked a pinecone as she walked, sighing deeply. Why did everything always seem to lead back to John? It had been several weeks since she'd talked to him. She'd stayed busy with the case, managing to avoid him, but one day she knew he'd confront her as to why she hadn't been to church.

She forced back his image and allowed a sense of determination to take its place. She'd help bring in the men who'd caused so much turmoil for the town of Windmere Falls and the surrounding area. Then she'd go back to Chicago and never have to see John again.

A drop of rain hit her on the forehead, and she looked up at the darkening sky, surprised at how fast the storm approached. Another bead of water dotted the end of her nose, and she stopped, wondering which would be quicker—turning

around and heading back toward town or continuing on to
Mrs. Norton's. Lightning splintered through a group of trees
beside her. Whatever she decided to do, it seemed the
chances of arriving at either place without getting drenched
were slim.

Lightning cracked ahead of him, and John eyed the incom-
ing storm clouds, nudging his horse to quicken its pace. The
last thing he needed today was to get caught in a downpour.
His meeting with Philip Norton had not gone well. Mrs.
Norton, a sweet widow who should have set the law down on
her only son years ago, had not helped matters. At twenty-
four, the only thing the young man had going for him was a
job with the railroad. Other than that, it seemed he took
advantage of his mother at every turn, spending his money on
frivolous things, then depending on her to support him.

Taking care of a congregation was proving to be difficult
work, and today he didn't have the answers. Or maybe it was
simply that Norton wasn't willing to face the reality that he
needed to take responsibility for his life. If he didn't, it
wouldn't be long before he ended up on the wrong side of
the law.

Norton wasn't the only person John worried about.
Something was not right with Sydney. She'd always had a
solid belief in God, but after almost two months in Windmere Falls, she still hadn't been to church, and she'd been
avoiding him.

Up ahead, someone crouched under the shelter of a
Ponderosa pine. A splash of rain hit his shoulder. On his

mount, he could reach town before the storm broke loose, but on foot, one would never make it in time. As he drew closer, his eyes focused on the figure. His heart pounded within his chest as he recognized the woman with long red curls falling around her face.

Sydney.

Lightning struck again. The crack of white light sent a chill down his spine as he saw the unmistakable trail of blood running down the side of her face. He had to get her out of here. Lightning could be deadly—he'd seen it first-hand years ago when a man had been struck and killed.

John jumped off his horse and covered the rocky ground between them. She leaned against the tree, her lips pressed together and a hand to her forehead, trying to stop the bleeding.

"Are you all right?" He pushed back a strand of hair to reveal a small gash on her temple.

She nodded. "Lightning must have struck one of the trees. A branch fell and hit me."

John took a handkerchief out of his pocket and pressed it against her head. "Sydney de Clermont, I do believe you've done it again."

Her green eyes peered at him from under thick lashes. "Done what?"

"Managed to scare me half to death. Your life is anything but uneventful. What in the world are you doing out here with a storm coming?"

Her eyes widened. "I was simply on my way to deliver a shirtwaist to Mrs. Norton."

"Do you always make personal deliveries?"

"Do you always ask so many questions?"

He ignored her remark, his pulse racing at her closeness. A strand of her hair tickled his neck. Her lips were close enough to kiss. His good intention of keeping their relationship on a friendship basis was going to be difficult at this proximity.

"I've missed you, Sydney." No matter the strong attraction he fought at seeing her, he wouldn't deny he cared for her, even if it could only be as a family friend.

He caught her gaze again before her lashes lowered and she turned away. He couldn't dismiss the faraway look in her eyes and wished again she would share with him what was bothering her. Pulling the handkerchief away, he saw the bleeding had slowed.

He glanced up at the sky, where angry black clouds churned. "We've got to get to some shelter. The Griffin place is the closest." He put her hand on the cloth. "Keep pressing this against the wound."

Sydney nodded and held it to her temple.

"I'm waiting for our town's fine deputy to appear." He grinned and led her to his horse. "It seems like every time I see you, he shows up."

Her lips curled into a smile, and John fought the surge of emotion. He hadn't accounted for the reaction his heart would make over such a simple gesture.

"Deputy Bennett certainly is one to speak his mind."

He couldn't read her expression. "Has he been bothering you?"

Sydney's melodic laugh contrasted with the continual rumbling of the approaching storm. "Contrary to the opinions of most, I can take care of myself," she said without a hint of bitterness in her voice. It would take a miracle to tame Sydney's heart.

She eyed his horse, her head cocked to one side. "We're both going to ride her?"

Without saying anything, he mounted, then pulled her up behind him, praying they'd make it before the heavens exploded—along with his heart.

Chapter 7

Arriving at the Griffin home, Sydney waited until John slid off the horse. When her feet met the ground, his hands lingered around her waist. Her breathing quickened, and for a moment, she wanted him to kiss her. She tilted her head back, blinking away the raindrops, and stared into his eyes, forgetting the rain and lightning and feeling only the thundering of her heart.

"John Langston, you better get in here out of the rain right now!"

Sydney turned toward the house, where a plump woman waved them inside with the flick of a white towel. "Hurry up! Jackson will take care of the horse for you!"

Sydney chewed the inside of her lip. Had she lost all control of her emotions? Here she stood in the middle of a rainstorm, soaking wet, and all she could think of was that she desperately wanted John to kiss her.

She entered the house in front of John, hating the fact that her limbs were shaking more from his touch than the cold.

"I'm sorry about the water," John said to Mrs. Griffin as

he set his hat down on the wooden deacon's bench and noticed the pool of rainwater dripping from his clothes.

Mrs. Griffin smiled. "Don't you worry one bit. I've got some coffee on, and if you sit in front of the stove, you'll both be dry as a hot summer day before you know it."

"Mrs. Griffin, this is Sydney de Clermont. We know each other from Chicago," John said. "She was delivering an order to the Norton place when she got caught in the storm."

The older woman stopped and wiped her hands on her white apron, smiling at Sydney. "So you're Miss Hunnicut's friend, the other young lady who opened up the new dress shop in town?"

"Yes, Ma'am." Sydney warmed at the friendly welcome that matched the atmosphere of the house. The parlor was tastefully decorated in a deep rose color and sprinkled with splashes of pink and gray. The smell of cinnamon, mingling with coffee, drifted in from the kitchen.

"I keep telling Miss Hunnicut I'll stop by one of these days and have something made for Jackson, my son," Mrs. Griffin said as they entered the kitchen. "He's an only child, and his father and I tend to spoil him."

Sydney pushed a strand of wet hair out of her eyes and sat down in the offered chair next to the stove.

"Why, Child, you're hurt!" Mrs. Griffin hovered above Sydney, examining the small wound on her temple.

"It's nothing really." Sydney sat up straight. "I was hit by a limb."

"At least the bleeding seems to have stopped," Mrs. Griffin said. "You need a damp cloth to clean it with."

"I'm fine, really."

John smiled. "There's no use arguing with Mrs. Griffin. She's not happy unless she's helping someone."

The older woman nodded as though in agreement. She took a cloth, poured water over it, then handed it to Sydney.

"Sarah!" a masculine voice called from the other side of the house.

Mrs. Griffin turned toward the open doorway. "That would be Hosea, my husband. John, pour Sydney and yourself a cup of coffee while I see what he needs."

Mrs. Griffin bustled out of the room, while John poured two cups of steaming coffee from the pot on the stove. Summer in Chicago would have never left Sydney longing for the warmth of a stove, but in the mountains of Colorado, one was vulnerable to the cold at nearly any time of the year.

She set her pouch down on the floor beside her, uncomfortable with the extra attention. John handed her the hot drink, and their fingers brushed, rekindling the emotions in her soul. She sighed, annoyed with herself. She wasn't here to swoon over John Langston. Mentally, she willed her heartbeat to slow down.

"You never told me where you were going this morning." She took a sip of coffee, then puckered at the bitterness.

John handed her a small dish of sugar. "I'd been out to the Norton place."

"Really?" Maybe her afternoon wouldn't be in vain after all. If she asked subtle questions, she might get the information she needed.

"I can't go into detail, but Mrs. Norton has been having problems with her son. I hoped to help."

A man in his mid-twenties stepped into the kitchen and leaned against the doorframe. "Did you see Norton's saddle while you were out there? Picked it up last week in Denver."

"Afternoon, Jackson," John said, then introduced Sydney to the Griffinses' son. "No, he didn't show it to me."

Jackson Griffin gave a low whistle. "Had it custom-made. Next time you go out there, you need to see it and all the fancy embroidery."

Sydney formed her next words carefully. "Sounds rather expensive."

Jackson nodded his head. "Yes, Ma'am. Sure wish I could afford something like that."

The fair-haired son of the preacher left the room, and Sydney's interest rose at the news. She'd gotten the exact information she needed. She'd already learned that Philip Norton had opportunity as an insider on the railway. His taste for expensive items could be a motive. Of course, rumors and speculation weren't enough. She needed hard evidence to catch those involved.

"The sad thing is, Norton's mother needs a new stove for the coming winter," John said. "Not something frivolous like an expensive saddle."

"I suppose ministers are always dealing with difficult situations."

"That's what I'm learning."

"Speaking of difficult situations, have you heard anything about what happened yesterday with the robbery?"

Sydney asked. "I was thankful to hear no one was hurt."

From what she'd gathered, the eyewitnesses all seemed to have opposing stories, and as in past cases, the bandits were gone before anyone could react.

John shook his head. "I spoke to the sheriff this morning. He told me that in spite of catching one of the four men, they were no closer than they'd been six months ago."

"The thieves must be smart," Sydney said.

"Yes, but the law will get a break, and the outlaws' days of freedom will be numbered."

Her eyes roamed the cozy kitchen where yellow curtains bordered a large window overlooking snowcapped mountains. A vase of fresh wildflowers adorned the table, and on the wall behind it, a needlepoint picture hung, depicting a shepherd with his sheep. *The Lord is my shepherd* had been neatly stitched in black. Her heart stung with guilt. She hadn't clung to her Lord as her shepherd; instead, she'd been like the sheep that had gone astray.

"How are services going?" she asked, broaching a subject she would rather leave untouched, but knowing it was an important part of John's life.

He set his mug on the table and leaned back in his chair. "It's a small congregation, but a growing one. Of course, I only plan to stay until Pastor Griffin recovers from his accident."

"And then what?"

"I'd like to find a place where I can work full-time. More than likely, back in Chicago."

Sydney raised her brows, surprised at his decision. "You'd choose the big city over all this?"

"I was born in these mountains and spent a good part of my growing-up years living in the Rockies." John circled the rim of the cup with his fingers. "The beauty of the land can't be compared, but for a long time, I've felt that God was calling me to work in the city."

She pressed her hands against the table. She'd feel perfectly comfortable around him—if only her reservations toward God didn't stand between them.

He turned to her and caught her gaze. "Why are you running from God, Sydney?"

She opened her mouth, but no words came. The question cut far deeper than she ever could have imagined. Why had she allowed herself to turn away from her belief in God? She'd been raised in a Christian home, valued right from wrong, and knew the Scriptures.

"I don't know, I—"

An older man hobbled into the kitchen using a wooden cane. "John, I heard you got caught in the rain."

John looked up, a fleeting shadow of disappointment crossing his face. He smiled at the man. "You're the one who told me things were never dull here. Pastor Griffin, this is Sydney de Clermont. I knew her family back in Chicago."

Thankful for the reprieve from answering John's question, Sydney smiled and shook the older man's outstretched hand. "It's very nice to meet you."

"The wife's fighting me on this one, but I'm taking the wagon into town now that the rains have stopped." He slapped his thigh with his hand. "The old leg's healing, and it's about time I got out of this place for awhile."

"Are you sure you're up to getting out?" John asked.

"I'm feeling better today than I have in weeks. Besides, I'm plumb tired of letting this leg get in the way of what I'm here for."

Sydney glanced at John, then stood and wiped her hands on her damp skirt. "Would you mind if I came with you? I need to be getting back into town."

"I've never refused the company of a beautiful woman." He turned to John and winked. "Another couple of weeks and I'll be ready to get back to work."

The reality of his statement hit her hard. Before long, John would leave the small town of Windmere Falls. She couldn't help but wonder how she'd feel when he walked out of her life for good.

John looked at her as she turned to leave, a sad smile across his face. "Seek Him and He will answer you, Sydney. And if you ever change your mind, Mrs. Griffin's offer of cherry pie is still open."

Chapter 8

S ydney snuggled down in her bed and pulled the thick quilt around her as the rain pelted against the window in heavy drops. Ruth worked downstairs finishing the hem on a dress, giving Sydney the few moments of quiet she needed.

She'd found André's Bible in the bottom of her trunk. All her life she'd looked up to her brother, idolized him, and tried to be like him. He'd always been there for her—until that fateful day when a stranger ended his life with the squeeze of a trigger.

What was she so afraid of now? Why had she chosen to run from God at the time she needed Him most? She thumbed through the brittle pages of the worn Bible, searching for a place to start. What had John said? Seek Him and He will answer you? How long had it been since she'd sought His will and guidance for her life?

Her decision to leave home and become a Pinkerton had been motivated by her heart seeking revenge for her brother's death—not a yearning bathed in prayer. Two years ago, she never would have made an important decision without praying, but somehow she'd let anger and hate take over her heart and draw her away from her heavenly Father.

The truth hit hard. André would never have wanted her to live her life away from God because of his death. Her brother wasn't perfect, but he had always taken his relationship with Christ seriously—holding no grudges over those who did him wrong.

She had done just the opposite.

"Oh, Lord, I've wandered so far from Your arms." The words came slowly as Sydney struggled to pour out her fears. Like a prodigal daughter, she let the tears flow freely.

Turning to the Psalms, she allowed David's heartfelt words to work like a salve on her wounded heart. The verse John quoted stood out in chapter thirty-four: *"I sought the Lord, and he heard me, and delivered me from all my fears."*

She hadn't sought the Lord and His presence in her life, and she had made major decisions without laying them at His feet. Her faith had faltered, and she felt unworthy to call Him Father. But one thing held true. She must stop running. It was time to come home.

Sunday morning arrived, bringing with it a slight chill in the mountain air. John finished the last swallow of lukewarm coffee and grimaced.

"Need a fresh cup?" Mrs. Griffin offered with a smile.

"That would be wonderful."

John took his breakfast dishes to the sink, while Mrs. Griffin refilled his cup. He'd spent a good portion of the night praying Sydney would realize that God waited for her with open arms. It was a good thing he would be leaving in a couple of weeks. He'd come far too close to kissing her yesterday.

She'd been so near he could smell the soft scent of roses in her hair. When she'd looked up at him, her green eyes wide and innocent, it was all he could do to ignore the longing of his heart.

"John?"

He turned toward the pastor's wife. "I'm sorry."

Her kind smile warmed him. "Is something on your mind?"

John shrugged a shoulder. "Living your ministry day to day is different from learning how to minister in school. It's easy to think you have all the answers, but yesterday I was reminded twice that I don't."

"No one does." Mrs. Griffin set the coffeepot on the cast-iron stove. "There are simply some things that books can never teach—and that holds true for love as well."

He choked on the coffee. "I never said anything about love—"

"Maybe, but I caught the way you looked at Sydney yesterday. She seems like a very sweet young woman."

John nodded. She was everything he'd ever dreamed of—except for one thing. "She's not the same person she used to be. We're headed down two different roads."

"Maybe what she really needs right now is a friend, then someday—"

He shook his head, trying to convince himself more than

Mrs. Griffin. "I don't think so. I'll be leaving soon, and she's building a life for herself here. There are a number of eligible bachelors in this town that will come courting before long. All I can do is pray she finds her way back to God."

"I'll be praying too." Mrs. Griffin glanced at the floor. "Time is running out, and church will be starting soon."

John followed her gaze to his sock-clad feet and laughed despite his somber mood. "I guess I'd better finish getting ready."

❦

Sydney surprised Ruth and her fiancé, Mark Chandler, by accompanying them to church. She'd chosen to wear her stylish plum-colored dress with gold contrasting damask more for confidence than for fashion.

The service was just beginning as Sydney slipped into the pew beside the engaged couple. From the front, she caught John's surprised glance and smiled, trying to settle the nervous fluttering of her stomach. How long had it been since she'd gathered with other believers and proclaimed her faith?

The atmosphere in the small church building was relaxed. John began with a prayer of thanksgiving over the news that Emily Duncan's operation in Denver had been successful. As soon as the little girl was fully recovered, she and her mother would return to Windmere Falls.

After the prayer, the congregation lifted up their voices in song, all proclaiming God's goodness. The words tugged at Sydney's heart. "Rock of Ages, cleft for me," and "The Lord is a rock in a weary land." A flood of unworthiness engulfed her. If God had welcomed her back into His arms, why did she still feel so undeserving of His love and mercy?

John began his sermon with a quote from the book of James on considering it joy when facing trials. His voice was gentle, yet she heard strength behind his words. He had listened to God's calling and followed—even when things had been difficult. He'd experienced not only the death of his mother, but his best friend. She and John had both faced choices. John let tragedy refine him and bring him closer to his heavenly Father. She turned her back on what she believed.

The closing song began, but all Sydney could think about was how unworthy she felt of God's grace and goodness. Easing from the pew, she slipped out of the small building.

John watched Sydney step out the front door at the close of the service. Members of the small church gathered around him, congratulating him on a fine sermon, but his heart was elsewhere. As soon as he shook hands with the last person, he told Mrs. Griffin he'd be late for supper and went in search of Sydney.

He found her in the small cemetery at the western edge of town, standing beside a granite marker where someone had recently left a bouquet of wildflowers. "I'd forgotten how you used to enjoy reading the headstones."

She turned to him, her face wet with tears. "We live for such a short time, don't we?"

"A mere vapor that appears for a little time, then vanishes."

"I've been so wrong, John." She sat on a wooden bench at the edge of the grassy area dotted with gravestones. She rested her chin in the palms of her hands. "I've held onto my anger over André's death, longing only for revenge on those who killed him."

He took a seat beside her, wanting nothing more than to draw her into his arms.

"I feel so unworthy." She looked up at him, her eyes glistening.

"We're all unworthy." He leaned forward to wipe away one of her tears. "God loves you, Sydney. Let the past go, and hold onto His mercy and forgiveness."

She hesitated. "I know God's forgiven me, but forgiving myself is what I'm struggling with."

"Christ gave Himself for our sins so He could rescue us from the evils of this world. He wants us to enjoy His freedom, not live under condemnation."

❧

Sydney twirled a blade of grass between her fingers. John was right. Christ's death was the only thing that could cleanse her from past failures. His love went beyond man's ability to forgive, and in the end, He paid the price with His life.

A soft breeze played with the hem of her skirt, and she lifted her gaze toward the heavens. White clouds billowed across an azure sky, rising to meet the mountains. It was a testimony of God's handiwork, a proclamation of His power and strength.

She turned back to John and placed her hand on his

forearm, allowing the growing sense of peace to bubble like a mountain spring within her. "Thank you."

He raised his brows. "For what?"

"Somehow I sense that you've been praying for me all along."

John nodded and took her hand, wrapping his fingers around hers. "I care very much. More than you probably realize. If you're still hungry, I'd bet Mrs. Griffin will have something left for us for dinner."

"I'd like that." Sydney stood, and he squeezed her hand before releasing it. As they walked side by side toward the parsonage, she could feel the lingering touch of his hand against hers and knew that, despite her efforts not to, she'd just lost her heart.

Chapter 9

John had been right about Mrs. Griffin's cooking. Sydney realized she would need to alter her dresses after four Sundays of the pastor's wife's wonderful meals. Her and Ruth's attempt at food preparation above the dress shop left much to be desired, so Sydney had savored every bite of today's menu of fried chicken with all the side fixin's. She would have requested a second serving of dessert if she didn't think she would appear thoroughly unladylike.

"Mrs. Griffin, this is the best apple pie I've ever tasted." Sydney took her last bite of the flaky crust.

"I'm surprised anyone had room after this afternoon's church picnic." Mrs. Griffin beamed at the compliment, then rose from the table and started carrying dishes into the adjoining kitchen. Sydney followed with a stack of plates.

"I can get these dishes," Mrs. Griffin said, turning to her. "You've had a busy day with all the preparations at church."

Sydney set the dishes on the counter. "I'm fine. Besides, I couldn't leave you to do all the cleaning up."

John stopped in the doorway of the kitchen. "Pastor

Griffin asked me to look at one of the horses. He's afraid she's colicky, and he wants my opinion."

"Then you get on out to the barn," Mrs. Griffin insisted, waving her arms in emphasis. "When you're finished, you can walk Miss de Clermont home. She's done more than her fair share of work today."

"Yes, Ma'am." John smiled and left the room.

Sydney's heart pounded as he disappeared around the corner. Sunday afternoon at the Griffins had become something she looked forward to. The past few weeks had only deepened the attraction she felt toward John—and from his growing attention, she was sure he felt the same. If only time didn't stand against them. He'd told her that any day he would receive word of where his next place of ministry would be, and while he had no idea where, one thing was for sure—it would be far from the small town of Windmere Falls.

"He's a fine man, that John Langston," Mrs. Griffin said, interrupting Sydney's thoughts. "Don't know what my Hosea and I would have done without him." Tears welled in her eyes.

Sydney touched the woman's shoulder, ignoring for the moment her own conflicting feelings. "I know these past couple of months have been difficult for you."

Mrs. Griffin continued washing the dishes, her gaze resting momentarily on the mountains that loomed beyond the small parsonage. "After the accident, Doc Wingert was afraid Hosea might not make it."

Sydney dried the plate Mrs. Griffin handed her. "It's not easy worrying about someone you love."

"I know I should put my trust solely in God, but I was

struck with how much I rely on my husband."

Sydney set the dish on the table and turned to the older woman. "God's blessed you with a wonderful man as your helpmate, and He will continue to give you what you need, no matter what the future holds."

"Look at me carrying on like this." Mrs. Griffin rinsed off another plate and shook her head. "I'm supposed to be the one ministering."

"Everyone needs a listening ear from time to time."

Mrs. Griffin wiped her hands on a dish towel and smiled as she turned toward Sydney. "You'd make a good minister's wife. You know how to listen without judging and how to comfort without throwing out advice."

"I don't know. . . ." Sydney ran her finger around the blue-flowered rim of the serving dish she held. She loved her work for the Pinkerton Agency. But lately, her gratitude toward God had strengthened, and she'd dared let herself imagine what it might be like to serve Him full-time—alongside John.

Mrs. Griffin's gaze softened. "You're a strong woman, and God has gifted you in ways you haven't yet discovered. You've found comfort in His faithfulness, and I know you have the ability to comfort others with the measure God has given you."

Sydney added the dish to the stack and sighed. *Is this Your answer, Lord, or the one I want to hear? Please show me what I should do.*

❧

An hour later, she took in a deep breath of mountain air as

she accompanied John down the tree-lined road toward town. She glanced at John and noticed he was watching her.

"You seem lost in thought," he said.

His smile made her catch her breath. "I'm simply enjoying the company."

They neared the schoolyard where an ancient oak tree stood, its heavy branches reaching toward the sky. Several boys played a game of catch in the grassy field beyond the schoolhouse, their boisterous shouts ringing through the late afternoon air.

"Do you mind if we stop for a minute?" she asked, wanting to prolong their time together.

"Of course not."

She rested on the wooden swing that hung from one of the tree limbs, her hands grasping the thick ropes that secured it to the tree. John sat nearby on a large rock, leaning his elbows against his thighs.

"I received a letter from my parents yesterday." She pushed back gently with the toes of her boots, then let the swing fall forward again.

"How are they?"

"They're doing well. I wrote them like you suggested." She might have been right in her fight toward independence, but not in the way she went about it. "I never should have left with so much bitterness between us. After receiving their letter, I feel a deeper measure of peace."

"God has a way of working situations together for good." John took off his hat and rotated it in his hands, catching her gaze. "Does that mean you'll be going back to Chicago soon?"

An expectancy rose in his voice. As much as she wanted to, she knew she couldn't leave. Not yet. She lowered her gaze. "I need to stay in Windmere Falls. . .for now anyway."

He sighed and placed the hat back on his head. "I suppose that's best. You couldn't leave Ruth after just starting a new business."

The boys' ball rolled across the schoolyard, stopping at John's feet. He picked it up and threw it in a long, high arc back toward the field.

"Thanks, Mister!" one of them called out after catching the throw.

"You might have missed your calling." Sydney's gaze lingered on John's masculine physique, grateful for the unexpected distraction. "I didn't know you were such an athlete."

"You haven't seen anything yet." He laughed.

The wind had picked up as the sun began its descent toward the mountains, and Sydney shivered at the drop in temperature. Her light cotton dress had been fine at the picnic this afternoon, but not anymore.

"I should get you back to town before it gets dark," John said.

Sydney stood, and the swing continued to dance in the wind behind her. "I left my wrap at the church. Mind if we stop there?"

A few minutes later, she waited as John opened the door of the small church, then left it open to allow the last rays of golden sunshine to fill the room.

"I'll be just a second," she said. "I think I left it up front."

John waited at the back of the building while she retrieved

the shawl. Wrapping it around her shoulders, she returned down the narrow aisle. At the last pew, she felt her left foot twist sharply.

"Sydney?" John grabbed her around the waist, stopping the inevitable fall.

"I'm sorry, I. . ."

She looked into his face, and his mouth curled into a warm smile.

"Sydney de Clermont, I do believe you've really done it this time."

"Done what?" Her heart pounded.

"I'm falling in love with you."

His lips met hers in a surge of passion she'd never imagined. His kiss felt firm, mingled with deep tenderness.

Sydney pushed away the reality of her situation. No longer was she an undercover agent with a criminal to catch. She only knew one thing as she let her heart respond to his deepening kiss. She was in love with John Langston.

Chapter 10

"Is she the one, Lord?" With a flick of his wrist, John skimmed another smooth rock into the stream and watched it skip across the water. Evening shadows settled about him, but he had a feeling sleep would be elusive tonight. Only one thing stayed fixed in his mind.

Sydney.

He'd wanted to kiss her for a long time. Then at the church, her emerald green eyes had smiled at him as she leaned closer, anticipating what was to come. He hadn't been disappointed when her lips touched his, and now that he'd tasted her sweetness—he wanted more.

Never had a woman stirred his soul like Sydney. He sensed an innocence about her, coupled with a deep strength that had captured him totally. He'd enjoyed the past few weeks they'd shared together getting to know each other. No longer was she his best friend's little sister. She was the woman he wanted to spend the rest of his life with.

He sat down on a boulder, staring out across the stream, a breeze tugging his hat. He'd tried to take things slowly, spending time not only enjoying her company, but praying for God's will to be done in his life. God hadn't meant for man to be alone. In the garden, He created Eve for Adam. A helpmate. Someone to share with, dream with, and grow old with.

He wanted a wife, needed someone to share his ministry with him. André's death might have caused her faith to waver, but she'd grown in the past few weeks after coming back into His presence.

He knew she had the qualities needed to take on the role of a minister's wife. The trials she experienced would help her minister to those in need. Sydney had a strength that would allow her not only to keep their home a place where others would feel welcome and comfortable, but to actually share in his calling.

John stood and skipped a final rock across the clear water. Pastor Griffin had gone to church without his cane today. The pronounced limp didn't stop him, and it wouldn't be long until it would be time for John to go. He needed to make his intentions clear—before it was too late.

Sydney lay awake for hours, still feeling the touch of John's lips against hers. She'd never allowed a man to kiss her before, but she'd wanted John to kiss her today—badly.

Now she wondered where they were headed and what she really wanted out of life. As a Pinkerton, she'd tried to prove to herself she could be a good detective, even as a woman.

She'd spent the past week convincing herself why she needed to tell John the truth about her role as a Pinkerton— and going over all the reasons why she shouldn't. What would John think when he found out the real reason she'd come to Windmere Falls? Could he love her despite the fact she'd deceived him?

It hadn't mattered to Mr. Chandler that Ruth was more than a seamstress. Her role as an undercover agent had done nothing to hinder their relationship. But what about John? Surely he was looking for a woman who was more qualified to play the role of a preacher's wife than a detective.

You'd make a good minister's wife.

Mrs. Griffin's words ran through her mind. Could she be the wife John needed? Whatever happened between her and John, there was one thing she wouldn't neglect this time. Lighting the small lamp beside her bed and being careful not to awaken Ruth, Sydney pulled out her Bible and turned to the book of Deuteronomy where she'd been studying.

" 'But if from thence thou shalt seek the Lord thy God, thou shalt find him, if thou seek him with all thy heart and with all thy soul.' "

This time, though the future loomed unknown, there would be no more running from His presence. She would seek the Lord and find God's wisdom and leading in her life—whatever that might be.

The next morning, Sydney accidentally poked her finger with a needle. She shoved the injured finger into her mouth to stop the flow of blood.

"Honestly, Sydney." Ruth let off the pedal of her sewing machine and grinned. "You've got to be more careful. That's the third time this morning."

Sydney gave Ruth a frustrated look and picked up the shirt she was mending from the floor. A night of prayer had given her the answer she sought but hadn't settled the flutter of nervousness inside.

Standing up, Sydney walked to the window before turning to her friend. "I'm sorry."

Ruth set her scissors down on the table and gave Sydney her full attention. "You've been restless all morning. What is it?"

"John," she admitted.

A smile spread across Ruth's face. "I knew something was brewing between the two of you."

Sydney played with a loose thread hanging from her sleeve. "Last night on our way back into town from the parsonage, we stopped at the church to get my shawl, and somehow I tripped. He caught me, and the next thing I knew I was staring into those stormy gray eyes of his—and he kissed me."

Ruth stifled a laugh. "I knew your clumsiness would come in handy someday."

"Ruth!"

"Seriously, finding Mark was the best thing that's happened to me. I just want you to be as happy."

Sydney's gaze roamed the floor, her stomach twisting tight. "I haven't told him the truth about what we're doing here."

Ruth stood and came toward her. "You've got nothing to worry about. I've seen the way he looks at you. That man doesn't care what you do for a living as long as it's decent and honest."

"But he's a minister, and our job is—"

"Decent and honest work that helps others. We're trained at what we do, and we're good at our jobs. He has to respect that, and if he doesn't. . ." She waved a hand into the air. "Then maybe he's not the man for you."

"But I want him to be, Ruth. I love him."

"Then I think it's time you told him the truth."

Sydney went back to the worktable and picked up the shirt she'd been hemming. "I've been praying about it, and I know it's time, but I'm still nervous. What was Mark's response when you told him?"

Ruth folded her arms across her chest. "After the initial shock of discovering I wasn't simply a seamstress, he laughed."

"Wonderful." Sydney shook her head, her nerves gathering momentum again. "I've imagined John concerned, disappointed, even angry. Now I have to worry about him laughing at me?"

Ruth smiled. "The initial reaction didn't last long. I honestly believe he admires me for my ability to do what I believe in."

"Speaking of Mark, aren't you supposed to meet him at the hotel for lunch?"

Ruth looked at the small watch pinned to her dress and gasped. "I'd no idea it was so late." She grabbed her shawl, then turned to Sydney. "Would you like to go eat with us?"

"No, you go enjoy yourself, I'll be fine. Besides, I could use the time alone in prayer. If this relationship is God's will, then I have to believe that somehow things will work out between the two of us."

Chapter 11

Sydney took the pair of trousers Gus Drummond handed her and examined the ripped pocket. Ruth hadn't returned from her lunch with Mr. Chandler, and the shop was empty except for the two of them.

"I hear business is going well." He leaned against the counter, his hat in his hand.

"Yes, but that's not why we came." What was it going to take to prove to this Pinkerton agent that she could do her job?

"I received a message that you needed to speak to me?"

She noted the impatience in his voice. "What do you know about Philip Norton?"

"He was one of the first suspects since he works for the railroad and was on the train during several of the robberies."

"He was on the train *each* time it was robbed," Sydney said. "I think it's an inside job and he's part of it."

"Do you have any evidence?"

Sydney shook her head. "Philip Norton's mother is a widow who makes a meager living by providing piano lessons for some of the local children and selling eggs to the mercantile. Mr. Norton does little to add to the family resources with his job and spends most of what he earns on booze and women. The problem is, he's spending a whole lot more than what he makes from the railroad—"

"Maybe there's a favorite uncle back East who died and left him a fortune." Drummond folded his arms across his chest and shook his head. "You have no proof, Miss de Clermont. All I'm hearing from you is gossip and rumors."

"Then what about this? Two weeks ago, a Mr. Philip Norton of Windmere Falls signed a deed for a silver mine in northern Colorado. He paid cash."

He raised his eyebrows. "Where would a brakeman for the railroad get that kind of money?"

"Exactly."

"Where'd you hear this?"

Sydney lifted her head and looked the agent in the eye. "One of the benefits of being a woman is that people will talk and share things they wouldn't dream of telling a man with a badge."

Drummond swallowed hard. "Okay, you've convinced me it's worth looking into. What do we need to do?"

"Find out everything we can about Mr. Norton. Besides the obvious lead of the silver mine, I understand he worked for the railroad in Kansas for a year. You have the connections to discover if anything suspicious happened while he lived there. And lastly, I need to find out where the cash came from that paid for the mine."

"You weren't able to get that information during afternoon tea?"

Sydney lowered her gaze into a scowl. "No, but I will."

"Sorry, that was uncalled for." The bell on the front door jingled and a customer walked in. "I'll be back in a couple of days to pick up my trousers, Miss de Clermont."

"I'll have them ready."

Drummond touched the brim of his hat and nodded to the woman who'd entered the shop before he hurried out the door.

An hour later, Sydney rushed through her tiny stitches, wanting only to finish so she could complete her work for the day and walk to the parsonage to talk to John.

Looking out the window, she saw Deputy Bennett approaching. Sydney prayed he was simply on his way to the gun shop or Doc Wingert's office on business and not coming to see her.

She closed her eyes and sighed as he stopped and entered the shop, letting the door close behind him. Why had she reminded Ruth of her lunch with Mr. Chandler? Now she'd be forced to handle the arrogant deputy alone.

"Miss de Clermont, good morning. It's a beautiful day, and you're looking lovelier than ever." He smiled, but his pleasant expression did little to lessen her dislike of him. "After all this time, may I call you Sydney? I feel like we've known each other for years rather than weeks."

"Miss de Clermont is fine," she said. "Did you need something mended? Perhaps a button fixed or a hem stitched?"

"Just two shirts that were ripped in the line of duty." He handed her the garments. "You know how dangerous life can be for a lawman."

Sydney stifled a yawn. More than likely he'd torn them himself as an excuse to come see her.

He leaned forward, and Sydney was thankful for the counter between them. "Miss de Clermont, the weather is beautiful today. I bribed Mrs. Worthington at the hotel to pack a picnic lunch. I thought the two of us could take a buggy ride up toward the falls."

Sydney held her temper in check. "Mr. Bennett, while I do appreciate the fine job you do as a deputy for this town, I have tried to make it clear that I have no interest in you romantically."

The deputy threw back his head and laughed. "Now surely you wouldn't say no to one of Windmere Falls's finest lawmen?"

"I did say no, Mr. Bennett." Her determination to avoid this man continued to grow. She'd already turned down invitations to dinner at the hotel and buggy rides. Why couldn't he understand that she had no desire to eat dinner with him—or do anything else with him for that matter?

"So you're playing hard to get?" He reached out and grabbed her arm. The lines around his eyes deepened. Her heart raced, and Sydney wondered if she would be forced to fight back physically against his blatant intentions.

"Mr. Bennett, I said no." She raised her head to meet his gaze. "Please remove your hand from my arm."

"Is there a problem here?" a male voice sounded from the doorway of the shop.

Relief flooded Sydney at the sight of John.

Bennett removed his hand and turned toward John, a

look of challenge in his eyes. "And why would you say that, preacher boy? I don't see a problem here. Sydney and I are just planning a private picnic up near the falls. You wouldn't have any objections to that, now would you—"

"I said I wouldn't be able to join you, Mr. Bennett." Sydney rubbed the spot that would no doubt leave a bruise.

"Sydney, are you all right?" John asked, not once taking his sights off the deputy.

She nodded. "Mr. Bennett was just leaving."

The deputy's hand rose in challenge. "I—"

"I believe the lady asked you to go." John's words left no question of his intent.

"You know, you need to be careful in a town like this, Langston." The deputy took a step forward and thumped the ends of his fingers against John's chest. "You don't know what kind of thugs might want to cause trouble for you."

"Is that a threat?" John kept his arms to his sides, his hands knotted in fists.

"Just a word of advice I give to any newcomer. Of course, I understand you'll be leaving soon, won't you?"

"Good day, Deputy Bennett."

She watched in admiration as John ended the conversation, refusing to back down to the deputy. She hadn't realized she'd been holding her breath until the door closed behind the deputy. She let it out slowly as he strode across the street in the direction of the saloon.

John touched her shoulder, running his hand down her arm where the deputy had grabbed her. "Has he done anything like this before?"

She shook her head. "Invitations to dinner and buggy rides, yes, but he's never touched me."

"If he ever lays a hand on you again—"

"I appreciate your coming to my rescue, but I can handle it myself."

"I think I've heard those words before." John took a deep breath, his chest rising. "I'm going to speak to the sheriff about this."

"Please don't." She shook her head again. "If anything, that will make things worse."

"I won't allow him to treat you this way."

"John, he's just an arrogant man who thinks he can get what he wants by pushing people around." Her independent will wanted to insist she could take care of herself alone, but she warmed at his protection of her.

"Promise you'll tell me if he tries to bother you again."

"I promise."

"I almost forgot why I came by." John tapped the brim of his hat against his thigh. "Mrs. Griffin wanted me to invite you to dinner tonight."

She nodded at the invitation that would give her the time she needed to talk to him. "I have a couple of errands to take care of around town, then I'll come to the parsonage."

"I'll pick you up here," John said. "Six o'clock?"

She set the shirts the deputy had given her aside. "I'll be ready."

❧

Thoughts of John tumbled through Sydney's head as she hurried across the street to the barbershop. The owner, Clarence

Porter, was an older gentleman who had been one of the original founders of Windmere Falls. When his wife died, he'd threatened to return back East, but Sydney didn't think he'd ever leave his Colorado home. She entered the small establishment and sneezed twice at the woody scent of cologne that hung in the air.

"Miss de Clermont." Mr. Porter looked up from behind the chair where he stood cutting a customer's hair. A cluttered assortment of soaps, oils, and scented bottles lay next to him. "How's business?"

"Going well, Mr. Porter. Thank you." Sydney smiled and held up the two plaid shirts the barber had ordered. "Where would you like me to put them?"

"On the back counter would be fine. Thank you." Clarence turned back to his client. "As I was saying, you wouldn't believe the price of Deputy Bennett's cologne. Had it shipped in from Paris. 'Course I've always said if a customer's willing to pay, then I'm willing to comply. I tell you, it won't be long before that man's headed toward the city. Doesn't seem to think much about the likes of us small-town folk."

Sydney set the repaired shirts on the table, listening to the conversation.

"Always been nice enough to me," the other man said. "Though you're right, he is a bit uppity. All them fancy clothes and such."

Mr. Porter picked up a straight razor with its shiny white bone handle and waved it in the air. "I bet that boy spends every dime he has on clothes and women. Even seen him with the schoolteacher a time or two, though I suspect he's not the kind of man who could ever settle down with just one woman."

Sydney cringed at the gossip. She didn't know Rachel Parker extremely well, but she knew the woman deserved better than Deputy Bennett. She headed for the front door. "Good day, gentlemen."

Expensive cologne wasn't the only thing out of character for the deputy. His clothes were of high quality, and on his right hand, he wore a gold ring. He could just be spending all of his salary, but the extravagance suggested a second source of income. And why would a man with expensive tastes stay in a small town in the mountains? He seemed better suited for Denver or Chicago. Unless his source of income was local—like the payroll of the Denver & Rio Grande.

She entered the dress shop, and her gaze swept to the shirts the deputy had asked her to mend. She'd barely looked at them before, but something had been familiar. Picking up the black shirt, she stifled a sneeze from the strong smell of men's cologne still lingering on the fabric.

One of the buttons caught the light. She gasped. The silver star pattern matched the one she'd found after the train robbery when she first arrived. Sydney ran her finger down the front of the shirt. One of the buttons was missing.

Chapter 12

Sydney lay the shirt down and sighed. She needed proof. A missing button wouldn't hold up before a judge—but a witness's account would. If her instincts were correct, she knew one person who might be able to offer that. Today wasn't the first time she'd heard rumors of something going on between Deputy Bennett and Rachel Parker. Mabel Hawkins told her a similar story. Trying to avoid being caught up in the gossip, Sydney had quickly changed the subject, not realizing the possible value to her case.

Mr. Porter's and Miss Hawkins's descriptions of Bennett as a womanizer proved accurate. Sydney had been certain all along that she wasn't the only person the deputy had set his sights on.

She carefully folded Miss Parker's velvet evening dress, with its gray silk lining and pearl buttons, and remembered the way she'd seen the town's schoolteacher coyly exchange glances with the deputy. She had ordered a number of new dresses in the past few weeks. If Miss Parker had been able to get close to him, Sydney felt sure that at one time or another the deputy had talked. And one thing she felt certain about Charles Bennett—his pride would be his eventual downfall.

She locked the door to the shop and hurried toward the school on the west end of town. The children were out for the summer, but when Miss Parker came by last week to choose a length of fabric, she mentioned plans to spend the next couple of weeks at the schoolhouse preparing for the coming year.

Five minutes later, Sydney knocked on the open door of the one-room building and was welcomed by the tall, willowy teacher.

"I hope I'm not interrupting anything," Sydney said, smiling. "I finished your dress."

Miss Parker looked up from a stack of books and motioned her to come in. "Not at all. It's good to see you."

Sydney made her way between two rows of double desks, where in a little over a week, students would return to their daily task of learning. Rectangular chalkboards hung along the back and side walls. A cast-iron stove sat in the center of the room, a necessity for warming the room during the long Colorado winter.

Sydney placed the dress she'd been carrying across the teacher's large wooden desk. "I just finished hemming it and thought I might catch you here and save you a trip into town."

Miss Parker ran her hand across the soft fabric. "It turned out beautiful."

"Planning to wear it somewhere special?"

The schoolteacher pushed her wire-framed glasses up the bridge of her nose, her cheeks turning a light tinge of red. "There is someone."

"Anyone I know?" Sydney asked.

"Yes, but we're trying to keep our relationship quiet for now." Her hands played with the folds of the dark blue fabric as she examined the bodice. "Since I'm a schoolteacher, he felt it would be wise if we were discreet."

"Of course. I understand."

Miss Parker held up the garment in front of her. The hint of a bruise peeked out from beneath the sleeve of the brown calico dress she wore.

Sydney leaned forward and touched her forearm. "What happened?"

"Nothing, I—" She turned away.

Memories of Deputy Bennett's iron grip on her own arm flashed before Sydney. "If you're in trouble, I know people who can help."

Miss Parker shook her head, clutching the article of clothing to her chest.

Sydney leaned forward. "Who's hurting you?"

The schoolteacher dropped the dress in a crumpled pile on the desk and walked toward the window, where oil lamps hung along the wall. She pressed her hands against the panes of glass. "He loves me."

"Not if he's hurting you. Tell me who it is, and I'll help you."

"You don't understand." She turned around and crossed

her arms in front of her as if shielding the world from hurting her. "Why are you asking me all these questions?"

"Because you're not the only one." Sure her assumptions were correct, Sydney pulled up her right sleeve, revealing the red marks the deputy had left behind. "Deputy Bennett wanted to take me on a picnic this afternoon. When I told him no, he grabbed my arm."

Miss Parker took in a sharp breath, her eyes wide with disbelief. "No! You must be mistaken. He promised to marry me."

Sydney cringed at the revelation and wished she'd been wrong about her assessment of the deputy. "Miss Parker, I have reason to believe that Mr. Bennett is a dangerous man."

"No!" She shook her head. "Why are you doing this to me? He loves me!"

"If he's involved in something illegal and you're covering for him, you could be convicted as well."

"I'm not covering for him." Anger flashed in her eyes.

"Think about it, Miss Parker. Is this the first time he's grabbed you? Do you really know what he's capable of?"

She turned away and stared out the window again. "It was an accident."

"I don't think so. I know you're a God-fearing woman. He wants more for His children than this." Sydney walked toward the window and rested her hand on the woman's arm. "God desires the relationship between a man and a woman to be one based on mutual respect. You deserve much more than a man who hits you to get his way."

"I don't know. . . ." Miss Parker's shoulders hunched forward, and Sydney saw a look of defeat in her eyes. "He did tell me a few things. . .one night when he'd drunk too much. . . ."

"What kind of things?" Sydney asked.

"He. . .he boasted about how the people of this town were a bunch of fools. How he was going to take them for everything they had and. . .and that the Pinkerton agent didn't have enough brains to figure out who was involved with the train robberies or the Ghost's identity."

"Did he admit to you he was one of the men behind the train robberies?"

She shook her head. "Not in those exact words, but he implied it. He must have realized what he'd said, because then. . .then he threatened me."

Sydney hated the look of pain that masked Miss Parker's face, but she couldn't stop now. She had to find out the whole truth. "Why did you keep seeing him?"

Miss Parker smoothed back her dark brown hair and walked toward one of the student's desks. Leaning against it for support, she turned to Sydney. "I know I've been foolish, but he could be so tender when he wanted to. He bought me expensive presents and told me he loved me. Truth is, I'm thirty years old, and I've never had a beau before. He made me feel special." She wiped away a tear. "If the school board knew the truth about our relationship, I'd lose my job."

"And he used that against you?"

Miss Parker nodded, clutching her hands together in front of her. "I shouldn't have told you any of this. If he finds out—"

"I won't let him hurt you."

Miss Parker stood and paced the room again. "You can't stop him. No one can."

"I'm friends with the Pinkerton agent in town. With what you've told me, they might have enough to convict him."

"I can't believe this is happening." Miss Parker struggled to take a deep breath.

"Would you be willing to testify against him?"

She shook her head. "Please don't ask me to do that."

Sydney whirled around at the sound of heavy footsteps.

"Charles!" Miss Parker cried out. "How long have you been standing there?"

"You little fool." Bennett's gaze riveted on Miss Parker. "What did you tell her?"

"Nothing!"

He stormed down the center of the room, his dark gaze lit with anger. Before she could react, he grabbed Sydney, his left arm hooked around her neck. The other hand held a gun to her temple.

Her eyes burned at the heavy scent of cologne and alcohol, and her lungs struggled for air as his grip tightened around her neck.

"Charles, please. Don't do this," Miss Parker begged, stepping toward him. "I didn't tell her anything. I promise."

"What did I ever see in you?" Sydney couldn't see Bennett's expression, but his voice sent shivers down her spine. "I can see it now, Rachel. Schoolteacher kills dress shop owner in a jealous rage. A perfect ending to your stupid mistake, don't you think?"

Sydney's mind reeled. *He's going to kill me!* Gathering every ounce of strength she could, she grabbed Bennett's right hand and pushed the gun away from her temple. His other arm tightened around her neck. *God, help me!* She bit into his flesh. Her fingers clawed for the gun, her left hand struggling to find the trigger guard.

As she twisted to face him, his elbow smashed into her jaw. The impact threw her off balance. *I'm no match physically for this man. Please, Lord, don't let me die this way!*

The gun fired, and the smell of blood and gunpowder filled the room.

The inevitable summons to Pastor Griffins's private study had finally come. The elder pastor was ready to resume his pulpit, and John would be leaving at the end of the week. He would miss the people he'd come to love in the church. Mr. and Mrs. Griffin welcomed him from the first day he'd arrived in the quaint mountain town. But there was one person he would miss more than anyone else.

He knew he wanted to spend the rest of his life with Sydney, but could he ask her to leave when she'd just moved here to start a new life? Would she even consider going back to Chicago with him?

John glanced at the small clock mounted on the kitchen wall. He planned to pick her up at the dress shop at six, but he couldn't wait that long. The time had come to tell Sydney exactly how he felt.

A soft breeze filtered through the trees as he walked along the dirt path toward town. The schoolyard was empty.

He'd be gone before the children returned for the fall semester. *Lord, only You know what the future holds for each of us, but I'd sure like to spend it with Sydney—*

A gunshot pierced the stillness of the afternoon. A woman screamed. John turned and bolted toward the schoolhouse.

Chapter 13

John's eyes widened at the sight before him. "Sydney?"

"I'm fine." She knelt beside Deputy Bennett, who lay still on the floor in front of her. Blood pooled beneath his left shoulder. "The gun went off when I grabbed it from him. He needs a doctor."

"I'll go." Miss Parker picked up a garment from the desk and threw it to the floor beside Bennett's body. "You'll need something to stop the bleeding. You can use this."

"He passed out, but I think he'll live." Sydney ripped off a narrow strip of fabric from the skirt and pressed it against the wound. "Now we'll add kidnapping and attempted murder to his list of crimes."

John worked silently beside Sydney, helping her wrap the wound to stop the bleeding. Five minutes later, the schoolteacher returned with Doc Wingert.

"You did a good job," the doctor said as he knelt beside his patient. "Looks like the bleeding has just about stopped. I need to get him to my office right away and prepare him for surgery. That bullet needs to come out."

Sheriff Masters entered the schoolroom. "I heard a gunshot. What's going on?"

"Charles tried to kill Miss de Clermont." Miss Parker sat at one of the desks, disbelief reflected in her eyes. "He put a gun to her head and. . .and threatened to kill her. There was a struggle, and the gun went off when Miss de Clermont tried to get out of his grasp. Then he fell to the floor and just lay there."

John turned to Sydney, the horror of the situation sinking in. Why hadn't he talked to the sheriff earlier? If he had, maybe all of this could have been avoided.

"I think I can prove he's one of the train robbers," Sydney said to the sheriff.

What business did Sydney have with the train heists? Yes, she'd been interested in the rash of robberies, but so was the whole town. Did the fact that their train had been robbed give her an added interest in the events of the past few months?

Bennett groaned and rolled over on his back, holding his injured shoulder. None of this made any sense. Had the deputy followed her here after he left the dress shop, intending to threaten and intimidate her? He never should have left her alone. Not after Bennett's aggressive advances.

"I'll testify against him," Miss Parker said to Sydney. "As long as you go with me."

"You know I will." Sydney stood to her feet with John's help.

"Guess we'll be making a quick trip to the doctor's office before the jailhouse," the sheriff said. "Never thought I'd see the day when I had to arrest one of my own men. I'll need a full statement from the women later, but for now I want to see this scoundrel behind bars as soon as possible."

"Do you need my help?" John asked.

"He can walk." The sheriff forced Bennett to his feet. "John, if you'd stay with the women for now, I'd appreciate it. This had to shake them up."

"Of course," he said.

Dr. Wingert and the sheriff left the schoolhouse, one on either side of Bennett.

John turned to Sydney. "Are you all right?"

"I'm fine." Sydney hated the fact that her instincts had been right about the deputy. "Miss Parker's the one I'm worried about."

The schoolteacher shook her head. "I think deep down inside I knew everything about our relationship was wrong. I just didn't want to see the truth." A sad but determined look marked her face. "I still don't know how I could have been so foolish."

"We all make mistakes," John said gently, his arm resting across Sydney's shoulders. "It's accepting God's forgiveness that makes the difference."

"I think I'm going to go home now." Miss Parker smoothed down her skirt. "My friend Mrs. Sanders has been trying to talk to me for weeks. I think she knew I was in over my head. Maybe it's time I took her up on that cup of tea and long chat."

"Can we take you home?" John asked.

"I'll be fine. A little quiet time with God wouldn't hurt either."

Sydney knew Mrs. Sanders was a strong Christian woman who would be able to minister to Miss Parker.

"Then you go on home," she said. "John and I will clean up here. Don't worry about a thing."

"Thank you for everything, Miss de Clermont." The teacher gave her a hug and said good-bye. "I never meant for things to end this way."

"I know." Sydney squeezed her hand. "If you need anything, please let me know."

Sydney watched until she disappeared out the back door. Healing may come slowly, but with God's help and that of her church family, it would come.

Realizing she was still holding the gun, she laid it on one of the desks and let John wrap his arms around her waist, pulling her tight against his chest. She could feel the pounding of his heart against hers.

"I still don't understand what happened here," he said.

"Apparently, Charles Bennett is one of the men who's been robbing the payroll." Sydney wondered if her breathing was labored as a result of Bennett's escapade or John's nearness. "Bennett had Miss Parker convinced that he loved her and would marry her someday. When he walked in, he overheard part of our conversation and thought she had given away some of his secrets."

"Like the fact he's a train robber?"

"Exactly."

John shook his head and pulled her closer still. "It could have been you lying on the floor. He could have killed you."

Sydney tilted her head back and gazed into his eyes, her

pulse racing at his nearness. "You were here just in time."

His mouth curved into a lopsided grin. "I don't know about that. Seems to me you had everything under control. You can take care of yourself, can't you?"

"Maybe, but you don't know how glad I was to see you come through that door." She took a deep breath, praying that God would give her the words to say. "We have a lot to talk about. There are some things I need to tell you before—"

"Before I ask you to marry me?"

Her eyes widened with anticipation. "Did you just ask me to marry you?"

"Yes, but there's one thing I still need to know. You haven't told me how you got involved in the arrest of the deputy."

"I was going to tell you everything tonight." *Lord, please let him understand what I'm about to say.* "My work as a seamstress is only a cover for my real job."

John leveled his gaze. "I still don't understand."

"A year ago, I was hired by the Pinkerton Agency in Chicago. This is my first case."

He took her hands in his and cocked his head. "Your first case?"

She took another deep breath, her nerves wound tight. She needed John to understand. "Catching the men responsible for the recent rash of train robberies."

His mouth dropped open. "So you're a spy?"

"A detective." Sydney laughed.

"From the looks of what happened today, you're a mighty good one."

She shook her head. She'd hoped to catch the rest of the

train robbery ring today. "There are still two men on the run, one of whom I think might be Philip Norton. He's been spending a lot of money lately. Money he didn't get from his job on the railroad."

"I can clear up that question."

"You can?"

"Norton does have a problem, but it's not robbing trains. It's gambling. He won the jackpot a few weeks ago in Denver, and he's been a bit extravagant with his spending. At the advice of Pastor Griffin, I've been talking with him."

"So he's innocent." Sydney bit her lip. Now they still had two men to capture.

"You never answered my question." He ran his thumb down the side of her cheek. "If this is what you want to do with your life, we can work something out."

A surge of joy raced through Sydney. "Mrs. Griffin told me I'd make a wonderful minister's wife."

"It isn't as exciting as chasing after thieves and bandits."

"Are you trying to talk me out of it now?"

John planted a kiss on her forehead. "Never, but I also won't ask you to give up something that's important to you."

Her heart soared with the realization that he truly loved her. "You're not asking, I'm offering. I was planning to talk to you tonight. I think God is calling me into a different line of work."

"One as Mrs. John Langston?"

Sydney nodded as John pulled her close and kissed her. She'd done more today than simply catch a thief; she'd caught the man who rescued her heart.

LISA HARRIS

Lisa lives in Texas with her husband, Scott, who is a high school principal, and three children. Lisa has been writing both fiction and nonfiction for the past four years and has had over fifty articles, devotionals, and short stories published. She and her husband spent several years living in Europe and West Africa as church planting missionaries.

Skirted Clues

by DiAnn Mills

Chapter 1

October 1890

This horse would be her demise. Moment Alexander studied the size of the raven-colored beast and realized she needed a stool to mount it.

"She knows you're afraid," Gus Drummond said with a chuckle.

"She?" Moment seized a quick glance at the horse to make sure of its gender. "Does she have a name?"

"Yep, Nightmare." He laughed again, but she saw nothing funny about the matter.

She trembled, but neither Drummond nor this insufferable Nightmare held any power over a determined woman. "Very well." She tossed her head. "I have an assignment, and I intend to follow through with it."

He crossed his arms over his chest and stood with his feet planted apart. "Do you need a hand up? I do say, you and Miss Hunnicut are right short little women."

Moment gritted her teeth. "Size has nothing to do with

intelligence, Mr. Drummond. Ruth already proved her mettle, and I will soon prove mine. No, thank you, but I don't need any assistance."

She peered around the dark stable, but in the early-morning hours with just a hint of orange slipping over the horizon, she couldn't see anything suitable for her to stand on. Moment sneezed. The cold weather always made her nose drip like a waterfall, and taking care of the matter sounded like a foghorn.

"God bless you."

"Thank you." At least the man had manners—at times.

Drummond cupped his hands. "Here, Miss Alexander, step up here."

Seeing no choice but to oblige the man, she stepped into his large hand. Gratitude for Victoria's riding skirt instantly washed over her. Her dear friend had several, along with boots, gloves, and the like for a proper ladies' riding attire. Out of sheer stubbornness, Moment elected to use a man's saddle, especially since most of the women here didn't bother with them. Nightmare shook her head, and Moment shuddered. In the next breath, she sat atop the saddle. Drummond would torment her forever if he knew she was not only afraid of horses but also heights. Taking a deep breath, she wondered what she was supposed to do next.

"You can't let her sense your fear," he repeated without a hint of teasing in his voice. "She'll take off and go just where she pleases—just like a few Pinkerton women I know."

"I'll overlook that last remark, and thank you for the lift-up."

He handed her the reins, then rubbed his auburn beard. "Have you ever ridden a horse before?"

Moment stiffened. "Not exactly, but I'm sure it's quite simple."

Drummond pushed his Stetson back on his head. "I will never, ever make those fellows in Chicago mad again." He inhaled deeply and took the horse by the bridle. "I'm going to lead you out to the road. Pay attention to me, or you'll end up stranded somewhere. If I didn't have work to do, I'd ride with you."

"I appreciate your concern," she replied. "But I have an assignment, and I wish to pursue it on my own."

"But you're shaking like a fall leaf, and I don't believe it's the cool weather. In fact, I wish you'd reconsider." He frowned. "Miss Alexander, you are scared to death, so admit it."

"I'm not afraid, simply. . .uninformed." She detested lying, but admitting the truth had its own set of retributions.

"Did anyone ever say you are more stubborn than a mule?" When she failed to reply, he continued. "All right. Here are some instructions. You pull the reins to the right when you want her to head right and left when you want to go left. Pull in both reins when you want to stop, but not too fast or sharp or she'll think you want to rear up."

Moment listened to every word. After all, her life depended on it.

"Do you know how to get to Brady Miller's place?"

She nodded and patted the map in her coat pocket.

"I hope you have a good sense of direction."

"I have excellent navigation skills." Nightmare pawed

the dirt floor, and Moment tensed.

Drummond stopped the horse. "Let me give you a little more information. First of all, a lady horse is called a mare, and the horse's name is Night."

Immediately, Moment realized what he'd done. A gentleman didn't play jokes on a lady, especially a frightened one. "Thank you for enlightening me."

"Then calm down. This is the gentlest horse I know. Don't disturb her sweet temperament by confusing her. Do you understand?"

A thousand rebuttals flew across Moment's mind, but she swallowed them all. No point making the man angry, even if he didn't know proper Pinkerton protocol. "What else do I need to know?" She remembered Victoria offering to teach her how to ride, but Moment couldn't bear to reveal her fear. At this moment, she'd much rather be taking lessons from Victoria.

"Your weight goes in the stirrups. These things." He pointed to the footrests. "Touch your heels to her side when you want her to go. I recommend you avoid trotting because, as inexperienced as you are, Night will jar your teeth out."

Moment's eyes opened wide. She hadn't expected this.

"Do you remember all I've said?" He narrowed his eyes. "Don't make me come looking for you."

"I'll walk first."

"I imagine you would. Brady Miller can be a bit feisty, and since he's a suspect in these train robberies, he might not appreciate you snooping around. Be careful."

The kindest two words he had spoken all morning. "I

will take heed, Mr. Drummond."

"And I want to see you the moment—where did your mama get that name anyway?"

Moment stiffened. "She wanted a thoroughly modern woman."

Without another word, he stuck his forefinger under the bridle where it fastened to the leather strap above the mare's nose and led her from the stable into the chilly morning air.

"Have a good morning, Mr. Drummond." She lightly touched the horse's sides, and the animal broke into what he had referred to as a trot. Moment figured by the time she returned to Windmere Falls, she'd be minus a few teeth.

A short while later, she basked in the solitude of the new day. Sunrise in this part of Colorado seized her breath. Shades of pink, yellow, and lavender spread across the sky as if an artist had brushed paint onto a navy blue canvas. Once the sun began its slow ascent across the sky, the mountains' fiery display of orange, scarlet, and gold would hold her captive. Chicago's art galleries in all their grandeur could not compare to this beauty.

Once, she'd termed Colorado as godforsaken, but through the summer months and now fall, it had become a bit of paradise. She welcomed the fresh scent of pine and open air, certainly unlike the assortment of city smells she'd grown up around.

Despite her city upbringing, Moment treasured the quiet where only melodic birds and chirping insects broke the tranquility. Once she closed this case, she'd have a difficult time boarding the Denver & Rio Grande back to Chicago.

Currently, she had only two problems: finding out if Brady Miller was one of the train robbers and tolerating the horse beneath her. Oh, how she longed to find out who had masterminded the five robberies.

"You and I will get along just fine." Moment patted Night on the neck. Perhaps she could convince herself that she enjoyed riding.

She expelled a heavy sigh. Truthfully, she felt quite dejected with her lack of progress on the case. Ruth had uncovered one of the suspects, the telegrapher Emmett Duncan, and Sydney had risked her life to learn Deputy Charles Bennett's role in the robberies. Victoria hadn't discovered a thing either, but she was too busy courting Will Bowen. Moment had much more to do than consider romantic interests, not that she begrudged Victoria her beau or Ruth and Sydney their marriage plans. Those things would have to wait. Right now, she wanted to pull this case together.

"But I should have solved this case a long time ago, instead of following one bad lead after another," Moment told the horse. "Could the Lord have a lesson for me here?"

When the horse didn't answer, she continued. "This little ride had better be worth it. I left poor Victoria minding the shop while I headed for the hills." She'd even started talking like these people.

Winter nipped at her heels. If she didn't nab her assignment soon, she'd be stuck cutting yard goods and selling dried beans until spring. Moment enjoyed the Windmere Falls Mercantile and their many customers. She even adored the cozy room above the store where she and Victoria slept, but she had an important job to do. After all, she was one of the Pinks.

A gust of wind nearly took her hat despite its being firmly fixed beneath her chin. Mr. Drummond warned her yesterday it might snow. She glanced at the clouds; no snow today. She'd heard enough tales about blizzards to give her a keen respect for inclement weather.

Without warning, Night lifted her front legs high, and Moment slid off the mare's back to the hard ground. Before she could blink and wonder if she'd been hurt, the horse raced down the pathway back toward Windmere Falls.

"Nightmare!" she yelled, shaking her fist at the fleeing horse. "I don't need you to get where I'm going." Moment stood and brushed off her skirt and sore behind. She pulled off her gloves with her teeth and retrieved the map from her coat pocket. Glancing about, she estimated Brady Miller's ranch to be about three miles ahead. She really didn't care if she met the man or not. All she wanted to do was look around, and she did enjoy a vigorous walk. She then concluded it would be at least an eight-mile trek back to town. She cringed at the thought of Drummond's deep belly laugh when he learned about this antic.

The farther she ventured, the more she wondered about wild animals. A couple of customers in the mercantile had mentioned bears, but they'd be hibernating by now. What about wolves? Moment shivered. Or wildcats? Or outlaws who never learned respect for women? Why hadn't she brought her revolver? That oversight was uncalled for. Why, Gus Drummond and Harry Fletcher would remove her from this investigation if they learned that tidbit. With every step, the landscape took on more of a sinister aspect.

"Oh, Lord," she said aloud. "I'm sure glad You're here with me."

She decided to consider the case instead of fret over wild animals and even wilder men. The succession of train robberies had even the Pinkertons scrambling. Ruth's exposure of Emmett Duncan, and the role he played at the telegraph office, stopped the gang from having firsthand knowledge about the gold shipments. Sydney's wit in matching the missing button from Deputy Bennett's shirt and his subsequent arrest ceased any further information to the thieves about what Sheriff Masters planned. But who was the Ghost, and what happened to the money? Someone had cleverly selected a group of men who were invaluable in the train robberies. This man, the Ghost, had insight to everything going on in Windmere Falls. At one time, he had control of the telegraph office and stayed a step ahead of the law. The recluse Brady Miller just might be the final puzzle piece.

Moment's feet started to ache. She'd borrowed riding boots from Victoria, and the sweet Englishwoman had a much narrower foot. If the weather had been a little warmer, she'd have gladly removed them. She moaned aloud thinking about the walk back.

She stopped in her tracks—paralyzed. A cougar stood directly in her path. Its amber eyes narrowed, and the animal looked lean and mean, a lethal predator. Moment's mind spun with what she remembered reading about cougars. For the life of her, she couldn't remember if they ate people. This one looked hungry.

Her neighbor's cat in Chicago ate rats.

"Scat, get out of here!" Her attempt at bravery squeaked out like a field mouse. Why could she handle herself when facing hardened criminals and clever villains but froze at the sight of most animals? "Go on home." Those orders always worked on her neighbor's tabby.

The ground below her held a few scattered rocks. With one eye on the cougar, she deftly gathered a few for weapons. She tossed one, and it whizzed by the animal's small broad head. "Go find your mama!" she shouted. Another rock bounced off its side. "Watch out; I'm coming through."

The cat screamed at her, and Moment screamed in reply.

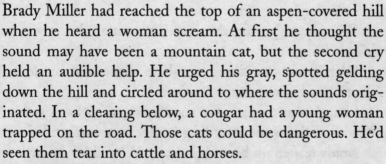

Brady Miller had reached the top of an aspen-covered hill when he heard a woman scream. At first he thought the sound may have been a mountain cat, but the second cry held an audible help. He urged his gray, spotted gelding down the hill and circled around to where the sounds originated. In a clearing below, a cougar had a young woman trapped on the road. Those cats could be dangerous. He'd seen them tear into cattle and horses.

Lifting his rifle, he aimed at the cougar and squeezed the trigger. The woman cried out again, but the cat lay dead. Brady rode down into the clearing, questions forming as he neared the frightened woman. He stopped his horse square in front of her.

"Thank you." She gasped for breath. "I was afraid it—"

"What are you doing out in the middle of nowhere without a gun or a horse?" he said, scowling.

His harshness must have startled her because she raised her chin. The fire in her brown eyes should have set the cougar running for the mountains. "I beg your pardon, Sir."

"Lady, this is no time for fancy manners. Don't you understand a cougar can kill you? What would you have done if I hadn't come along?"

A lock of light brown hair, near the same color as the cougar's hide, fell from under her hat. She frowned and tucked it behind her ear. When she peered up at him, he caught sight of a patch of orange freckles across her nose. Suddenly, Brady found this sassy lady incredibly funny.

"What are you laughing at?" The young woman pressed her lips together the instant she made her demands.

"You."

"Sir, you are insufferable. I didn't come all this way to be ridiculed."

"What are you doing out here alone and on foot?" Maybe she'd answer him this time.

She glanced toward the mountains, then back at him "My horse threw me after I'd gone for a morning ride."

Brady leaned on his saddle horn. Why didn't he believe this lady? "I don't recall seeing the likes of you in Windmere Falls before. Are you new?"

She silently challenged him. "I've lived there since late spring. My friend and I operate the mercantile."

"Do you always take off on foolish notions?"

"What is your name, Sir? I surely don't want to forget your bad manners."

"Brady Miller. I own the land you're standing on."

Chapter 2

B rady Miller lived up to his reputation. Drummond said he preferred solitude, but what the Pinkerton hadn't said was that Mr. Miller's personality had the drawing card of a cougar. She didn't like his horse either. The animal had a white-gray coat with gray spots and legs, and its mane and tail were a blend of the gray and white. The horse's eyes looked peculiar, reminding her of a woman with no lashes.

If he hadn't been so obnoxious, she'd have thanked him for saving her life. Instead, she wanted to fling dirt in his face and give his hat a toss into the treetops. But she needed information to solve the case. In particular, she needed evidence to prove him part of the train robber gang.

"Mr. Miller, I apologize for riding across your land without permission and for disrupting your cougar."

His handlebar mustache gave his face a perpetual frown. She studied him carefully, wondering if this face was among the many mug shots compiled in the Pinkerton files in Chicago. She hadn't seen him before. In fact, she hadn't seen a single criminal face in Windmere Falls until Ruth and Sydney completed their work and had two men arrested.

Mr. Miller leaned on his saddle horn, and a slow grin inched across his face. He had a wide smile that could have been pleasing under other circumstances. At least he had released his frown. "You don't shake up easily, do you?"

Was he passing out a compliment? She caught a sparkle in his dark blue eyes, the same shade as his bandana. "Not usually. Animals frighten me more than anything else."

"A woman needs a gun out here." He dismounted and strode toward her.

"I agree." Moment forced herself to be friendly. But as he approached, a twinge of apprehension swept over her. She could swing a mean punch if need be. Living with nine brothers had taught her how to take care of herself. "I have a good revolver, but I left it in Windmere Falls. Looks like my forgetfulness nearly cost me my life."

"You're right there." He glanced at the cougar. "Believe I'll take his hide with me."

The thought sounded repugnant to her. "And I'll be heading back to town. Thank you again, Sir."

"You're looking at a long walk, Ma'am."

"Miss Alexander. Moment Alexander, to be exact."

He lifted a brow.

"I know, it's a bit different." She managed a smile.

"Do folks call you Mo for short?"

That remark did it. Brady Miller had been rude, sarcastic, and crude, but insulting her name pushed him over the tolerable edge. She arched her back and swung around toward

Windmere Falls. This man had to be guilty, and she'd work night and day to prove it.

Because you let him anger you doesn't make Brady Miller a thief.

Moment recognized the voice. How many times had God let her know when she allowed personal feelings to get in the middle of a professional decision? How many more times had she allowed folks' reactions about her name upset her?

She didn't slow her steps, but she did resolve to return to Mr. Miller's ranch when she had a gun, a horse, and a few riding lessons.

"Miss Alexander, you don't have to stomp away all mad. Why not let me take you back to town?"

She continued to walk, but she did vow to restrain her tongue a bit. "You have a cougar to skin. Besides, it's a lovely morning for a walk."

"Until you meet up with another cougar. . .or a bear. . .or a nest of rattlers. Even outlaws are known to roam these parts."

Moment swallowed hard, but she refused to give in. She was a Pinkerton. Granted, she'd made a few mistakes this morning, but climbing up behind a possible criminal on an odd-looking horse would not be her next one. "No, thank you."

"I won't tease you about your name."

"No, thank you."

"You don't give me much choice."

Uneasiness squeezed at her heart. This time he had her attention, and once more she wished she had a revolver.

Although she despised guns and preferred to use her wits and training, weapons could be invaluable in the face of danger. The sound of hoof beats alerted her to his proximity.

"If you won't ride with me, then I'll escort you to Windmere Falls."

She inwardly grimaced. How grand to spend the next three hours with this ill-mannered fellow. But at least she could talk to him and possibly learn a little more about his ranch. He might even brag about a few things; most men did.

"It's not necessary, but the company is welcome."

Brady Miller didn't hold much stock in women. His experience proved the fairer gender always wanted to change something about a man or, worse yet, deceive him. Women said one thing and meant another. They were helpless creatures, prone to tears, talked too much, and could cost a man plenty of money. So far he'd delivered Moment Alexander from the claws of a cougar and listened to her chatter. That's all the involvement he intended, except escorting the woman back to town where she belonged.

If he'd been looking for a pretty face, she might have caught his eye, but he wouldn't call Miss Alexander pretty so much as cute—like a new puppy. Brady chuckled to himself. He doubted if she would appreciate his comparing her to a dog. She walked a little oddly, but once he observed her feet, he surmised that those fancy riding boots must be too small. She wore a white, high-buttoned shirt with mounds of lacy stuff and a dark riding skirt. The latter appeared to be the only sensible item about her.

"How big is your ranch, Mr. Miller?"

Women and their idle prattle. He rode up to her side. "About two thousand acres."

"And what do you have there?"

"Cattle and horses."

"Sounds like a lot of work to me." She tipped her freckled nose up to peer at him.

"Yes, but it's worth it. I have good ranch hands."

"How many?"

"About ten."

"Do you have barns and such?"

She must not have spent much time on a ranch. "Some scattered here and there. Do you always ask so many questions?"

She shrugged. "Only when I'm trying to get to know somebody, and we're spending miles together."

"Didn't folks already tell you about me?" Brady knew his reputation, and most people considered him a bit strange because he didn't take to socializing.

She hesitated. "They said you liked living alone and preferred cattle and horses to people."

"That's me, and I don't particularly like folks riding on my land."

"Why?"

"That's my business."

They continued in silence. The woman's strange walk turned into a limp. He started to say something about climbing up behind him again, but he figured she'd start firing more questions into his ear.

"You're carrying a fine-looking Winchester," she said.

"It does the job. How did you make its acquaintance?"

"I have nine brothers. They taught me how to handle a gun."

"And you're a good shot?" Brady had yet to see a woman who could hit the broad side of a barn.

"Fair. I can hold my own."

"And still you forgot to bring your revolver?" He couldn't help but wonder how a person could head into dangerous territory without a weapon. She didn't make sense.

"I already admitted that wasn't a smart move." She stopped in the middle of the road and sat down. Before he could form another word, she tugged off her boots. "Don't say a word. My feet really hurt, like I'm stepping on porcupine quills."

Brady chuckled. "I'd lend you mine, but they won't fit." He leaned over to take a better look at her stockinged feet. They looked swollen. "Should have broken those in."

"There're a lot of things I should have done this morning."

Her sharp words amused him. He pointed in a westerly direction. "Right around the ridge over there is a stream—a bit cold, but it will help the swelling."

She slowly nodded, as though contemplating his suggestion. He swung down and led his horse toward the ridge. She picked up her boots and followed.

"The good Lord gave us two feet to walk on and a mind to use," Brady said. "So think real hard about riding the rest of the way to town." When she refused to respond, he silently labeled her stubbornness as stupidity.

At the stream, the clear water gurgled around moss-covered rocks. Soon this area would be covered in snow.

He glanced in and saw a trout swim by. If not for Miss Stubborn-Sore-Feet, he'd have fishing on his mind.

"Sit down and dangle those feet in the water." He anticipated a shriek when her feet touched the cold water—matching the sound when she met the cougar. In an instant, she removed her socks and plunged them into the icy water. Brady averted his eyes for modesty's sake.

Miss Alexander sucked in her breath but did not utter a word.

"A little cold?" Brady stifled a laugh, although he did admire her spunk.

"They're numb," she said through chattering teeth. "How long must I do this?"

Most women were gullible. "A couple of hours."

"I'll be dead by then. You forget, Mr. Miller, I have nine brothers. They pulled every nasty trick they could think of, and I don't fool easily." He suddenly felt sorry for her. Her feet must be blue by now.

"How about a few more minutes? Then we can dry them off." He jerked off his bandana. "If you don't want to ride behind me, then I'll walk and you ride."

She shook her head. "I won't be taking advantage of a man who saved my life. I can walk the rest of the way without my boots."

Brady studied her pert little nose and mouth. Yes, she was as cute as a puppy but more woman than he cared to consider. He liked her—freckles, sore feet, and bullheadedness. He imagined she held her own with those brothers. "Then let's sit a spell on the riverbank and let those feet rest.

Pull 'em out of there." Again, he turned his head while she dried her cold feet with his bandana and slipped back on her socks. "The sun is warming things up a mite."

"Mmmm," she responded, but he could hear her chattering teeth. Without asking permission, he shrugged off his coat and draped it over her shoulders.

"Thanks." She offered a faint smile.

"How are things in Windmere Falls? I don't get there much." As much as he detested thinking up conversation, it would help pass the time.

"Good. The ladies are putting together a bazaar for sometime in November. The telegraph office is looking for a new operator. The restaurant hired a new cook. She makes wonderful pies, but some of her meals need help."

"Is Reverend Griffin still preaching?"

"Yes, and the church is growing too. He had a hunting accident but recovered nicely."

"It's been awhile since I visited there. I probably ought to consider it." He eased into silence while he contemplated Preacher Griffin. The man had led him to the Lord a few years back, but Brady had a rough time facing folks each Sunday. He did better reading his Bible in the privacy of his home. Guilt cut at his heart, but he pushed it away. One of these days he'd be a regular church-going man again.

Miss Alexander picked up a rock and skimmed it across the wide part of the stream. He watched it ripple and grow.

"You must have grown up on a farm."

She smiled, a warm comforting gesture that gave his heart a little flip. "Sure did, back in Illinois. Papa grew corn and wheat, then we had milk cows."

"Illinois is a little different from Colorado."

"I like Windmere Falls," she said. "But what really bothers me is the train robberies."

"I thought the sheriff arrested the thieves."

She snuggled deeper into his coat. "They did, but the authorities believe more are involved."

Brady lifted his hat and combed his fingers through his hair. The robberies didn't concern him, except stealing was downright wrong. "I heard the Pinkertons were involved in the investigation."

"That's comforting."

He pulled at his mustache. "In my opinion, the law around here should settle the matter and leave those fancy city detectives where they belong. In the old days, we strung up thieves and murderers. That sent a good message to the rest of 'em to behave themselves or get out."

"I understand, but—"

"This is a man's country, Miss Alexander. City slickers are not for us. It would take a lot for me to respect them Pinks."

"I heard they were well trained before being sent into the field. Some of the outlaw gangs are meeting their end through the work of the Pinkertons."

Brady tossed a stone atop the stream. What did a woman know about tracking down criminals? "Maybe so. Maybe the outlaws are simply getting lazy."

Chapter 3

For certain, Brady Miller didn't care much for the Pinkertons. Moment found his reasoning a little amusing, a consistent male opinion. He knew nothing about the history of the detective organization, and even if she were in the right frame of mind to enlighten him, she might anger him and he'd cease talking. The Pinkertons had successfully stopped a number of train robberies since the 1870s. She'd read back reports of how the investigations uncovered inside jobs as well as stopped outlaw gangs. For now, she'd act the part of a lady in distress—which wasn't hard—until Mr. Miller slipped up. Moment could only imagine his ire when he learned a lady Pinkerton outsmarted him.

"You're quiet, Mo," he said, chuckling. "Maybe I should enjoy it and not get anything started."

Moment swallowed the irritation threatening to surface. "If you insist upon calling me Mo, you will most assuredly rile me."

"Living with nine brothers make you gutsy?"

What she'd like to say to this man. "Tough and mean too."

He laughed and tilted back his hat. "You forgot clever, and I remember you said you were a fair shot. I bet you're a real Annie Oakley."

She dampened her lips and masked a grin. "Truthfully, I don't like guns, but I know how to use them."

"What about a little target practice?" The smirk on Mr. Miller's face needed taking care of.

Moment took her time in responding. "All right, but not for very long. I need to get back to town."

"What are the stakes?"

Your confession to all of those train robberies. "I have no idea. What is this worth to you?"

"When I beat you, then you ride behind me to Windmere Falls."

"And if I win?"

"I'll buy you supper."

Sharing a meal with a potential criminal who had the finesse of a tobacco-spitting mule sounded more like the bad end of a pitchfork. She imagined most women threw themselves at his feet, but not her.

"I believe you strike a fair deal." She attempted to stand, and Mr. Miller offered a hand to assist her. Her feet still ached. No matter what the outcome, she would never struggle with Victoria's boots again, neither would she complain to Mr. Miller.

"What are we using as a target?" she asked.

He grinned again, an obnoxious smirk. "Do you have a preference?"

Moment glanced about her. She simply wanted to show

him her ability to hit something. "We could use one of these leaves against a tree."

He snatched up a scarlet one and stuck it atop a loosed piece of bark. "How far back?"

She shrugged. "Fifty feet?"

"Why don't you stand at twenty-five, and I'll shoot at fifty? I sure don't want to take advantage of a woman."

Did he think she'd cry? "No, thank you. I want to be equal."

"Suit yourself, Mo."

If he called her Mo one more time, she'd send a hole through his fancy hat. He must have sensed her anger, for he quickly retracted.

"Miss Alexander," he said, leaning her way, "would you like to take the first shot?"

She reached for his Winchester, a model 1876. At least she was well familiar with this rifle. For a moment, she let her mind linger on days gone by when she and her brothers nailed bull's-eyes to the back of one of Papa's barns. They teased her unmercifully until she could handle an old shotgun that more often than not sent her sprawling to the ground. It was her way of getting even when they asked her to go riding.

He backed off plenty from the tree. "Are you ready?"

"Yes, Sir." She eyed the center of the brittle leaf. Holding her breath, she squeezed the trigger. The thundering echo broke the peacefulness of the morning, and she watched the leaf crumble into dust. "Looks like beginner's luck." Moment tossed Mr. Miller a demure smile. She walked toward him and handed him the Winchester. "Your turn. I'll stick up another leaf."

He scowled and took his place. In the next instant, he had shattered the leaf.

"We're even," she called out.

"No, we're not." A muscle twitched in his right cheek. "We'll go another round, this time a little farther back."

Three more rounds, and each held their own.

"Are you ready to quit?" Moment asked. She'd made her point, and she really needed to get going.

Mr. Miller lifted the rifle to his shoulder. "Very few men have ever beat me, and now I'm looking at a half-pint of a woman who shoots better than I do."

Moment laughed, no longer able to conceal her mirth. "You haven't lost, Mr. Miller. We're tied."

"Same thing."

"I'm sorry."

"No, you're not."

With his admission, she laughed until her sides ached. Finally, she could talk again.

"I must get back to town. Although this has been great fun."

"Are you going to ride behind me?" he asked, a sparkle lighting his eyes.

"No. I actually enjoy walking, and I'm capable of making it by myself."

"I don't doubt it, but I'm still escorting you."

"Then we're back where we started," she said.

"Looks like it."

Moment snatched up her boots and moved toward the road. "Why not tell me all about yourself?"

Brady believed if he lived to be a hundred, he'd never meet another woman like the one walking alongside him on the road to Windmere Falls. Moment Alexander had looks, skill, spunk, and a witty sense of humor. Too bad she was of the female persuasion. Couldn't trust them, and he didn't intend to make exceptions. Except, the lady beside him, limping with her sore feet and wearing a winner's smile, sure did tempt him.

"What made you come to Colorado?" he asked. Might as well get to know her.

"A job."

"Couldn't you find work in Illinois?" *What about a husband?*

"Not like I wanted."

He'd heard of women wanting to become doctors, lawyers, bankers, and some ran successful ranches, but a mercantile? "What makes your store special?"

She tossed him an impish grin. "I don't own the business; I simply work there for a man who moved to Denver. I like Windmere Falls. It smells fresh and clean, not at all like Chicago, and I like living without the noise and people."

"I understand." And he did know how the wide, open spaces calmed a person's soul. He'd been to a few large cities, and the likes nearly wore him out. "So you boarded a train and came out here all by yourself?" Now he was asking questions and chirping like a bird.

"I came with my friend, Victoria Barrett-Ames. We both

work at the store and live above it."

"That's nice, Mo, real nice."

When she glared up at him, he hastily amended her name. The light in her brown eyes indicated a lot of fire beneath. He chuckled and focused his attention on the road. "I'm surprised you aren't married."

When she didn't respond, he realized he'd touched on a sensitive subject. "I'm sorry. Didn't mean to pry."

"He died of a bullet wound about four months after we were married," she said, not once lifting her gaze to meet his. "That was over two years ago."

"Sometimes new territory helps a person work through sorrow," he said after several minutes.

"I dealt with it there, and God has given me strength to build a new life for myself."

Brady admired Moment Alexander. She hadn't led the sheltered existence of so many females. Of course, he met few in his hermitlike existence.

"Ouch."

"Step on a rock?"

"Yeah, but don't go celebrating, I'll live." She limped some but continued.

"We're only about a mile from Windmere Falls." Then he did something totally unexpected and absolutely uncharacteristic. "Would you like supper tonight?"

She hesitated, and in that instant, he regretted the invitation. The whole town would be talking. Brady Miller had not only set foot in town, he'd escorted a lady to supper. Hopefully, Miss Alexander would decline and he'd head back to cowhands and cattle. He understood them better anyway.

"I think supper would be lovely, under one condition." She squinted against the bright sunlight.

"And what's that?"

"I don't have to wear boots."

He grinned. This should be interesting. "I don't care if you go barefoot."

She gave him an abrupt nod. "Don't tempt me."

"You're having supper with Brady Miller?" Gus Drummond's eyes widened. "What did you do, bribe him? Or was it the fact you're scared to death of horses?"

Moment wiggled her shoulders. She refused to tell him that Mr. Miller didn't know about her fear. "Neither. I simply used my feminine charms." She glanced about the mercantile to ignore his amusement and to see if they were truly alone. Victoria assisted a gentleman in the front of the store who needed matches and tobacco. No other customers. "Mr. Miller is rather peculiar, and I intend to follow up on a few comments he made."

"Like what?" Drummond rubbed his whiskered chin.

"Why he doesn't want anyone on his land and why he stays to himself. I understand some men prefer an isolated life, but I intend to learn all I can."

"I agree. He knows I'm a Pinkerton, and my attempts to befriend him weren't well met."

She offered a smile. "He informed me of his feelings toward the Pinks too—thinks the law here in Windmere

214

Falls should handle local problems."

"Except, the law here hasn't been able to. Anything else?"

"He's a crack shot." *Besides calling me Mo, he can be rather likeable.* Moment quickly dispelled her thoughts. A Pinkerton didn't have time for such nonsense, especially if a romantic interest interfered in her work.

"Stay on it, Miss Alexander. Criminals don't expect women to nail 'em."

The bell above the door jingled, and Jackson Griffin walked in. He waved at them and then turned his charms on Victoria.

"Talk to me tomorrow," Drummond said. "Might as well have a word with Jackson. Wish all the young men of this town had his respect for the law."

"True. His father is proud of him." Moment walked to the front of the store with him. She wanted to close a few minutes early. The idea of thinking through the past few days' happenings while soaking her bruised feet sounded more appealing than a few extra coins in the cash register.

"How's everything with you, Griffin?" Drummond offered his hand, and Jackson Griffin grasped it.

The young man had a little-boy grin complete with dimples. That was the best way to describe the preacher's son. He just seemed out to please everyone around him.

"I'm fine, Sir, just fine. Thanks for askin'." Griffin's blue eyes looked clear—what Mr. Fletcher back in Chicago termed honest eyes. He tipped his hat. "Afternoon, Miss Alexander, Miss Barrett-Ames."

"What do you need today?" Victoria's delightful English

accent wafted over the store. She lifted her chin and stood poised with her hands clasped in front of her, as though ready to serve tea.

"Rifle shells, please, Ma'am. I'd like two boxes."

"My goodness," Victoria said with her lingering smile. "Last week you purchased two boxes of shells. You must be doing quite a lot of hunting these days."

"I sure am, Ma'am. Huntin' is one of my favorite things to do, and I do like bringing in venison for the winter ahead. Since my father's accident, Mama wants me to be extra careful. Unfortunately, my aim's not too good, and I waste a lot of shells."

Drummond clapped him lightly on the back. "Well, you keep trying. I'm sure your shooting will improve."

"Maybe you could give me some tips," the young man said. "I could use a little help."

"Be glad to. Stop by the hotel tomorrow, and we'll work out a good time. You still working between the church and the lumber mill?"

"Yes, Sir." He paid his bill and politely said good-bye before leaving the store.

"What a fine young man," Drummond commented as he turned to Moment. "Too bad you aren't having supper with him. He'd be a sight better company."

She ignored the barb and proceeded to straighten the licorice and cinnamon sticks on the counter. "Does Mr. Griffin always pay for his purchases in cash?" she asked.

"Oh, yes," Victoria replied. "I believe he has too much integrity to ever ask for credit. I mean, I know many very good people can't pay, and I'm not in the least being conde-scending to them. But Mr. Griffin is a prize customer—mannerly and pays in cash."

"And his habits and those like him keep us in business," Moment said. Still, all those shells looked suspicious, and she found it hard to believe a young man could be such a bad shot.

Chapter 4

Moment stepped out of the telegraph office into drizzling, cold rain, the kind that chilled a body to the bone. For an instant, she thought she was back in Chicago, but her nose and ears quickly apprehended the dismal thought. Wrapping her shawl tightly about her, she ducked the rain and hurried into the mercantile adjoining the building.

"What uncomfortable weather," Victoria said from the rear of the store. "I'd rather spend the day around a cozy fire with a good novel."

"Oh, but reading doesn't bring the store a profit." Moment stole a glimpse at the source of Victoria's business. "Are you playing with the new shipment of ladies' hats?"

"I'm displaying them with the yard goods in hopes of enticing our ladies to make more than one purchase."

Moment tilted her head to admire Victoria's ability to arrange items so they'd catch the customers' attention. She had a yellow-ribbon bonnet near a yellow and green flowered print. "As always, it looks splendid."

Victoria scooped up a small brimmed hat decorated with a bird nest and feathers in shades of purple. She rested it on her head, allowing a few blond tendrils to frame her face. "What do you think?"

Moment studied the hat for a moment. "It looks perfect for a proper English lady." She swept her hand to the floor in a royal gesture. "Lady Victoria Barrett-Ames."

Victoria laughed and artfully placed the hat back on the shelf. "How kind of you not to insult my favorite millinery showpiece."

Moment wrinkled her nose in response.

"Did you have Mr. Drummond send the telegram?" Victoria asked. The women could talk freely with no one in the store.

"Yes, and now I wait. Patience is not one of my finer virtues. Mr. Drummond kept me waiting at the hotel desk for nearly an hour."

"I imagine you engaged the desk operator in a fine conversation."

Moment refused to answer the familiar teasing about her ability to talk with anyone about anything. "I sent the questions directly to the Denver office. If Mr. Miller has been a part of any criminal activity, they'd have the information."

"I thought Mr. Drummond said he didn't have a record."

"He did. I'm simply checking again." Moment picked up a cinnamon stick. "I'll pay for it," she said before Victoria scolded her about eating the merchandise. "I wanted to know about his parents or any siblings. I also pulled out a map this morning and checked the perimeters of his ranch—the

Double Horseshoe. It runs alongside the railroad closer than I thought. The location alone is reason enough to investigate him further. I'd like to know how he acquired it. Also, I want a rundown of all his ranch hands."

"How do you plan to obtain the names?"

"I thought about checking with Mr. Bowen to see if any of the ranch hands deposit money at the bank, but I decided not to pursue it."

Victoria blushed. "Are you wanting me to gather the information for you?"

Moment shook her head. If Victoria didn't grab hold of her senses soon, she'd be planning a wedding like Ruth and Sydney. Admittedly, Will Bowen, the owner of the bank, possessed all the traits of a gentleman, and if Moment seriously considered her friend's best interests, then he suited her well.

"I think not. I don't want anyone knowing we're Pinkertons, and Mr. Bowen would want to know why I wanted the information."

Victoria nodded. "I understand. So what are you going to do?"

"Swallow my pride and ask Mr. Drummond to find out for me." She shrugged. "Or see if Mr. Miller reveals any names."

"I nearly forgot. You had supper with him last night. Tell me all about it, Lady Moment Alexander." Victoria perched herself on a stool and folded her hands in her lap. With her white lace blouse and deep blue skirt, she looked quite the prim young woman.

Moment couldn't help smiling. The meal had been pleasant according to her standards, but Mr. Miller had more closely resembled the time she dressed her shabby dog in her brother's shirt to have tea with her doll. "The evening progressed rather interestingly," she finally said.

"Tell me more. Mr. Drummond said he was a recluse, and then he invites you to supper?"

Moment giggled. "If I hadn't been working and afraid I'd anger him, I'd have laughed out loud. The restaurant's special was pork chops, potatoes, gravy, bread, and green beans. Oh, the cook had apple pie too." She shook her head. "Normally the food is quite good, but not last night. Well, poor Mr. Miller must have never taken a woman to supper, because he was extremely nervous. He dropped his knife twice, spilled a glass of buttermilk, and dribbled gravy down his shirt."

Victoria shook her head with a frown. "How humiliating for you."

"Not me, him! He tripped over his words until he gave up, and I did all the talking."

Victoria smiled.

"I didn't learn all I needed—why he doesn't want anyone on his land and especially the names of his ranch hands. If one of them is up to no good, I could at least get a profile from the Chicago or Denver office and hopefully link it to Mr. Miller." Moment placed her hands on her hips. "He has a hint of a drawl. Not much, but enough to lead me to believe his parents may have been from Missouri or Kansas."

"When will you see him again?"

Moment thought back to their parting words. Even if the man robbed trains, he still had spent a wretched evening, and she'd felt genuinely sorry for him. His tanned, rugged face had been a perpetual shade of red. The two had managed nicely on the road back to town—well, certainly better than over tough pork chops and salty gravy. "I'm not sure. I might have to venture his way again."

"On a horse?" Victoria's eyebrows rose in obvious disbelief.

"If I have to. I learned enough about Mr. Miller to know there's more behind the man than a stoic facade."

"I think you like him," Victoria announced in a lilting voice.

"Why ever would you say such a thing?"

"I think you are intrigued by his cowboy nature." Victoria reached out to touch Moment's arm. "And it's time you progressed with your life."

"I'm working as an investigator for the most prestigious detective agency in the world. I believe what I'm doing indicates advancement with whatever God intends—not another man." *And certainly not the likes of Brady Miller.*

Every time Brady allowed his mind to wander, he remembered sharing supper with Moment Alexander. He'd been miserable, out of place, and felt like a fool. To make matters worse, the food tasted like cow patties. At first, the words formed in his mind for some kind of conversation, but when he opened his mouth, they twisted around until he couldn't speak at all.

That ought to teach him. The next time a pretty face

turned his head, he'd run the other way. The two would have done better eating bacon and beans and drinking bad coffee over a campfire. Brady recalled the noise of the restaurant's dining room. How could a man eat with all the voices and clamor of silverware and dishes? Miss Alexander talked plenty, but the woman behind them had this high-pitched laugh that reminded him of a screech owl.

Miss Alexander had been gracious by not pointing out his foolhardy attempts at sophistication. She'd smiled and chatted on whenever he stammered.

"Do you want those cattle moved to the lower pasture?" one of his hands asked, interrupting his painful memories.

With the question, relief flooded Brady's mind. For a moment, he thought he'd been swept back into the preceding night. Thinking about it made his head pound. Immediately, the sound of bawling cows and whistling hands drew him to the present. "Yeah. Won't be long before we have new calves."

"You feelin' all right?" the same man asked. "You look a bit peaked."

"Sure, Sam. Got some matters on my mind."

"Does it have anything to do with the cute gal you spent the day with yesterday?" With those words, Sam grinned and then spun his mustang around and rode toward the herd.

Brady was glad he didn't have to respond. Not only did he have a certain cute gal under his skin, but now his ranch hands knew it too. If he could forget last night, he'd surely do so. Of course, it did his pride good to have a woman interested enough to ask genuine questions about his life and ranch. Normally a woman pestering him about things sent him running, but he kinda liked this one.

When he heard a shout from the west, Brady remembered why he'd been out riding yesterday before meeting Miss Alexander. He'd heard gunshots in the wee hours of the morning. The shots had echoed from a westerly direction. None of his ranch hands knew of their origin, but they'd heard the shots. If someone had camped on his land, they best be gone before nightfall, and he'd better not find a dead cow full of buckshot. In any event, he needed to inspect some fencing up that way.

Within the hour, Brady picked his way over rocks toward higher ground. It wound around the hills and finally down to a fertile valley. The cattle liked the choice grazing here, but autumn freezes had taken care of the grass. He knew of a few caves in the area, although the thought of encountering a bear looking for a hibernating den didn't set well. Maybe his cautious nature had gotten the best of him, but he had learned a long time ago the poison of ignoring what was happening around him. He'd sworn then to always keep both eyes open, and every time he suspected someone might be using him, he repeated the same vow. If a group of boys were using one of his caves for drinking or some other nonsense, he'd end it.

The closer Brady rode to the secluded area, the more apprehension settled on him. He pulled out his rifle and readied it. Within a half mile, he dismounted and led his horse around to the top of a hill that sheltered the roof of a cave.

Boot tracks seized his attention. Brady tied his horse to a sapling and bent to examine the prints further. They looked fresh, as though made this morning. From the indentation of one, he saw the right boot had a hole above the heel. He scrutinized the area surrounding the tracks. The man looked to have hunched down for some time, shifting his weight to the front of the boot, overlooking the top of the cave. Creeping further, Brady peered over the ledge and saw remains of a smoldering campfire. Two, possibly three, men were involved. They hadn't tried to cover up what they were doing, which indicated they would be back.

Brady considered contacting Sheriff Masters, but he'd feel right foolish if all he'd witnessed were a couple of boys skipping school. He stole another look at the boot prints. Those were the tracks of a full-grown man.

Listening for every crackling leaf, he kneeled motionless over the cave's opening. Certain he was alone, he gathered up the reins and moved down to the cave opening. The men had either been there for a long time or often frequented the place. What he didn't know was why they were there or when they planned to return. Why bothered him more than when. In walking across the campfire area for a third time, he determined three men had been there.

Maybe he'd bring a couple of his hands up here and wait for them. Realizing he couldn't do much more, he led his horse from the campsite. A shot rang out, and Brady grabbed his left shoulder as blood spurted between his fingers. He dodged under a layering of rock and peered out. Nothing. He glanced down. The gaping hole was dangerously close to his heart. Either the man on the other end of the rifle aimed for his heart and missed or aimed to scare him. Brady fired a shot, expecting another one headed his way. When several long minutes passed, he crept from his hiding place and managed to mount his horse. Blood flowed down his chest like a crimson river.

❧

Moment had no sooner closed her eyes than a loud banging at the door startled her. She glanced at Victoria, who instantly sat up in her bed.

"Who is it?" Moment called out into the darkness.

"It's Drummond." The flat timbre of his voice gave her concern.

Curious and a little afraid, she grabbed her wrap and headed to the door. "I'm hurrying. What's wrong?" She flung open the door that led to the outside stairway leading down to the mercantile.

"The sheriff contacted me about an hour ago. Looks like Brady Miller got shot."

"How badly is he hurt?"

"Doc says he's going to be all right. One of his ranch hands brought him in late last night."

"What time is it now?"

"About five-thirty. I thought you might already be up."

"Not until six," a sleepy Victoria called.

Moment tried to focus. She trembled, willing her nightmares to flee. The night Thomas died, she'd been awakened early, before six. A bullet wound. The similarities were too real, too frightening. She ushered her thoughts to the present. "You must have something you want me to do. I'll get the lantern."

"No, don't draw attention to us. I wouldn't want Mabel Hawkins to see me here. I'd like for you to visit Miller this morning, sort of a goodwill call. See if he will tell you more than what he told the sheriff."

"Which was?"

"Said he'd been riding on the west side of his ranch when someone shot him."

"Did he see anyone?"

Drummond shook his head. "No. He made it back to his place, and when the fellas there couldn't stop the bleeding, they loaded him in the back of a wagon and brought him here."

"What kind of gun?"

"Rifle, a Winchester. I saw the bullet before handing it back to Sheriff Masters."

"Half the men in this town own a Winchester." She expelled a frustrated breath. "All right. I'll dress and pay Mr. Miller a call." Moment closed the door. Her mind whirled with memories of Thomas.

"Moment, do sit down. I know exactly what you are thinking." Victoria swung her feet to the floor and escorted Moment to the bed.

"This is not Thomas," she soothed.

"I know."

"Mr. Miller will recover. Mr. Drummond said so."

"I know." Moment's voice sounded weak. She hated remembering. . . .

Victoria wrapped her arm around Moment's shoulders. "You have grown fond of him in two meetings, haven't you?"

In the blackness, her friend's words moved Moment to weeping.

"Surely not. I believe the coincidence of the shooting unnerved me for an instant. I'm rather tough, you know."

"Of course," Victoria said softly. "Would you like for me to go with you?"

Moment shook her head. She needed to do this alone— face the demons laughing at her fears. "I'll be fine. He might not want to see me after our supper problems. I plan to see him friend to friend, which is precisely what we are."

"All right. I'll be here waiting when you return."

Moment leaned her head on Victoria's shoulder. "Thank you. Will you pray for Mr. Miller?"

"I already have."

Before the sun could announce a new day, Moment made her way a few buildings down to the doctor's home and office. She tried not to think about Thomas and those early-morning hours years ago. He'd worked as a policeman in Chicago until a drunk shot him. It was mid-February, and a thick layer of snow and ice lay on the ground. Thomas had been trying to help the man find shelter.

With a deep breath, she let herself into the office. "Doc Wingert?"

"Yes, I'm in the back."

"I hear you have a friend of mine back there."

"Depends." She imagined the doctor frowning and scratching his head. "I have two ranch hands and a fella here shot in the shoulder."

"Mr. Miller?"

"He's the man. Come on back. He's been a hard patient—complaining about everything. Maybe the sight of a pretty face will sweeten him up."

Moment made her way across the wooden floor. Planting a smile on her face, she gazed at Mr. Miller. "Good morning."

In the lamplight, he lifted a brow. "Hello, Mo. At least I know you didn't try to kill me. You're a better shot."

"Thanks, but the name is Miss Alexander, unless you want a hole in the other side."

"I believe you've met your match," one of the ranch hands said. He glanced at Moment. "My name is Sam, and this is Clay."

"Pleased to meet you, gentlemen. Are you making him behave himself? Because if you're having a difficult time, I might give you a few ideas."

Mr. Miller grinned. "I thought you were supposed to make me feel better."

"Oh, I am. I've come to hold your hand and spoon-feed you nasty-tasting medicine."

He raised a brow. "How did you know I was here?"

"News travels fast."

He grimaced. "Right now, I want my gun so I can go hunting."

Chapter 5

Moment heard the anger in Mr. Miller's voice. She stared at the blood-soaked bandages and saw pain etched around his eyes and forehead. For the first time, she hoped he didn't have a part in the train robberies. If he'd been involved in the plan to rob the local train, then why had he been shot? Brady Miller didn't sound like the Ghost to her.

The thought sent her senses spiraling, and she attempted to steady them by telling herself a thief could bleed and hurt as well as an innocent man. As a committed Pinkerton, she had a case to solve, and identifying criminals could not share a room with sentiment. Unlike the courts, she viewed Mr. Miller as guilty until proven otherwise.

Victoria's earlier words returned. Did she feel something for this man lying so helpless before her? The thought twisted in her mind and refused to let go. She'd believed no other man could take Thomas's place, and until this very minute, she hadn't wanted to consider another. *I can't lose my heart. My devotion belongs to my work. . .nothing else.*

"You're not the ideal patient." She dragged a chair to the bedside.

"Amen," Doc Wingert said.

Mr. Miller scowled. "When can I go home?"

"You need rest." Doc picked up a bloody instrument and dropped it into a pan.

"I can sleep at home." He turned his head to look at his shoulder, and his face paled.

"Mr. Miller, you can't move your head without hurting," Moment said. "Riding in a wagon back to your ranch could not be good for you."

"Thank you, Ma'am," Doc said, gathering up soiled rags. "Tomorrow I might agree to getting rid of him—as much as I'd like to send him home now—but he's lost a tremendous amount of blood, and I want to watch him."

"What am I supposed to do?" Mr. Miller's eyes closed. "I have work to do."

"Precisely why I'm not cutting you loose." Doc Wingert addressed the two ranch hands. "Why don't you head over to the restaurant for breakfast? Once you're done, I'll let you know when you can take him home tomorrow. Remember what the sheriff said. No one's to know about the shooting."

The two hands wasted no time in leaving the doctor's office. Moment wondered if their stomachs were the deciding issue or if her presence made them uncomfortable. Probably both. Doc lifted the basin full of dirty instruments and rags. "Miss Alexander, I'll be in the next room tidying things up. Let me know when you leave."

She nodded and watched him walk away.

"It's not right you're here," Mr. Miller said without meeting her gaze.

"Why?"

"First of all, I'm red-faced about the other night."

"You shouldn't be. The food wasn't the best, but I don't see how you could be to blame."

He pressed his lips together. "You know what I'm talking about."

She sighed and offered a smile. "I hadn't given it another thought."

"Well, I have."

"Is that how you got shot? Thinking about our supper?" She meant for the questions to sound humorous, but her training had taught her to take advantage of every instant, including this one.

"Not exactly. I've asked you this before, but how did you know about the shooting?"

She didn't want to lie. "Mr. Drummond."

"Am I in the way of you two?"

Moment wanted to laugh. She purposely hesitated to answer. "We're friends, and he felt a need to tell me about you."

"I'd just as soon keep this information quiet."

"I understand. What did happen?"

He hesitated, and for a moment, she thought he might refuse to talk. "I was riding on the western side of my ranch when someone got trigger happy."

He'd given the sheriff the same story. Moment waited.

"He may think he got by with it, but he doesn't know me

very well. Trespassing is one thing, but ambushing a man is another."

"I'm sure Sheriff Masters will find him."

"Like he found the train robbers?"

Realizing this conversation held little merit, Moment bent her words in another direction. "Would you like for me to contact anyone about this?"

He gave her a startled look. "There's only me and the Lord; besides, I'm not dying."

She stood and pointed to his wound. "Looks like the bullet hit rather close to your heart."

"Poor shot." Suddenly a spasm of pain wrenched his rugged features.

"I'm sorry, Mr. Miller. You need your rest, and you surely won't get your strength back by talking to me."

"Didn't mean to run you off."

"You're not. I need to tend to a few things before the store opens. Would you like for me to visit you later?"

"Sure, and thanks for stopping by."

She bid him good-bye and left the room—a little more shaken than she cared to admit. Brady Miller looked a lot less intimidating this morning than he did the day he saved her life from the cougar. Drummond described him as a feisty recluse, but Moment saw a different side of him, one she'd like to get to know.

Brady fought the sleep tugging at his senses and dulling his mind. He'd been awake since the afternoon before, and he didn't feel quite like resting until he sorted out a few things.

The biggest matter plaguing his mind was who shot him. To his recollection, he didn't have any enemies. Admittedly, he let folks know he didn't want them on his land, and his gruff mannerisms discouraged those who wanted to socialize. Still, he didn't think he'd made anybody mad enough to try to kill him.

Or maybe the man who shot him didn't care if he was Brady Miller. Maybe his curiosity at the cave nearly got him killed because someone didn't want him snooping around. Were they stealing from him? That made no sense at all, for cattle and horses were all Brady had worth taking, and those couldn't be kept in a cave. Or perhaps those train robbers were involved in this, and they hid the money in the cave. After all, he'd stumbled onto the hidden spot a couple of years after he bought the land.

Brady blinked. The sheriff ought to know about his suspicions. But if he had made a mistake, he'd look like a fool. Best keep his thoughts to himself and let Sheriff Masters or that city-slicker Pinkerton figure it out.

As soon as I can ride, I'm going back to take another look.

An incessant throb pounded from his upper shoulder down into his chest. With a deep breath, he captured Miss Alexander's pretty face in his mind's eye. In the beginning, he termed her as cute, but she had lovely features. This morning, she'd not worn a hat, and he was privy to all that thick brown hair pinned up loosely. He might try asking her to supper again. No, he wouldn't. Memories of his stammering tongue halted him.

Brady couldn't hold off sleep any longer. Once he rested,

he'd talk Doc Wingert into letting him go home.

The morning sped by at the mercantile. Victoria and Moment found no time to discuss the investigation until mid-afternoon when Drummond made an appearance. The broad-shouldered Scotsman had a good-natured side to him. Over the months, he'd shaken some of his animosity toward Mr. Fletcher for sending him women detectives. He could still be gruff—but more tolerable than back in the spring. At times, Moment recalled how rude he'd been to Ruth and Sydney, but when they proved their mettle, he praised their work. Now she wanted to show him she had the Pinkerton ingenuity too.

Glancing at the counter where Victoria filled a rancher's order, Moment felt a bit of sadness for her dear friend. She may look the part of a spoiled, well-bred Englishwoman, but she had a clever mind. Unfortunately, she had turned up nothing in the case, and Moment knew it bothered her considerably. Matters didn't help when Drummond insisted upon calling her Miss Vicky. Secretly, Moment didn't mind Mr. Miller shortening her name to Mo, but to Victoria the nickname was an insult.

The bell jingled above the door, and Ruth walked in wrapped in a pale blue shawl, her cheeks glistening in the chilly air.

"You look positively radiant," Victoria said after she completed the rancher's order. "I daresay it must be love."

"It is," Ruth said. "I wanted to tell you that we've set a date."

Moment laughed. "I could tell on your face when you walked in. Oh, tell us when!"

"We've decided on a Christmas wedding. I know Sydney won't be here, but I am hoping you two can be."

"Most certainly I will," Victoria said. "This will be such a delightful holiday. Please, let me help with the preparations."

"And I will be here too," Moment added. "I'm not a great seamstress or creative, but surely there must be something I can do."

"Having you both at the ceremony is all I want." Ruth giggled. "Although, I'm sure once the plans are started, I'll be overwhelmed. I can't sleep at nights as it is. Alice Duncan wants to make my dress, which relieves a heavy burden from me. She insists that all I have to do is find a picture. Can you believe that?"

"And how is Mr. Chandler handling this?" Moment asked, picturing him with his dark heavy brows solemnly taking his vows.

"He's managing, but I believe he will be glad when the wedding is planned and over."

"I suggest we begin with your dress," Victoria said. "Do you know what you want?"

"That's one of the reasons I'm here. I came to select fabric—nothing fancy. I want to wear it afterward to church."

"I see." Victoria hugged Ruth's shoulders. "Mr. Chandler put the sparkle in your eyes, and God placed His love in your hearts."

Tears welled in Ruth's eyes. "Thank you. You two are the best friends in the world. I just wish Sydney could be here."

"Maybe she will surprise you," Moment said.

"That sounds nice." Ruth bent in closer. "How's your investigation going?"

Moment sighed and gave herself a pause to reflect. "My suspect got himself ambushed and shot yesterday."

Ruth frowned. "Maybe he's not your man."

"I'm beginning to wonder. There's a lot of work to be done yet."

Another customer entered the store, and Victoria hurried to greet her, while Moment showed Ruth the yard goods.

"I can't choose," Ruth finally said. "At least I don't have to purchase the fabric today."

Moment loved watching Ruth's excitement. How wonderful to feel the tingling of love. It had been a long time since she'd indulged in those light-headed remembrances of yesterday. "Why not think about it? In the meantime, we may be receiving more yard goods."

Ruth replaced a bolt of pale blue fabric. "I agree. My mind is moving faster than a hummingbird's wings."

Moment inhaled deeply and took a glance about to see if anyone could hear their conversation. "Ruth," she began, "do you know the particulars about Pastor Griffin's hunting accident?"

Her friend blinked and hesitated, as though searching through her wealth of memories to remember the details. "I believe the pastor and Jackson were trailing a deer when Pastor Griffin slipped on an embankment, and his rifle went off. Jackson went for help." She looked at Moment curiously. "I know your mind. How do you think the accident connects with the train robberies?"

"I'm not sure it does," Moment said. "I'm just wondering about Jackson."

"Jackson? He's every mother's dream."

"Sometimes I think he's too good to be true."

"You could ask the sheriff or Doc Wingert."

"I will," Moment said. *Very soon.*

By the end of the day, Moment had not found the time to visit Mr. Miller. Once the mercantile held the "Closed" sign in the window and the door was securely locked, she grabbed her shawl and walked toward Doc Wingert's. Her mind spun with the investigation and how she truly felt about Mr. Miller. Deep in her heart, she wanted to believe in his innocence, even if those reasons were selfish and the thought of loving another man frightened her immensely.

With a deep breath, she strode past the gunsmith and met Jackson Griffin coming from the establishment with two rifles and a revolver.

"Looks like you're going to be busy," Moment said. "Hunting again?"

The preacher's son glanced her way. He frowned and then in the next moment, flashed a bright smile. "Good evenin', Miss Alexander. Yes, I plan to do a little more hunting."

"I didn't think you could hunt with a revolver." Curiosity piqued her interest.

"Oh, the revolver." His left eye twitched. "This is for protection. I got it for my father. Can't be too careful these days with all the goings-on. I heard Brady Miller got shot real bad yesterday."

How did he find out? "How horrible. Is he going to be all right?"

"I'm not rightly sure." He pointed to the doctor's office. "See if Doc Wingert is in. I'm sure he could tell you about it."

She purposely shivered. "The streets of Windmere Falls aren't safe for anyone. I hope Sheriff Masters puts an end to this soon."

"I agree." He shifted. "Well, I'll be seeing you."

"Tonight at church?"

He hesitated. "Naturally, Ma'am. You know me, I never miss church."

Moment watched the young man place the guns in a wagon and drive out of town—away from the parsonage.

Chapter 6

"Good evening," Moment said in the doorway where Mr. Miller lay. His pale skin revealed his pain and loss of blood, but he did look more rested.

"You mean I've slept all day?" He craned his neck to see outside through the solitary window in his room. His eyes widened. "The sun's setting."

"You must have taken the doc's advice," she said. "Are you up to a visitor?"

He frowned. "I'm pretty ornery right now."

"That's nothing new."

He offered a wry smile, and she moved to his bedside. "I told Sam and Clay to be here no later than the afternoon, and I haven't seen hide nor hair of them."

"Good. You need to stay here at least tonight. Besides, Doc said tomorrow afternoon."

He attempted to lift his head from the pillow, but obvious discomfort forced him back.

"See what I mean? I bet I could get Doc to tie you to the bed."

"I thought you were on my side. I have a ranch to run."

She enjoyed the bantering more than she'd ever let him know. "How long have you been a rancher?"

"About ten years here."

"Where before that?"

He swallowed hard, and she realized she'd overstepped his privacy line. But if he answered, she'd learn more about him.

"Texas. I didn't have a spread there."

Curiosity needled her. "What did you do?"

"I was a sheriff."

If he had thrown a rock at her stomach, she could not have had a more fierce inner reaction. Bound by her training as a Pinkerton, she couldn't let him view her feelings.

"So you traded law for cattle and horses?"

"In a manner of speaking." He turned away from her. "I don't feel much like talking." His stoic demeanor alerted her senses. This topic clearly upset him.

"All right." Dread washed over her. "Shall I leave you alone?"

He kept his attention away from her. "Probably so. I'm not much company."

Moment smiled. "I'd like to visit in the morning, if you don't mind."

"Suit yourself."

She left Doc Wingert's office wondering about Mr. Miller's life in Texas. There was one way to find out if he told the truth. Gus Drummond.

She found the Pinkerton man at the restaurant and relayed her brief conversation with Brady Miller.

"We looked for a criminal record on him, not the other way around," he said. "I'll send a wire first thing in the morning." He swirled the water in his glass. "You realize we may have the wrong man?"

Moment nodded. "I have another suspect."

"Who?"

"I'd prefer to keep his name to myself until I find out more." She rose from her chair. "I'm going to be late. Church starts in a few minutes."

He pointed a finger at her. "Don't get yourself killed over this. I need to know what you've learned."

She mustered her most charming smile and then left the restaurant. Picking up her pace, she hurried to the other end of town to church. Moment needed to pray for wisdom. As rough as Mr. Miller appeared, deep down she felt he could not possibly be one of the thieves—and she also felt the town had been duped by Jackson Griffin. How did she prove to all of Windmere Falls that he was not the town's favorite son?

Lord, I need guidance here. Please give me discernment and wisdom. And, Lord, if I'm wrong, hit me with lightning or something.

When the service ended, Moment's heart seemed heavier than before. She spotted Jackson heading for the rear door and knew she had to follow him. Without informing Victoria, who chatted away with Ruth and Alice Duncan about the upcoming wedding, she exited the building. Some of the parishioners mingled outside, but Jackson walked past them, calling out familiar greetings, and headed up Main

Street into town. Moment stayed close enough to watch and far enough not to arouse his attention. His step picked up, past Doc Wingert's office, the mercantile, barbershop, and on until he swung a left at the hotel. In the shadows, she crossed the street to avoid the saloon. He stood outside the establishment, whistled twice, then strode on to the rear of the livery and along the railroad tracks.

Moment slipped to the side of the same building and waited. She heard nothing for several minutes except the night sounds of insects and a barking dog. Just when she felt like giving up, she made out the forms of two men standing by the tracks. Their low-pitched voices urged her forward until she moved to the livery and crouched at the corner of the building.

"Where you been, Jackson?" The man's voice was foreign to Moment.

"Behaving myself. It's hard to get out of the house when your father is the local preacher."

The man laughed. "But you're out tonight. Did the prayer meetin' let out early?"

"Naw. I didn't feel like being sociable. I needed a drink, and being around those people all the time makes me want to get crazy drunk."

The skin on the back of Moment's neck prickled.

"We're having a little party tomorrow night in the usual place. Want to come along?"

"You bet. About nine o'clock? Going to have a little target practice?"

"I imagine so. I've been winning a fair amount of money

since you haven't been around."

"That won't happen tomorrow." Jackson laughed. "Any women there?"

The man chuckled. "Yep. Don't you worry; we'll have a good time. Got a few minutes? I want to show you my new stallion."

The voices drew closer, and so did the likelihood of being exposed. The silvery cast of a half moon shone directly in her path. Moment pressed her back and hands against the side of the livery and crept to the front. A splinter lodged in her palm. She bit her lip to keep from crying out. The two men sounded as if they were right behind her.

"I'd like to talk a little business after I show you my horse," the one man said.

"Sure. This will be the most excitement I've had all day. I'm going to be in the market for some good horseflesh in a few weeks. Riding the preacher's broken-down mare is humiliating."

Moment sucked in her breath. She'd be discovered in the next instant! If she didn't fear having her heart fail, she'd crawl into a stall until they left.

One of the men snatched up the lantern and struck a match.

"Why, Miss Alexander, what are you doing here?" Jackson held up the lantern.

"Swing that away from my eyes," Moment said, shielding her eyes. "You're blinding me."

"I'm sorry. You surprised me being in the livery at this hour."

"I wanted to check on a horse that I'd ridden earlier in the week." She detested lying, even to a deceiver. "I walked from church and neglected to think about light."

"It's always here at the door," he said.

"Thank you. I suppose my negligence comes from living in Chicago." She peered around him to the man in the shadows. "Who's your friend?"

"Excuse me." Jackson stepped aside. "This is Robert Wingert."

Doc Wingert's son—one of the roughest men in town.

"Pleasure to meet you." Moment noted the man's dirty clothes and foul, alcohol-soaked breath. "I'll leave you gentlemen to your privacy. I'm finished."

"Are you certain?" Griffin's manners were impeccable. "We don't want to run you off."

"Oh, yes. I've had quite a tiring day." She ambled past them, the splinter cutting into her palm like a knife. "By the way," she said over her shoulder, "I hope your hunting gets better."

"Thank you, Ma'am." His voice held a tight edge.

Moment grinned in the dark. Aside from having to stand dangerously close to a horse, the evening had been quite productive. She wasted no time getting back to the mercantile and up the stairs to her and Victoria's room. Her dear friend would be sending Drummond after her soon.

Brady attempted to sleep, but his rudeness to Moment picked at him. In fact, he'd been like a hungry, mangy animal a good bit of the time. Folks knew to leave him be, but the Bible didn't condone such behavior. If he thought on it real hard, he couldn't come up with a single incident where Jesus displayed a bad mood and ran someone off. He remembered the moneychangers in the temple, but they were in a heap of trouble. Moment hadn't done a single thing to provoke him, other than be kind and pretty.

His mind drifted back to another woman who had been sweet and pretty. She and her brother had visited him often at the sheriff's office. Darkness crowded his thoughts while his mind wove a tale that nearly cost him his life—and the lives of those entrusted to him.

That's why he couldn't get close to Moment Alexander or any other woman. Deadly mistakes had a way of haunting a man.

Shoving aside thoughts of her warm brown eyes, he again focused on who had shot him. Brady had spent six years making sure folks were safe, and he'd learned a lot about the criminal mind. Every activity, response, and reaction mirrored the person, and when he looked at things in their way of thinking, he could figure out the motivation. Greedy men wanted something, and they'd go to any extent to get it and keep it. What frustrated him was what had the shooter been doing in that cave to risk killing a man for?

The unsolved train robberies darted in and out of his thoughts. That cave ran deep, and it was the perfect location to hide guns, ammo, and even money. In one breath he considered going to the sheriff or Gus Drummond, and in the next he feared them learning about his failure as a lawman.

With all the prayers sent heavenward for release from his past, Brady still harbored the guilt. Up until a few days ago, he'd been content with his dour reputation. But then a cute-as-a-puppy little lady who wasn't afraid of him set claims on his heart.

The door to the doc's office opened, and Robert Wingert stumbled inside. Brady had quickly sized up Doc Wingert's son last night when he came home drunk. Instead of taking to his room, he moved up next to his dad and opened a conversation with a slur of cursing about never having any money. The doc ignored his son instead of tossing him out in the street where he came from.

"You ain't dead, huh?" The drunken young man leaned against the door. "Thought you'd got shot too close to the heart."

"I'm going to make it," Brady said. "Don't suppose a smart fella like you might know who shot me?"

Wingert laughed. "My friends are all better shots. If you were snooping around something of theirs, they'd of made sure you were dead."

"Keep on the lookout for me, will you?"

"What's it worth?"

"Name your price," Brady said.

Wingert suddenly sobered. "Three hundred in gold."

"That's fair."

Robert Wingert knew who shot him.

Moment waited two days for Gus Drummond to get back with her about Mr. Miller's days in Texas. In the meantime, she stopped by to see Mr. Miller the afternoon he went home. To her surprise, the man apologized for his rudeness. His words simply added more to his credibility, but she'd feel much better once Drummond relayed the new information.

It was Friday evening, and the mercantile rang with customers. She and Victoria hadn't taken a midday meal, and both of them were tired and hungry. Finally the last customer took his bundle and left. Victoria hastily turned the window sign to "Closed" and locked the door.

"Let's straighten in the morning," Moment said. "I don't want to think about doing this tonight."

"A splendid idea. Shall we see what the restaurant is serving? Hopefully the meat isn't leather soaked in gravy."

Moment lifted her gaze. "Victoria, I never thought I'd hear you make such a remark."

Her friend rubbed her temples. "Even Lady Barrett-Ames has her instances of indiscretion."

Before Moment could respond, a pounding at the door caused them both to moan.

"We're closed," Moment called out. "Sorry."

"It's Drummond."

As weary as she felt, she desperately wanted to hear what he'd learned. She opened the door and then locked it behind him. "Did you receive a telegram?"

He nodded. "This one will shock you, 'cause it sure did me."

Moment tapped her foot on the floor. "I'm waiting. Victoria and I are headed for food and sleep."

He nodded at Victoria. "Ah, Miss Vicky, do you find

yourself in a vile temperament when you are hungry?"

"Worse, Mr. Drummond. Please don't patronize me."

His eyes twinkled, yet he said nothing and pulled a piece of paper from his coat pocket. "Brady Miller was a sheriff in Texas for six years—a good one I might add. He originally came from Missouri, then settled in West Texas before taking the job. Says here he was only eighteen years old at the time he started."

"Interesting," Moment said. "Why did he leave?"

"A woman destroyed him. Once I started reading this, I remembered the particulars. A brother and sister used Miller to cover up for rustling cattle and horses. The sister would take up his time while the brother hit the ranchers. The town thought Miller was involved until he proved the sister and brother were in it together. He resigned after their arrest and conviction. Then he moved here to Windmere Falls, although the town didn't want him to leave."

"No wonder he stays to himself," she said.

"My thoughts too." Drummond folded the paper and stuck it back inside his pocket. "I don't think Miller is a part of the train robberies. It doesn't fit his way of doing things."

"I agree." Relief calmed Moment's nerves.

"What about the other suspect?" Drummond asked.

"You didn't say a word to me about someone else," Victoria said, clearly annoyed.

Moment sighed. "I'm not ready to give you any names, but I will soon."

"Why not?" Drummond asked.

"I want to be absolutely sure. If I told you his name, you'd send me packing back to Chicago."

He stared at her curiously. "You going to tell Mr. Miller you're a Pinkerton?"

She wondered if the man could read her thoughts. "I'm considering it."

"You've lost your senses," he said.

"No, I haven't. Think about it. The shooting took place on his ranch, and the location of his property is what pulled him in as a suspect in the first place. I don't think he's telling the whole story."

"Moment," Victoria began, "what have you uncovered about the train robberies?"

"Nothing yet. Just a feeling that won't leave me alone. Maybe Mr. Miller has been tracking them. You know how he feels about trespassers."

"If you're right, why didn't he tell the sheriff?" Drummond asked.

Moment shook her head. "Ponder on it for a minute. If in his mind he made a fool of himself as a sheriff, the idea of sticking his neck out to solve a train robbery might not appeal to him. Why humiliate himself again?"

Drummond studied a far corner of the room. "You're making sense."

"Which is why I think I'll tell him who I am. You've got to admit, he's warmed up to me more than anyone else in this town."

Victoria touched her finger to her cheek. "You're forgetting one thing. If a woman betrayed him before and you tell him that you're not who he thinks you are, he isn't going to trust you either. In fact, he may despise you for the deceit."

"I'll have to take a chance."

Chapter 7

Two weeks passed, and Moment still deliberated whether to tell Brady Miller about her job. To make matters worse, she hadn't been able to keep track of Jackson Griffin. If she hadn't been afraid of horses, she could have followed him when he rode out of town. Her fears disgusted her, even more so since she'd been thrown.

Pushing her thoughts aside, she tried to concentrate on the piano prelude before church started. At times she thought if she prayed any harder, the whole world would know her dilemma. How many times had she stated that her future with the Pinkertons came before any man?

"Are you saving this, or can I sit with you?"

Moment instantly recognized the male voice. "Mr. Miller, how good to see you. Of course you may sit here."

Victoria slipped her a half-smile and scooted down the pew. "I'm Victoria Barrett-Ames," she said, extending her gloved hand. "Moment and I share a room over the mercantile."

He nodded. "Brady Miller. It's a pleasure to meet you."

He seated himself next to Moment.

"How are you feeling?" She noted a sling held his arm against his chest.

"Better. I'm impatient, wanting to be as good as new."

Pastor Griffin limped to the pulpit. She needed to concentrate on his sermon, but with Mr. Miller beside her, she'd need more than a little grace this morning. She saw a few other curious glances too.

Pastor Griffin based his sermon on Jacob, the deceiver. Moment felt her face redden and her stomach twist in a peculiar way. She had to tell Mr. Miller about her job when the service was over and face the consequences.

"Would you like dinner at the hotel?" he asked once the last hearty amen had been spoken.

"I'd be delighted." Moment cringed. She sounded like Victoria without the English accent.

"Appreciate it." He loosened his collar. "The last time didn't turn out so well. Should we ask your friend?"

Moment swung a look at Victoria, who had heard every word. "No, thank you. Ruth and I are working on wedding arrangements." She flashed a charming smile.

You could have left out the wedding arrangements.

As they made their way from the building, several people welcomed Mr. Miller and invited him back for the evening service. At one point, Moment saw Jackson Griffin studying her. They hadn't spoken since he found her in the livery. She didn't care for him, not one bit.

Pastor Griffin beamed when he saw Mr. Miller. "Been a long time," he said. "I'm glad to see you here."

"Thanks. I've missed church for too long." He smiled, and she knew he meant it.

"What happened to you?"

"I headed in when I should have headed out."

The pastor expelled a heavy sigh. "Best you watch where you're going."

"Excellent advice, and I will." Once outside, he plopped his hat back on his head, and they strolled toward the restaurant.

"I'm glad you came today." Moment wished she'd worn her lacy blue blouse with the pearl buttons.

"Me too. I need to start coming regular."

She felt herself smiling from the inside out.

"You sure look pretty today. I was afraid I'd be standing in line to talk to you."

Slow down, heart, before he hears you. "Takes a man to save me from a cougar to get my attention." Moment couldn't believe her boldness.

"Good, 'cause I'd like to talk to you about something."

"And I'd like to discuss a matter with you."

She lost her appetite while waiting for him to state what was on his mind. Her favorite—chicken and dumplings— tasted bland, while the folks around her complimented the cook. Mr. Miller appeared more relaxed this time; now she was the nervous one. He pushed back his plate and crossed his arms on the table.

"Do you mind if I talk while you finish?"

She nodded and reached for her coffee. Curiosity had given her chill bumps.

He cleared his throat. "I'd like. . .I'd like to tell you a little about my past."

Moment pushed her plate aside. "Is there enough privacy here?"

He smiled, his dark blue eyes gazing at her face. "That's why I chose this table." He hesitated. "I have a reputation for not taking to folks, and although I know it's not right, I'd like to tell you about it."

"Are you sure you want to?"

He lifted his cup to his lips. "Yes, I am. After hearing Preacher Griffin speak on Jacob and his habit of deceiving folks, I realized you needed to hear the truth about me. I told you about being a sheriff in Texas, but I didn't tell you why I left."

Moment's stomach fluttered. Guilt hit her again.

He leaned closer into the table. "About ten years ago, I fell in love with a woman who used me. She and her brother were cattle and horse rustlers. She'd keep me busy, and he'd steal from the neighboring ranchers. I finally caught on and arrested them. Afterwards, I couldn't face the people of the town and resigned."

The same story Drummond told. "I'm really sorry." Tears pooled in her eyes, especially when she considered what she had to tell him.

"I have a reason, Mo, I mean Miss Alexander. This last week I've been thinking my bitterness is eating me up inside, and God most likely wants me to start acting human again. Today's my start." His simmering gaze revealed his feelings. "You're different. I've been rude and cantankerous, and you let me have it right back with a smile. So I'd like to ask you something."

"Of course, go ahead."

"Would you mind if I come courtin'?"

Every nerve in her body ceased to react. Brady Miller wanted to come courting?

"If you're not interested, I understand. I haven't been the most pleasant cowboy."

"I would like that very much," she said through a ragged breath. "I need to tell you something about me."

"This must be the day for confessions." His smile nearly melted her resolve.

Her heart beat faster, and she felt warm, extremely warm. *Lord, I need Your help. I have to tell him, but I'm afraid.*

Suddenly he leaned back in his chair. "Now, if that don't beat all."

"What?" She didn't want to turn and stare at anyone.

"There's the sheriff, Preacher Griffin, Jackson, and Gus Drummond. Wonder why they don't send the Pinkerton back to Denver?"

For the first time in her life, Moment was speechless. She quickly prayed for help. "You don't care much for the Pinkertons, do you?"

He shook his head and narrowed his eyes. "It was a Pinkerton who told me about the goings-on in Texas."

"Mr. Miller." She moistened her lips. "What I've been trying to tell you is. . .I'm a Pinkerton, sent here on an undercover assignment."

He stared at her in silence for several minutes, then

frowned and pulled out a few bills from his pocket. Throwing them on the table, he left the hotel.

Brady stomped from the hotel and into the biting cold November wind. She'd lied to him. Women were all alike, pretty faces and deceivers. A man could lose his mind. He'd nearly done so once and almost did again. *Lord, did I hear wrong? I thought You said this woman was different.*

He'd left his horse at church. The longer he walked, the angrier he got. Moment Alexander most likely had been on his land looking for clues about those train robbers. For all he knew, she suspected him. Clenching his fists, he thought about what a fool he'd been. If she had been interested in him, it was to gain access to his land.

"Mr. Miller."

He heard her call his name, but he kept right on moving.

"Please. Let me explain."

When he refused to give her his attention, she ran up beside him and grabbed his good arm. "You're being a stubborn mule about this. If I didn't care about you, then why did I tell you about myself?"

"I don't know. What were you doing on my land that day?" He walked faster, hoping to dispel the anger raging through him.

"Looking for you."

He stopped and glared at her. "You mean you thought I was one of those thieves?"

She stood as tall as her small frame allowed and nodded. "But after I got to know you, I realized differently."

"How comforting. I bet you thought my little speech back there was amusing."

"No, I didn't. Please. Don't leave angry. Can't we talk about this?"

"No."

She shook her fist at him. "Fine, be miserable and cantankerous. You are the most judgmental, mule-headed man I've ever seen!"

"At least I'm honest." With those words he picked up his pace to the church. Snatching up his horse's reins, he headed back to the Double Horseshoe where he belonged. He vowed to never look at a woman again. They were more trouble than a she-bear with cubs.

Moment watched Brady Miller ride toward his ranch. A single tear slipped from her eye and slid down her cheek. It felt cold in the blustery wind. How could one ill-mannered man touch her to the point of tears? He could be rude and obnoxious—and he could be caring. The deep sound of his voice emitted strength and warmth, and the sound of his laughter tickled her. A godly woman couldn't fall in love in such a short time—or could she?

Lord, take care of him. She prayed her deceitful actions wouldn't stop him from coming back to church.

Turning her back to the wind, she walked home. Her thoughts centered on Mr. Miller and how she could rid him from her heart and mind. Thankfully, Victoria planned to be with Ruth and Mrs. Duncan all afternoon; Moment needed the time to deliberate her mistake with Mr. Miller and decide how to nail the train robbers. If she failed in her relationship with the rancher, at least she could complete her assignment.

Sitting alone and sipping on coffee, her thoughts centered on Jackson Griffin. He had the town fooled; she was sure of it. The night she'd followed him and overheard his conversation proved it. Every time she heard his syrupy "Yes, Sir" or "Yes, Ma'am," she bordered on being sick. The whole town looked up to him. No one would believe his real nature.

Moment caught her breath. Mrs. Griffin! No one understood the strengths and weaknesses of a person like a mother. Setting her mug on the table, she decided to pay Sarah Griffin a little visit. The woman might not easily tell it all, but she might with a little prodding.

Within a few minutes, Moment stood at the door of the parsonage. She hoped the younger Mr. Griffin had plans. She had an inkling he could find plenty to do on a Sunday afternoon that didn't involve his parents.

"Afternoon, Miss Alexander," Pastor Griffin said and ushered her inside. "How can I help you?"

"I wondered if Mrs. Griffin is busy. I wanted to talk to her." Moment didn't want to deceive either of these precious people—in fact, she didn't want to mislead anyone.

Pastor Griffin took her heavy shawl and led her into the parlor, where she seated herself in a comfortable sofa. Mrs. Griffin bustled in, and judging from the spot of flour on her nose, she must have been baking.

"I'm keeping you from the kitchen," Moment said with a smile. "I see a telltale sprinkling of flour on your nose."

"Oh, dear." The portly woman brushed at her nose. "I'm sorry."

"I am the one interrupting. Could we talk in the kitchen?"

Mrs. Griffin gave her a sideways glance. "I don't often do baking on a Sunday afternoon, being it's the Lord's Day, but tomorrow morning is a funeral for an elderly church member who has a large family."

"Please. I'm used to nine brothers and a busy mother who never had enough baking done. I'd feel much better if we talked there."

Mrs. Griffin smiled, and in the next breath they were in the kitchen tending to apple pies. Moment rolled up her sleeves, intent on helping.

"I couldn't let you—"

Moment waved the comment away. "I want to, really. This is one part of home I miss."

"All right, Dear. Let me tie an apron around you. Wouldn't want to soil your pretty dress." She handed Moment the rolling pin. "Did you say nine brothers?"

"Yes, Ma'am." She laughed. "They were a handful, still are."

"I can only imagine. Jackson is our only child, and he has his moments."

"With Jackson? He's the model son." She studied Mrs. Griffin's face and saw what she anticipated—a cloud of sadness.

"No one is perfect. Even the best of men have a flaw or two."

"I agree," Moment said. "Is he here? I'd be humiliated if he heard us discussing men's flaws."

Mrs. Griffin shook her head. "He went visiting friends somewhere out of town."

Moment continued to roll the pie dough to fit the size of the pan. "I'm sure you are very proud."

"Most of the time." The woman's words were nearly a whisper. Moment didn't need to prod her any further; she had her answer.

Moment stayed until time for the evening service for two reasons—she enjoyed Mrs. Griffin's motherly ways and she wanted to see if Jackson returned. He didn't.

All during the opening music of the evening service, she thought about him. She'd learned enough not to trust a single word he said. The idea of hurting his parents once she proved his involvement in the train robberies didn't sit well. And yet he had to be stopped before more innocent people were hurt or killed. Moment must follow him, which meant riding a horse. Waiting on him to make a mistake while in town had proved ridiculous. A wise Pinkerton understood criminals were clever—often more clever than those who hunted them down.

I rode a horse once; I can do it again. The mare hadn't been at fault when it threw her. Victoria said Moment had pulled too hard on the reins. She had no excuse but fear, and with God's help she could overcome the panic rising in her whenever she encountered a horse.

When the truth was laid bare, Jackson Griffin probably had a hand in Mr. Miller's shooting. She didn't want to think about Mr. Miller—not now, tomorrow, or the next day. She'd destroyed anything they could have ever had. In his eyes, she shared the same characteristics as the woman he sent to jail in Texas.

The younger Mr. Griffin walked down the aisle, his heels clicking against the wooden floor, and took his place on the front pew. He smiled and played the role as always. She wondered what his tune would be when he looked at the world from behind bars.

Pastor Griffin made his way to the front of the church. He announced they would continue to talk about Jacob and the cost he paid for deceiving those around him. Moment focused her attention on the message and hoped she didn't weep with the emotion welling inside her.

Lord, I thought You wanted me in this job, but now I wonder if my desire came from wanting justice for Thomas's death. Help me find a way to end the train robberies and to do Your will.

God and God alone would squelch her fears and bring justice to Windmere Falls.

Maybe when the smoke cleared, she might try to talk to Brady Miller again.

Chapter 8

Moment watched Jackson for the next ten days, and he outwitted her every time. Even with her determination to follow him on horseback, he still eluded her. She nicknamed him the snake—able to wiggle in and out without much notice. Three times she convinced Drummond to escort her to the livery in an effort to make friends with Night. When she finally gathered the nerve to pet the horse's nose, she found it velvety soft. But the mouth was large, and she'd never forget sliding off the mare's back. Drummond showed her how to bridle and saddle the horse, especially how to tighten the cinch.

Amidst all her problems, her heart lingered on Mr. Miller. He'd been back to church, but he sat in the back, obviously to ignore her. She wouldn't beg for his attention. Victoria had found her weeping and offered a comforting shoulder. The unfairness of it all made Moment short-tempered. Why had she fallen for a man who despised her? The most difficult part to accept was that he had a right to loathe her.

Thursday morning saw the second snowfall. In the distance, snowcapped mountains rose up like fortresses against the sky, but in Windmere Falls the temperatures were much milder. The powdery flakes reminded her of the upcoming holidays, including Ruth's wedding. Normally snow and the thought of spending time with family and friends excited her. Not this time. Surely God must be disappointed in her.

Whenever possible, she kept her attention focused on the storefront window in hopes of seeing Jackson Griffin walk by on his way to the livery. He kept the pastor's horse there instead of at the parsonage, most likely because he didn't have to explain his whereabouts. This particular morning, while the snow dusted the ground like a baker sprinkling flour, she spotted Jackson crossing to the opposite side of the street and heading for the livery.

"I've got to go," she said to Victoria. Snatching up her coat, scarf, and a rifle, she hurried after him.

"Where?" Victoria asked.

"To end the train robberies."

"You need Mr. Drummond."

Moment didn't have time to reply. She kept far enough behind Jackson not to alert him to her plans. As suspected, he entered the livery and, shortly afterwards, left riding his mare out of town. Moment hurried inside and quickly saddled Night. Her fear of the horse had not vanished, but the anticipation of finding evidence linking Jackson to the robberies seized control. Luckily, the horse prints were easily followed in the snow. She trotted Night until she realized she might trail too close to him.

Without warning, her gaze swept ahead to where the road climbed and disappeared into a thicket of pine trees. At the top of the road, Jackson sat erect in the saddle. He paused, then turned right. Moment pulled slightly on the reins, and Night stopped. Without moving a muscle, she waited until she felt certain he could not view her. Slowly she rode up the hill. This time she intended to find the evidence needed to arrest Jackson Griffin.

Brady shrugged on his coat. The memory of Moment Alexander and what she'd started to mean to him burned in his heart and mind. He'd poisoned himself against women, and those thoughts did not come from God. What did come from Him dealt with love, forgiveness, and grace. Nothing else compared to those free gifts. That's why he headed to the barn for his gelding and planned to ride into Windmere Falls. First, he intended to see Miss Alexander and apologize in hopes they could start a relationship. Secondly, he'd pay Gus Drummond and Sheriff Masters a call. He'd found someone had stashed guns, ammunition, and explosives in the cave on his land, and since it was close to the railroad, he figured the train robbers were involved. No point in trying to take care of the matter by himself. His pride had shattered with the understanding he needed God and Miss Alexander in his life.

The ride into town gave him more time to think. God had snatched him right out of his private ugly world and reminded him about the joy of living. He'd always had a peculiar temperament, but that didn't give him a reason to be downright mean. Those days were over, whether Moment Alexander wanted him or not.

Brady stopped at the mercantile. Nervousness nipped at his heels, and it took a word of prayer to step inside.

"Good morning, Mr. Miller," Miss Barrett-Ames said in her proper English accent. She wore the silliest hat Brady had ever seen, but he would not make a comment.

"Is Miss Alexander here?"

"No, she's not." The woman removed the hat and placed it with a host of others. "She left quite abruptly this morning, and I'm a bit frightened for her."

Alarm sounded in his brain. "Did she leave alone?"

Miss Barrett-Ames nodded and moistened her lips. "I know she told you about working for the Pinkertons."

"Yes, Ma'am. Does this have anything to do with the case she's working on?"

"I'm positively convinced it does. She's been watching someone for days, and I think she spotted this person earlier. In fact, she took her rifle."

"What about Drummond?"

The woman frowned. "Moment is an independent sort. She wouldn't tell me or Mr. Drummond who she suspected."

"Would she be on foot or horseback?"

"You could check the livery. But if Moment rode out, she would have to be definite about her evidence."

"Why's that?"

Miss Barrett-Ames sighed. "She's deathly afraid of horses. Remember when you found her and she walked back to town?"

Realization hit Brady like an avalanche. "How would I know which horse she took?"

Miss Barrett-Ames rushed to the back of the store and picked up a coat. Hurrying toward him, she swung the sign in the window to "Closed." "I know which one."

"I wish I had some way of tracking her," Brady said as they walked briskly toward the livery.

Miss Barrett-Ames hesitated. "The only thing I know is the investigation revealed the train robbers might be using your land, since it is in close proximity to the railroad."

The cave.

"I'll have to take a chance." Brady picked up his pace. "Pray for me, will you? I need direction. Would you let Drummond and Sheriff Masters in on this? One of them might have an idea where she went."

"Most assuredly, Mr. Miller."

Inside the livery, Night was missing along with the mare's saddle and bridle. Brady felt he raced against time and a stubborn woman.

Lord, keep her safe and help me find her.

Once he headed back toward his ranch, he spotted two sets of horse prints. He'd seen them on his way into town but hadn't put much stock in them. Now the prints were starting to fade with the continual snowfall. If he didn't find Miss Alexander soon, he faced losing her. The longer he ventured, the more he saw the trail led to the cave. He didn't know what training she'd received as a Pinkerton, but he hoped caution stood at the top of the list.

Moment followed Jackson through a narrow path that wound around and up to the hills. She worried about the sound of snapping tree branches that brushed against her. More so, she feared sneezing in the cold and alerting him to her position. Repeatedly she grabbed her nose and prayed for God to keep her presence secret. The higher she climbed, the colder the weather turned. Perhaps she should have been up-front with Victoria. At least the horse's feet were silenced in the snow. Finally, she dismounted, grabbed her rifle, and led Night after the tracks. She'd found the horse amiable and not fearsome as before. If she worked on it, Night could be a friend of sorts.

A voice called out, and Moment stopped. She recognized the voice from the night she followed Jackson to the livery. Robert Wingert.

"Jackson, I thought you weren't coming."

"We got business to tend to." Jackson's words slurred.

"You drinkin'?"

"It's cold. Got to keep warm."

Moment held her breath. His drunkenness is what kept her from being discovered.

"Head in here. The fire's warm. Hope you didn't drink the whole bottle."

Jackson laughed. "Most of it, but there's a little left, and I got another in the saddlebag."

Night nudged Moment. Instead of shrieking in fright, she rubbed the mare's nose as she'd seen Drummond do. Patience, she told herself. Those two would drink themselves into a stupor, and then she'd take a better look.

The snow fell harder, and a gust of wind whipped around the trees, decidedly colder. The longer she stood there, the colder it felt.

The men's voices grew louder and echoed around her.

"Are you ready for this next job?" Jackson's friend asked.

"I've been ready. Looks like it's just me and you, Robert."

"We can handle it. Is the preacher behaving himself?" Wingert laughed.

"Depends. As long as I'm in church, he leaves me alone."

"You should have killed him when you had the chance."

Jackson cursed. "He's my father. I do have a little decency. If he hadn't found out what we were doing, he wouldn't have a bum leg. My aim's better than that—and you know it."

"That's the price you pay for being the Ghost."

Jackson Griffin's the Ghost! Moment's mind raced with the truth. His deceit and cleverness had worked up until now. She remembered the sadness in Sarah Griffin's eyes. Did she know her son had shot his father?

Suddenly, a hand clamped over her mouth.

Chapter 9

I t's me, Miller," Brady whispered. Instantly her body relaxed.

"What are you doing here?" she shot back when he removed his hand.

"Following you. I went to town looking for a lady Pinkerton, and after talking to your friend, I picked up your trail."

Miss Alexander pointed to the cave area. "Jackson and Robert Wingert are down there."

He nodded. "I heard every word."

She smiled, and if they hadn't been in such a precarious situation, he might have kissed her. "Who would believe?"

"No one but a Pinkerton." Brady touched her arm. "Is it too late to say I'm sorry?"

She studied his eyes, and he received his answer. Her face flushed, and the patch of freckles darkened. She hastily looked away. "Your timing could have been better."

"Suppose so. Now that I'm here, I want you to do something for me." When she didn't reply, he pressed on. "Ride back to town for Drummond and the sheriff."

"I'm not leaving you," she said over her shoulder.

He reached for her chin, forcing her to look at him. "Look, Mo, I care about you, and I don't want you hurt. I'll watch these two until you get back. From the sound of them, they'll be sleeping off a drunk soon."

"We can take them." He saw determination in her eyes.

He shook his head. Convincing Moment Alexander to step back and allow a man to handle the situation proved harder than he thought.

"I'm a better shot than you," she said. "I've been trained for this kind of thing."

Perhaps if he got her out of harm's way, he could surprise Griffin and Wingert and disarm them without risking her safety.

"All right." Brady pointed to an area opposite where they crouched. "Head over there, and I'll signal when it's time to close in."

Without another word, she crept away.

Thank You, God. Brady knew he'd have bound and gagged her before setting her in the path of danger. When he saw she had positioned herself by the pine, he set his plan into action. She couldn't see the men, which was exactly what he wanted. By maneuvering around the hill to the cave's entrance, he could surprise them both.

The path downward was blanketed in snow. He measured each step and balanced his rifle. Griffin and Wingert may be drunk, but their aim could be just as deadly. Within about twelve feet of the clearing, Brady slipped and lost his footing.

"I should have killed you when I had the chance," Griffin shouted.

Brady braced himself, realizing he'd seen his last snowfall. Regrets darted across his mind. *Well, Lord, it's just You and me.*

The crack of a rifle burst through the crisp air. He lifted his head and saw Griffin clutch his right leg. Blood spurted through his fingers and jeans. In the next instant, he fell. Miss Alexander stood behind Griffin and Wingert, rifle raised.

"Don't move, or you'll be the next," she said loudly. "Mr. Miller, you all right?"

He snatched up his rifle. "Yeah. Guess I owe you."

She laughed. "Not bad for a Pinkerton, huh?"

Brady realized he and Moment Alexander were headed for an interesting life. He had saved her from a cougar, and she saved him from a bullet.

December twenty-fourth marked the nuptials of Mark and Ruth Chandler, with a lively party afterwards. Moment leaned into Mr. Miller—whom she now consented to call Brady—and he responded by planting a kiss on her nose. Whether it was the magic of the season or the wedding, she and Brady had gotten along splendidly ever since the train robbers' arrest. In short, they'd found a precious love.

Moment glanced at Pastor Griffin and his sweet wife.

The two looked at peace, although their only son sat in jail awaiting sentencing. From what she had learned from Mrs. Griffin, Jackson had been rebellious for years. How sad for the couple, but at least the truth was in the open. The burden they'd carried for years had been lifted.

Doc Wingert's downcast gaze tore at Moment. His son shared a cell with Griffin. She prayed the town's doctor would once more find joy in his life, especially with Pastor Griffin counseling him.

Victoria caught her attention and waved. Poor thing. She'd come all this way to help solve a crime, and to no avail. Will Bowen wrapped his arm around her waist. Maybe she'd find love in Windmere Falls like the rest of the lady Pinkertons.

Brady brushed a kiss across Moment's hair.

"We're next," he said. "I love you, Moment Alexander, for as long as I live."

She snuggled against his jacket. "I believe you need a Pinkerton woman to protect you."

"I do," he whispered. "I'm not good at putting fancy words together, but would you consider marrying this cowboy?"

Tears pooled her eyes. Brady would always fill her with surprises. "I'll marry you tomorrow."

"Thank you, Darlin'. As much as I'd like to marry you tomorrow, I know women want to plan things nice. How does February sound to you?"

"Perfect."

"Together, we'll handle anything thrown our way, beginning mid-March with a trip to Denver."

She peered up into his rugged face and his beloved dark blue eyes. "Did you accept the job with the Pinkertons?"

"Had to." He smiled. "I couldn't let my Mo outdo me."

DIANN MILLS

DiAnn lives in Houston, Texas, with her husband Dean. They have four adult sons. She wrote from the time she could hold a pencil, but not seriously until God made it clear that she should write for Him. After three years of serious writing, her first book *Rehoboth* won favorite **Heartsong Presents** historical for 1998. Other publishing credits include magazine articles and short stories, devotionals, poetry, and internal writing for her church. She is an active church choir member, leads a ladies Bible study, and is a church librarian. She is also an advisory board member for American Christian Romance Writers.

Victorious

by Kathleen Y'Barbo

Dedication

To the prayer warriors,
without whom this book would have never been finished.

Wait on the LORD, and he shall save thee.

PROVERBS 20:22

Chapter 1

January 1891

As he warbled the last line of "Rock of Ages" and then took his seat, Gus Drummond tried in vain to ignore the swaying blue feather on the pretty Pinkerton's Sunday hat. Doubtless he'd see the feather, and the fair-haired Pinkerton beneath it, at close range come the end of Sunday service, for he'd avoided her all week.

With some swift detective work on his part, he'd managed to slip out of the hardware store when she wasn't looking, and he'd avoided her at the hotel by consuming his meals in his room. He'd even taken to walking rather than chance a meeting with the woman at the livery.

How like the Lord to show His sense of humor by placing her across the aisle from him at church this morning.

Ever since she'd come to his office last Tuesday morning asking for the train robbery case to be reopened, he'd seen right through the ruse. Obviously, she was sweet on the banker and buying time in Windmere Falls by creating a situation to be investigated where there was none. It was common knowledge she had orders to board the first train back to Chicago once Moment Alexander and Brady Miller's march down the aisle was over.

He'd listened, sort of, to the female Pinkerton's ideas and given her the only answer he had. The case was closed, and she'd best tell Will Bowen good-bye, then pack her lace and linens and catch the first train back to Chicago. Or, preferably, give up the ridiculous pursuit of a man's career and head back to England, where, no doubt, some duke or prince pined away for her.

When that woman bit into a topic, however, she seemed to chew it until nothing was left. In this case, her topic was the identity of the Ghost, and she didn't care that the man who'd confessed to being the fellow in the flour sack mask now sat behind bars awaiting the hangman's noose.

No, she dismissed that little piece of evidence with a wave of her gloved hand and informed him she intended to get to the bottom of the investigation with or without his help. Typical hardheaded female.

Still, the memory of high color staining her face as Miss Vicky stormed out of his office caused Gus to smile. One thing about this Pinkerton, she took her job seriously. If only she didn't expect him to take *her* seriously.

And as much as he hated to admit it, she *was* right about the fact that the rest of the loot, a good half of the take, hadn't been accounted for. To Gus's mind, however, the gold had been spent long ago on high living and low women, but he had no proof. It unsettled him a bit that the little

Englishwoman thought better of his conclusion and intended to prove him wrong. If she hadn't stated that fact in front of the sheriff, he'd be long gone, sitting in his place in Denver spending the winter in his own warm bed and planning that cabin he would build come spring.

His gaze dropped from the feather to the fancy hat and finally to the bothersome woman beneath. As pretty as a new pony, Miss Vicky had chosen an outfit of chestnut brown trimmed in lace dyed to match her eyes.

A sane man would have looked away when those eyes met his across the aisle, but every bit of his sanity had fled when the Pinkertons in petticoats came to town. With a polite nod, he ignored Miss Vicky's frown and transferred his attention to the bowler-hatted dandy on her left. Irritation rose and stuck in his gut.

Whatever possessed the woman to take a shine to the citified banker? Looks, money, and social standing most likely, but could Bowen make camp in the Llano Estacado or track a renegade desperado? With his lily-white skin and soft hands, he'd be sunburned and lost before he hit the edge of town. No, that wasn't right, Gus amended. Will Bowen would pay one of his flunkies to do the work for him while he sat in his office and counted coins.

Gus stifled a snort of amusement and shifted positions, forcing his mind back to the task at hand. He'd learned if he kept his knee pressed against the pew in front of him, the splinters caused just enough affliction to keep him awake until the reverend finished his business and turned the crowd out to meet the afternoon.

Somehow, though, his thoughts kept leaving the trail and heading off in the direction of the blue feather. Before he knew it, the closing hymn had been pounded out on the dilapidated organ and that feather dangled just under his nose.

"Mr. Drummond?" The Pinkerton peered up at him from beneath the brim of her hat. "May I have a word with you, please?"

Brady Miller and Moment Alexander filed past, and Gus nodded in their direction. He owed them more than a passing greeting, but the Pinkerton woman had his spleen in such an uproar that he'd hardly provide tolerable conversation for these nice folks. He'd have to make amends outside if the opportunity presented itself—that is, if he could rid himself of Miss Vicky and still manage to be civil.

The object of his irritation yanked at the sleeve of his coat. "Excuse me, please," she said, "but we've a bit of *business* to discuss."

Once again, he ignored her to watch the faithful trod outside only to see more trouble headed his way. Right behind the newly engaged Pinkerton couple, Mabel Hawkins, passable organ player and all around busybody, glared at the little circle in which he stood.

Gus stifled a groan. Doubtless she'd stir up some sort of trouble come Monday morning, most likely setting him in the midst of some sordid love triangle with the Englishwoman and her banker friend. He pictured her narrow eyes and thin lips as she repeated the story, embellishing it a bit more each time until it reached epic proportions over the Monday washday special of beans and rice at the hotel.

To his mind, Miss Mabel read too many dime novels, and the last time the pastor approached him with concern after hearing one of her tales about him, he'd told the man so. If only the life of a Pinkerton were half as exciting as the one Miss Mabel claimed he had.

"*Mr.* Drummond."

There was that feather again, this time so close it nearly tickled his nose. He stared at it a second, then braved a glance into the face of its owner. Once again, bright red stained Miss Vicky's cheeks despite the relatively cool temperature of the morning. Once again, she looked like one of heaven's most elegant angels, lost among the mortals and ready to fly home without warning.

Thoughts of Miss Mabel evaporated.

Her soft pink lips puckered with hostility just like his mother's used to when he'd stuck his finger in the pudding before the meal had been properly served. Quite the character, his Scottish-born mother, as was the lady Pinkerton. Those pink lips began to move.

"A *word* please, kind sir."

Gus broke into a smile that would have made Mama proud as he curled his fists and fought the urge to pluck the blue feather right off her brown hat. "Why, of course."

"Thank you," she said on a soft breath as her features relaxed and her beauty increased.

"And that word," he said before he could change his mind and tell her all she wanted to know and more, "is no."

Gus looked past her, open mouth and all, to the slick-haired banker who stood waiting like a calf on a tether. Several possible responses to Bowen's bland greeting occurred to him, none of which were acceptable beneath the roof of God's house.

Squelching the need to say them anyway, Gus tipped his Stetson and pressed past the well-matched pair to follow a grinning Miss Mabel outside. If he couldn't win, he'd walk away.

He walked away.

Victoria gathered her irritation and her reticule and turned to follow the impossibly stubborn lawman outside. She'd allowed him to believe he had escaped her too many times this week, reasoning that if she gave him the privacy he desired, he'd have time to do some serious thinking on the topic at hand.

Obviously this had not been the case.

"Shall we, Miss Barrett-Ames?" Mr. Bowen's arm linked with hers, punctuating the request with a slightly possessive tug to bring her sharply to his side. "After all, the temperature is unseasonably mild and the day is still young, as are we."

Victoria turned her attention away from the broad back of the retreating Pinkerton to the handsome banker. An impertinent response lay on the tip of her tongue, but she swallowed it along with most of her anger.

After all, William Bowen was the closest thing to a gentleman Windmere Falls had to offer, and she did enjoy his company. What harm was there in being cordial in return?

Still, she wriggled out of his grasp and busied her fingers with the ribbons on her bonnet. Above all, she was a

Pinkerton woman, and until she'd heard otherwise, she must conduct herself as if she were on assignment at all times. What good would it do to allow a bit of fancy to sway her when she had a case to complete?

And, no matter what Gus Drummond and the other three ladies believed, this case was far from closed. She could only pray that word would not get back to headquarters before she had her proof. At least she had until Moment's wedding next month.

"Miss Barrett-Ames, did you hear me?"

The banker's perfectly formed features were stricken with worry, and his full lips closed over a line of perfectly white teeth to offer a frown. Victoria moved instantly to repair the damage her inattention had caused.

"Of course," she said, as she lightly placed her hand over his, "although I must insist you call me Victoria."

The banker smiled as if she'd given him the most exquisite of gifts. "Only if you will address me as Will." Without waiting for an answer, he lifted her fingers to his lips, then abruptly grasped her elbow, leading her down the aisle toward the sunlit street. "Now, I've taken the liberty of having Cook prepare a repast for two, and I thought we might saddle the horses. There's the loveliest little spot where we can build a fire and enjoy our meal up past. . ."

His words disappeared as Victoria's thoughts intruded. While the Sabbath was not a day to spend in pursuit of the Ghost, it could be a day to leisurely seek a clue or two.

Perhaps Will, with his vast knowledge of the Windmere Falls citizens and their respective financial situations, might have some insight into possible suspects. Dare she mention to him that the ringleader of the gang might still be at large? She pondered this as he led her down the steps of the church toward his buggy.

". . .and I know how your countrymen love scones with their tea, so I felt obliged to have Cook. . ."

Victoria's concentration slipped once more when the sunlight hit her eyes. Blinking to retain her vision, she halted her steps. Oblivious, the banker continued speaking as he strode toward his buggy.

Gus Drummond stood with Moment and Mr. Miller, pretending deep conversation when she knew he'd been watching her as she emerged from the church. Their gazes met, and as her eyes found their focus, he had the audacity to wink.

"Quite the impertinent one, that Pinkerton fellow. I declare, it seems as though he's got something besides law work up his sleeve."

She turned to see Mabel Hawkins standing to her left, just out of Mr. Drummond's line of sight. "Indeed," Victoria said with a conspiratorial nod. "He certainly does."

Miss Hawkins's smile broadened. "So you agree that there's something funny about Mr. Drummond then?"

"Something funny?" Victoria studied the woman and the idea all at once. He *had* seemed strange each time she'd sought him out to discuss the train robbery case, and he *had* acted less than professional in his responses. Actually, his response had been no response at all.

Her Pinkerton's mind set to putting the clues together.

There was a substantial sum of money missing, the case was due to be closed without finding that money, and Gus Drummond was most vocal in his opposition to continue searching for it.

An idea most bizarre and yet not totally far-fetched began to form. Out of the corner of her eye, she saw Moment climb into Mr. Miller's wagon. Perhaps she should share her suspicions with her dear friend. Then Moment smiled, and Mr. Miller wrapped an arm around her waist. Crime fighting with her friend would have to wait, Victoria decided.

She whirled around to face the most informed female in Windmere Falls. "Tell me everything you know about Mr. Drummond."

Chapter 2

Victoria took careful note of Gus Drummond's face as she stepped away from the crowd to speak to Miss Hawkins. To borrow a phrase from the man himself, he looked like he had swallowed a bug. She smiled. He was irritating on a good day, but he certainly had an unusual way with the English language.

"And so when I heard we had us a Pinkerton in our midst, I figured he would be rounding up those bad fellers in no time." Miss Hawkins leaned toward her. "Well, I say he coulda caught those robbers if he'd a wanted to."

"What are you saying, Miss Hawkins?"

"Well, when that Pinkerton feller first come to town, he kindly kept to himself, 'cept when he paid a call to the sheriff. All of a sudden, he was at the church every time the doors were open, and he and the reverend was thick as thieves." She paused. "Now we all know what come of the reverend's boy and his no-account friend."

"Yes, but I don't see how that—"

Miss Hawkins put her hand on Victoria's arm and drew

her closer. "A man don't just give up his ways and go to church lessen one of two things has happened. Either he's found the Lord or he don't want somebody else to find him out." She gave Victoria a conspiratorial wink. "I reckon our Mr. Drummond fits into one of those two categories."

"I believe we all do." Victoria took a deep breath and tried to remember why she had credited Mabel Hawkins with owning any information that might help in the case. Instead of finding an answer, she found Mr. Drummond staring at them, and she waved. His response was to turn his back and focus his concentration on the reverend.

Of all the nerve. If she hadn't been raised a lady, she would go over there and—

"Victoria, dear, we really should be going."

She tore her gaze away from the uncivilized Pinkerton to see Will Bowen walking toward her. He looked so handsome in his well-cut suit and bowler hat, and his manners were impeccable. The fact that he never missed a church service and owned one of the finest stables of thoroughbreds she'd ever seen also did much to endear him to her heart. Why on earth did she let Gus Drummond affect her when she had a wonderful friend in Will waiting for her?

"Of course," she said. "Perhaps we can talk again soon, Miss Hawkins."

"I'd like that," the woman said as she looked past Victoria to Will. "Maybe we'll talk about something more interesting than that double-minded Pinkerton."

"Double-minded?" Victoria peered up into Will's handsome face. "Would you give me just a moment with Miss

Hawkins, please? I promise I'll tarry no longer than necessary."

Will smiled, a glorious smile that lit his entire face. "Of course," he said. "I only ask that I have your full attention for the remainder of the afternoon. For that, I would wait indefinitely."

"Will, you are a dear, and you have my promise I shall dote on your every word."

"Then I shall hold you to your promise, and I shall await you with great anticipation. I suppose I can bide my time by contemplating the pastor's words. The day is certainly fit for thinking on the Lord." He leaned toward Miss Hawkins and took her hand. With great flourish, he kissed it and then repeated the process with Victoria, tarrying a bit longer and making eye contact as he released her fingers. "As always, Miss Hawkins, it has been a pleasure. Victoria, I am patient but I am human, so don't keep me long." She watched him stroll toward the buggy. How very blessed she was to have a true gentleman interested in her. Dare she allow the feelings budding within to find the light of day? Perhaps with Will she might finally find a man who—

"Miss Barrett-Ames, I do declare you're plumb smitten with that banker fellow."

Victoria turned her attention back to Miss Hawkins, fully aware the woman had read her expression and guessed the direction of her thoughts. As a Pinkerton, she'd just committed a serious breach of protocol.

"He's a wonderful man," she said in as neutral a tone as she could muster.

"He is that."

Victoria regained her focus on the investigation. "Forgive me for changing the subject, Miss Hawkins, but I believe you mentioned you were concerned that our Pinkerton man might be double-minded."

Miss Hawkins nodded. "All I'm saying is I believe a Pinkerton's gonna get his man if he wants to. Talk around here's that he brought in some help to get those boys caught, but I ain't seen no sight of any other Pinks around here. Ain't nobody new come down since you and Miss Moment and the other two ladies showed up. Now I might have seen some things in my day, but I don't believe I'll live to believe that you four ladies are the backup for that big old Scotsman over there."

Victoria giggled and then forced a serious expression. "It does seem a bit far-fetched, doesn't it?"

"It does indeed," she answered. "And that's why I'm saying I think that Pinkerton man's got something up his sleeve." Again, she leaned toward Victoria. "You can't tell me the boys who admitted to the robberies had the time or the brains to get rid of all that money."

Victoria adjusted her hat and shook her head. "Well, it does seem to stretch the imagination a bit."

Finally she'd found someone who agreed with her assessment of the situation. If only it were someone a bit more respected than the town gossip. Still, the facts were the facts. An astonishing amount of money was missing, presumed by law enforcement to have been spent. All those responsible for the crime were said to be behind bars, and the case was declared closed.

Mr. Fletcher's last letter had insisted Victoria only remain in Windmere Falls long enough to attend Moment's wedding. By the end of February, she would be on a train to Chicago, the sole person who believed justice had not been done in this situation.

The worst part of it was that Moment, her best friend in the world, doubted her theory. If only she could find some proof.

"And so I told the reverend that if I had the proof, I'd go straight to the sheriff, but no, he says to me—"

"Excuse me, Miss Hawkins. Did you say the reverend has proof of your theory?"

She shook her head and rested her hands on her hips. "Lands no, Honey. I know you're not from around here, but don't you English ladies know a body can only talk about one subject until a more interesting one comes along? Now what I was saying was that I saw Alice Duncan yesterday and she told me—"

"Forgive me, Miss Hawkins, but I really must go. I'm afraid Mr. Bowen will give up and leave, and I'll miss a wonderful afternoon. Do come and see me at the mercantile, won't you?"

With that she made her escape, heading for the buggy where Will waited. He stepped out to help her settle comfortably on the seat. Before climbing in and taking the reins, he tucked what looked to be an authentic sable spread over her lap.

"To keep you warm." He smiled. "I'd like you to accept it as a small token of my affection."

Victoria ran a hand over the lush fur and recognized it as Russian sable, a favorite of her grandmother, the duchess. Back in England she owned several coats of this quality, but here in the American West she'd seen nothing of the kind. Even in Chicago, furs of this caliber were a rarity.

Her Pinkerton training sounded a warning. How would a banker living in tiny Windmere Falls manage to acquire such a beautiful fur? Dare she consider Will Bowen might be capable of acting as the mastermind behind the string of robberies?

"Really, that wasn't necessary. I'm afraid I could never accept a gift of such value. It wouldn't be proper," she said as she cast a wary eye upon her companion.

"I disagree." He offered a wink, snapped the reins, and urged the mare into a trot. "Actually, I had an ulterior motive."

"Oh?" Victoria waved to Moment and Mr. Miller, then pointedly ignored Mr. Drummond, who continued to ignore her. She gathered a handful of the luxurious spread and buried her fingers in the fur. It did feel heavenly. "And what might that be?"

"Well, I don't think it would be too presumptuous of me to assume that you are used to the finer things in life."

Victoria froze. *How could he know that?* She had been careful not to draw any undue attention to herself or to act in any way that might cause the citizens of Windmere Falls to think she was anything other than a shop girl.

"You look surprised." His smile melted most of her fears. "Forgive me. I suppose I should explain myself."

"Yes, please do," she said as evenly as possible.

He shrugged. "You see, I've known for quite awhile who you really are."

If Will Bowen knew her to be a Pinkerton, she'd just acquired either an ally or an enemy. Slipping one hand beneath the throw, she reached into her reticule and wrapped her fingers around the pistol she'd thus far only used in target practice back in Chicago.

"I'm making you nervous." He rolled his shoulders and sat up straighter on the seat. "Perhaps I should start at the beginning."

Victoria nodded.

"I don't know if you realize this, but I'm not actually from Windmere Falls."

"I guessed as much."

"I grew up back East. New York, actually. My father was a furrier by trade." He cast a sideways glance at her. "He did quite well for himself. He insisted I seek the education he had not received. In time, I went off to university at Oxford."

Oxford. Her father and brother's alma mater. "I see," she said, hoping against hope the connection ended there.

"And I took a liking to polo."

Victoria swallowed hard. Polo had been a favorite sport of both Papa and Charles. During his time at Oxford, Charles had captained a team two years in a row. What were the odds, though? Still, if he knew anything about her past, she had to consider he might know about her present situation as well.

"Of course." Her gaze drifted past him to check for

other travelers on this road. Unfortunately, they were alone.

Will pulled the buggy to a sudden stop and turned to face her. "I can't tell if you're following me, Victoria."

"Please just state what you mean," she said as she tightened her grip on the pistol.

"I rode with your brother, Victoria." He grasped her free hand in his and stared at the robin's egg blue glove before lifting it to his lips. "I know who you are."

Gus Drummond's gaze scanned the horizon searching for the fancy buggy that held the banker and his date. He tried not to think that his suspicions might be correct, but any investigator worth his Pinkerton badge could tell that Victoria Barrett-Ames was just biding her time until the banker asked her to open a joint account.

To think that she might actually try to involve him in her plan to lure the banker into matrimonial bliss really galled him. Why didn't she just tell the fellows up in Chicago the truth and keep him and his office out of it? Just because her friends had all snagged themselves husbands didn't mean Miss Vicky had to do the same.

After all, the robberies were solved and the money was spent. What more was there to talk about?

Gus stalked back to the hotel with a little more attitude than a man fresh from church ought to have. By the time he reached his room, he felt good and convicted. The next time he saw Victoria Barrett-Ames, he wouldn't let her trample on his joy. No, sir, the one Pinkerton who failed to catch a crook wouldn't catch him acting anything but nice.

Chapter 3

Victoria held fast to the pistol hidden beneath her skirts and contemplated her options. She must determine exactly how much Will Bowen knew about her life after coming to America.

As if he'd guessed her thoughts, he tightened his grip on the reins and swung his gaze back to meet hers. "Your secret is safe with me, Victoria."

She toyed with using the direct approach, questioning Will as she had learned to do with a potential suspect, then decided against the hard approach. It never seemed to work for her in practice anyway, and she'd never tried it on anyone except her instructor. He laughed every time, causing her to do the same.

Pasting on a casual look, she released her grip on the pistol and allowed it to slide back into its place inside her reticule. "Will, I have no idea which of my many secrets you've guessed. Please do enlighten me."

With a flick of his wrists, he set the buggy back into

motion. "I wrote to your brother to tell him I had chanced upon his sister in the Colorado wilderness." He let the statement linger between them a moment before commenting further. "I'm sure you understand I had your best interests at heart."

"Indeed." Victoria held her feelings in check, but just barely. If Father and Charles were to discover the job she'd described to them as a secretarial position had turned into actual crime fighting, one or both of them would be on the next ship headed west. "Dare I ask what my brother's response might have been?"

"His first response was the same as mine." Will gave her a sideways glance. "He expressed surprise at our finding each other in a country of this size. Of course, while he attributed it to luck, I admit I must ascribe this to the mysterious workings of the Lord. Perhaps He intended me to protect you while offering some civilized companionship."

She relaxed a bit more. Yes, perhaps the Lord had placed her in Windmere Falls for this very reason, although the thought of a Pinkerton in need of protection from a civilian did cause her to smile.

"You have a beautiful smile, Victoria."

"Thank you." She rested her hand on the thick sable blanket and pondered her next words carefully. "Did my brother happen to mention anything else about me that you'd like to share?"

Again, he slid a glance her way. "Is there anything in particular you're concerned about? I assure you I have been completely circumspect in my correspondence with your brother. Above all, we are both gentlemen, and you are Charles's sister."

He looked completely flustered, a reaction that both charmed and pleased Victoria. Perhaps the banker did have an interest in more than a friendship. Would that be so bad?

"Did he mention anything about my being employed?"

Will shrugged. "He told me you'd been doing secretarial work in Chicago. He expressed surprise at your change of location."

"Secretarial work, yes, that's right." Again, she paused to size up the situation. While she felt an instant trust for Will, something kept her from revealing her true mission in Windmere Falls. Perhaps it was her Pinkerton training, or maybe it was the fact that once she admitted she was a Pinkerton, she would then have to admit she was the only one in their group to fail in her mission to catch the person or persons responsible for all the robberies.

A notion occurred to her, and she filed it away to discuss with Moment at the first opportunity. With Will's connections in banking circles, perhaps he could be of some help in locating the missing funds.

She would have to do a cursory check of his background, just a basic report to assure her of his credentials. Once that was accomplished, perhaps she and Will would become the crime-fighting team she'd hoped she and Moment would be.

Or perhaps she and Will would more closely resemble the soon-to-be-formed team of Moment and Brady

Miller. The thought made her blush. It also intrigued her immensely.

※

Monday morning just after first light, Gus joined the sheriff at a table near the front window of the restaurant and ordered the breakfast special. "You're up early, Luke. Anything going on I should know about?"

The sheriff nodded. "Well, I don't know if it concerns you, but last night we had us some suspicious activity at the saloon, the livery, and the telegraph office."

"Is that right?"

"Just some fooling with the locks and such. Nothing stolen outside of some horseshoe nails and such. Probably kids up to no good." He shifted positions and speared a piece of sausage with his fork. "You looking to head back to Denver soon, Gus?"

"Looks like we ought to have all the loose ends wrapped up by the end of the month, but you never know." He tucked his napkin into his shirt collar and sipped at the worst coffee this side of the Mississippi. "No matter what, I aim to sleep in my own bed come the spring thaw."

Sheriff Luke Masters laid down his fork and shoved the sugar bowl toward him. "Three, four big spoonfuls of this and you won't even taste the bitterness—much."

Gus nodded and lifted the bowl to pour a healthy amount of sugar into his cup. "Why'd I let you throw the only good cook in town into the jailhouse? If I didn't know better, I'd think you trumped up those charges just to get a better cup of coffee over there."

The sheriff grinned. "Who could predict he'd have warrants that would get him sent to Denver? Guess we'll never eat good in this town again." He paused to shovel the last bit of runny eggs onto a corner of his toast. "You said you were tying up the loose ends in that train robbery case?"

"That's right," Gus said as a plate of eggs, sausage, and toast was set before him. "Looks like we caught the lot of them. Now all I've got to do is file the paperwork and wait for the judge."

"You sure you got 'em all?" Sheriff Masters asked.

Gus choked down his bite of breakfast and gave the sheriff a look intended to show he'd heard just about enough of what he was about to hear.

"I see." The sheriff jerked his napkin from around his neck and tossed it on the table along with payment for his meal. "I hear tell not everybody's sure all those men were caught." He paused. "You sure don't look like you're too worried about it."

Gus stifled his rising anger and let his fork drop. "What're you getting at, Luke?"

"Nothing," he said. "Except I have to wonder how a collection of fellows who don't seem to be the smartest group of men managed to pull off all those robberies *and* find time to spend all the loot." He pushed back his hat to scratch his head. "Just don't quite seem possible, although I'd have to take the word of a Pinkerton man over the opinion of a lowly sheriff, wouldn't I?"

"I reckon you would, Luke," Gus said slowly, "but I wonder if there's something else you're wanting to say."

The sheriff stared at him for a minute and then stood. "I believe I've about said all I need to."

"I believe you have," Gus responded as he returned to his breakfast.

Before the seat beside him had time to get cold, the prissy Pinkerton Victoria Barrett-Ames had settled herself into it. Today she wore green, a frilly frock with ruffles at the neck and a hat that looked even more absurd than yesterday's feathered fiasco.

"Good morning, Mr. Drummond," she said.

Rather than speak, he nodded. Let her think he was too busy eating to talk.

"I've a favor to ask."

"A favor?" He grumbled under his breath at the woman's ability to draw words out of him despite his intention of silence.

She folded her hands on the table and offered him a smile. "Just a small one."

"Then call me Gus if you're going to ask me a favor." The smile edged up a notch, and Gus's heart sank. This Pinkerton was as pretty as sunrise on a spring morning. Whatever she asked, he'd probably do it. "But I'm not re-opening the case and that's final."

"While that remains to be seen, Mr. Drummond, that's not the favor I wish to ask." Her smile broadened.

Gus let his fork drop again with a satisfying clatter and steepled his hands before meeting her gaze. What in the world was this woman up to?

"Miss Vicky, I'd agree to just about anything right now if it meant I could finish my breakfast in peace and quiet."

"Now don't say anything you don't mean."

Her tone was playful, but the look on her face told another story. He decided to proceed carefully. "Is this business or pleasure?"

She cupped her hand against her chin and leaned toward him. "Business," she whispered.

He pushed away from the table and stood. As pesky as this Pinkerton in petticoats had become, he might as well get this showdown over with sooner rather than later. He would have to let the kid down gently, maybe give her a little encouragement that there were a lot of things a pretty lady could do with herself before he told her the plain facts. Not everyone was cut out to be a Pinkerton.

Discretion being the better part of valor, he decided to take the woman and the discussion elsewhere. No sense letting the whole town see the Englishwoman in tears.

He groaned. One thing he couldn't abide was a tearful woman. Every last one of his six sisters could reduce him to a babbling fool with their feminine tears. For that reason, he'd fled Scotland and vowed to remain a single man.

Women were just plain trouble—and the worst of the lot sat next to him. The first sign of tears from those eyes and it would all be over.

Maybe he should stay right there in full view. He looked past the lady Pinkerton to see Mabel Hawkins bearing down on them, winding her way through the Monday morning crowd like a wet hen heading for cover.

What a conundrum. Should he take his chances with Miss Mabel or risk Miss Vicky's tears? Both choices sounded about as appealing as slow dancing with a porcupine.

When Miss Mabel waved, his decision was made.

"Why don't you and I take a stroll?" Gus practically lifted the female Pinkerton out of her chair and onto her feet. As gently as he could manage, he linked arms with her and set her to walking toward the nearest exit. "It's a beautiful morning, and this place is a bit crowded for my liking."

The Pinkerton stumbled, and Gus caught her, steadying her arm as she set her silly hat to rights.

"But your breakfast, you haven't finished," she said. "Oh, look, there's Miss Hawkins."

The overly chatty organist called out a greeting, and Gus answered with a polite but firm hello and good-bye all in one breath. Stepping aside to allow a couple of hungry cowhands to enter the restaurant, he prayed while he counted the seconds until Miss Mabel had them in her grasp.

His prayers were answered when he saw through the front window that she had found someone else to visit with this morning.

"Thank You, Lord," he whispered before ushering Miss Vicky across the street toward the livery and a quiet spot where they could speak privately.

He'd have to remember that little blessing in his prayers tonight. If only the Lord would allow him one more blessing, that of being free from the tangle of the last of the Pinkertons in petticoats. Unfortunately, when he cast a glance beneath that silly green hat to the source of his irritation, he realized he just might miss her.

Their casual banter often ended up in heated debate, and he'd learned the lady could match wits with the best of them in conversation. A man who didn't know better might even think a sharp mind lay beneath that fancy hairstyle and foolish hat.

He shook off the silliness and led her to the side of the livery, where he pointed to a bench half-hidden from the road. Gus took up a position against the wall of the livery and lightly rested his fingers on his revolver. From the street, the casual observer would not see the lady but would have a clear view of him.

Miss Vicky arranged her flouncy skirts and settled her purse onto her lap. A light breeze danced around them, skittering across her feather and sending it into motion. As he had yesterday at church, Gus turned his attention to the feather rather than the lady beneath it.

"I'd like to state my request and be on my way. Moment will be wondering where I am."

"So whatever this business favor is, your friend isn't in on it then?"

For purely investigative purposes, he studied her face. It didn't take a Pinkerton to tell that this woman had something to hide. But then, didn't they all?

Something slammed against the side of the barn, and

Gus went for his pistol. Miss Vicky jumped to her feet, producing a gun from her lacy purse.

"What?" she whispered. "Surely I'm not the first Pinkerton you've seen with a pistol."

Another thump inches away from the side door prevented him from answering. Gus touched a finger to her lips and pointed toward the door. With care, he reached for the latch and pushed. The door swung in on silent hinges and he peered inside.

Nothing but horses and straw in sight.

Out of the corner of his eye, he saw something dart across the shadows and disappear into an empty stall at the end of the stable. He gestured for her to stand still and then crept toward the stall.

To her credit, Miss Vicky kept her silence and stayed rooted to the spot. At least she could take orders from a superior officer. Perhaps their conversation on her career change, if it happened today, would be a short one.

Gus moved slowly, sticking to the shadowy side of the space until he reached the stall door. It stood half-open, hiding whomever or whatever might be standing behind it. He reached for his pistol and placed his palm on the door. Something shuffled in the straw, and he looked over his shoulder to see if Miss Vicky had moved.

Good. She hadn't.

Another shuffling sound, this one seemingly coming from behind the door where he stood, told him he and the lady were not alone in the stable. He raised his pistol and took another step forward.

The mare in the stall nearest the door whinnied, and Gus jumped, collecting his wits just in time to keep from firing his pistol. He whirled around to see Miss Vicky petting the animal and frowned.

Then he felt the cold steel against the back of his neck.

"Drop the gun and turn around real slow, Pink," the deep voice said.

Gus's gaze darted to Miss Vicky, who stood scratching the mare's ears like she hadn't a care in the world. What a time for him to be without a real Pinkerton as backup. Just wait until he told the guys back in Chicago how their petticoated Pinkerton performed under pressure.

If he lived that long.

Chapter 4

Victoria heard the gruff voice and knew it couldn't belong to Mr. Drummond. Hiding her pistol in the folds of her skirt, she turned to get a better view of the big Scotsman. Cloaked in shadows, he appeared to raise his hands in a gesture that resembled surrender.

Her senses on alert, she nudged past the mare. Mr. Drummond's revolver glinted silver as it hit the ground and skittered toward the center of the aisle. She moved a bit closer, catching his attention when she reached a spot only a few feet way.

The Pinkerton's expression, visible despite the dim light, warned her to stop. She ignored him to creep into a position where she could see the situation more clearly.

Behind him were two men, a nervous-looking fellow with a pistol and an oversized man with a rifle. The barrel of the rifle rested against the back of Mr. Drummond's neck, and a white sack dangled from his hand.

A white sack.

Her detective's mind began to race. Could one of these

men be the Ghost? Had the money been hidden in the livery all this time?

There was only one way to know for sure.

The reality of the situation assaulted her. Unlike the practices she and the other ladies had performed in Chicago, this was a real crime in progress. No instructor would appear to order the scene stopped. The criminals were real and so were the bullets in her gun—the gun she had prayed she would never have to use.

Focus on the task at hand, Victoria. Remember your training. Don't ponder the possibilities; just aim and pray.

Blood pounded at Victoria's temples as she debated which of the men to aim for. If she hit the one with the sack, she might be credited with catching the elusive Ghost, but she might risk allowing Mr. Drummond to be shot in the process. If she took aim against the other man, the fellow holding the money might get away.

"Fetch that lawman's gun," the man with the rifle said. "We ain't got all day."

Lord, what do I do? I can't possibly shoot anyone.

As the man reached for Mr. Drummond's gun, Victoria took a deep breath and raised her pistol. With Drummond's gun in hand, the nervous fellow darted toward the stable door. Victoria dove into the nearest stall and landed in a pile of hay and horse manure.

"Say good-bye, Pink," she heard the man say.

Before she realized what she'd done, Victoria jumped to her feet and released two shots from her pistol. The first hit the man with the rifle just below the knee, sending him sprawling to the floor. The second merely winged the nervous fellow on the arm, but the subsequent blood caused him to faint.

Covered in straw and horse dung, she handed Mr. Drummond his revolver and stored hers in her reticule, then reached for the bag. The contents shifted, lifting Victoria's hopes that at least part of the money would be returned. She turned the bag up and prepared to watch gold pour out. Instead, out came horseshoe nails, horseshoes, and various pieces of tack.

"Mr. Drummond, I heard a couple of shots. What happened?"

Victoria stood to see the sheriff barge into the livery through the side door. Drummond stepped between her and the lawman and gave her a warning glance. As the ranking officer on the case—and the only one not under cover—it fell to him to handle any contact with the law. Quickly she let the bag fall from her fingers.

He clapped the sheriff on the back and pointed him toward the stable, where the two thugs sat in the corner. "Miss Vicky and I were just having ourselves a private conversation when these two gentlemen decided to pull their weapons, Luke. I believe they just might be the two fellows you went looking for this morning."

The sheriff peered into the stable. "Good work, Pinkerton," he said. "Looks like you caught the fellows who've been plaguing the livery."

The nervous one moaned and clutched at his arm while the other remained motionless and pale. Neither seemed permanently injured. God must have directed the shots because Victoria certainly could claim no part other than pulling the trigger—and she had no real memory of doing that.

"Nice shooting, Gus," the sheriff said. "A couple of inches either way and these fellers would be sitting in a pine box instead of a jail cell come this afternoon."

A couple of inches. Pine box.

The bile rose in Victoria's throat.

"Why don't you see the little lady home and then stop by to fill out the paperwork?" He tipped his hat to Victoria. "You all right, little lady?"

Victoria tried her best to affect a helpless female stance, enabled in part by the unsettled state of her stomach. "I'm fine, thanks to this big strong Pinkerton."

"Very funny," Mr. Drummond said under his breath as he led her out of the livery.

"Indeed."

"If you hadn't been petting horses, I might not have given up my gun so easily." He cast a sideways glance in her direction. "I figured I could take one before the other one got a shot off. I was just afraid that shot might hit you instead of me."

"Thank you."

He tipped his hat but said nothing further.

Matching his long strides with difficulty, Victoria met his gaze. The big Scotsman wore a bit less of his usual formidability, but then a close encounter with a bullet would do that to a person.

A bullet.

Victoria's knees threatened to buckle. She'd not just shot one man, but two. Considering she had never even fired the thing at a living target before today, she'd done a fair job. Neither man had been seriously hurt, and the criminals had been captured before either did serious harm.

Oh, but what if she had missed? What if her incompetence and lack of formal Pinkerton training had caused a fellow agent to be hurt—or worse?

She squared her shoulders and pushed away the awful thought. Until now her image of a Pinkerton centered on saving lives, not taking them. She'd even entertained the notion that God was proud of her career choice. Now that He had seen her wound not one but two of His creatures, dare she believe He still held that opinion?

Perhaps the gentlemen in Chicago were right. Perhaps a lady didn't possess the temperament necessary for proper crime fighting.

No, Moment, Sydney, and Ruth certainly proved that wrong. And what of the famous Kate Warne, the lady Pinkerton who saved President Lincoln from an attempt on his life just prior to his inauguration? Without Kate's successful foiling of the assassination plot, Abraham Lincoln would never have become president.

Stories of Kate Warne and others like her had fueled Victoria's desire to become a Pinkerton. Dare she now give up on her dreams merely because she'd been forced to use the weapon she disdained?

Mr. Drummond nudged her side with his elbow. "A

penny for your thoughts, Miss Vicky."

Why did the ruffian insist on calling her by that dreadful name? Worse, how could she tell someone as insensitive as he of her concerns? Another person might offer words of comfort or advice, but what would Gus Drummond have to offer?

Most likely a sarcastic comment or a derisive laugh at her expense. Better to keep silent rather than share her thoughts with her fellow Pinkerton.

A chill wind danced past and caused her to shiver. Looking up at the sky, she saw the portent of rain, possibly even snow. Would spring ever come?

She pretended an interest in the items for sale at R & S Fashions across the street. The beautiful frock and matching hat in the window reminded her of the sorry state of her current ensemble, and she stifled a groan.

"I'll say it again. A penny for your thoughts."

"I'll keep my thoughts to myself for now, if you please."

"Suit yourself." He chuckled. "Not that you need my permission to do that."

They walked along in silence for a moment until Mr. Drummond stopped abruptly at the stairs behind the mercantile and turned to face her. She took a step back to gain a bit of distance and peered up into a blinding ray of sunlight. Blinking, she shaded her eyes and waited for him to come into focus once more.

"This isn't easy to admit." He wrapped a big hand around the stair rail leading up to Victoria and Moment's second-floor rooms. "I owe you a debt of thanks."

His honesty took her by surprise. So did her heart's reaction to the look on his face. Where she had once seen disdain, there now appeared to be a genuine respect. Or was it merely an illusion caused by the blinding light of the morning sun?

Victoria stepped into the shade covering the first riser of the stairs. Her position brought her nearly eye level with his chin, a definite advantage over her usual height deficit. If only she could conquer her fears as easily.

She dared another look at him. Whatever she'd seen—or imagined she'd seen—was gone, replaced by the old Gus Drummond's usual countenance.

Perhaps someday she would discover what lay behind the gruff lawman's ill-tempered disposition. Right now it was all she could do to stand in his presence. For that matter, standing at all was becoming quite the ordeal.

Why did she have to shoot those men? Couldn't God have thought of a better plan?

"You might want to sit down until your knees stop knocking."

His smile mocked her as he reached for her elbow, but her knees thanked her as she relieved them of their responsibility and settled on the step. Before she could protest, Mr. Drummond landed on the riser beside her, crowding her against the rough wooden rail.

"The first time's the worst," he said. "Not that it gets any easier."

Victoria scooted as far as possible from the Pinkerton and wrapped her arms around her knees. "I don't know what you're talking about."

"Shooting someone. It's hard but it's part of the job." He reached for her hand. "I don't believe God gives the responsibility to anyone who would take it lightly."

Rather than respond, she stared at the hand enveloping hers. A scar ran across three knuckles, and a light dusting of cinnamon-colored freckles could barely be seen. These were the hands of a capable lawman. Hers, by comparison, looked frail and inadequate.

Like her.

"That was some fine shooting though," he continued. "Neither will forget they met up with a Pinkerton anytime soon. What you're feeling now, it'll pass."

Victoria sighed. "Indeed."

Mr. Drummond squeezed her hand and then released it. An awkward silence fell between them as she realized she missed the warmth of his touch.

"You say that a lot. 'Indeed.' "

His affectation of her native inflection made her laugh. When their gazes met, she averted her eyes and studied her fingers. "Do I?"

"I'm of a mind to ask you a question."

"Ask away."

"What leads a woman who doesn't like shooting to be a Pinkerton?"

What indeed? If she attempted to answer the question properly, they'd be here all winter.

"One might argue a case of foolishness was to blame, but I prefer to think the Lord had something to do with it," she said instead.

"What sort of foolishness?"

She shook her head. "The sort that a man wouldn't understand."

"You might be surprised what a man will understand." His gaze softened. "I do have six sisters. Why don't you give me a try?"

Where was the gruff lawman who'd made it his business to irritate her? She tried to picture him living in a house filled with sisters and failed.

Silence once again reigned between them as Victoria looked away. Mr. Drummond's shoulders moved, brushing hers, and his fingers once again wrapped around her cold hands. When she looked back toward him, he had leaned so near that their noses nearly touched.

For a long moment, neither moved. The absurd thought that her nemesis might actually kiss her popped into Victoria's head.

Strange, but the idea held some appeal. Actually, it held great appeal. She puckered her lips and waited. He seemed to be doing the same.

Victoria closed her eyes.

An instant later, the whistle of the morning train from Denver sent her skittering to her side of the stairs. Her face hot with shame, Victoria snatched her hands from his grasp and buried them in the folds of her skirt.

To his credit, Gus Drummond looked as flustered as she did. "I believe all this started when you interrupted my breakfast," he said. "Something about some business you wanted to discuss with me."

Victoria cleared her throat and attempted to speak. "Yes," she finally managed, "actually I have a favor to ask."

"Considering I owe you my life, I suppose I can take on a favor from a fellow Pinkerton." He paused and looked as uncomfortable as she felt. "As long as you're not asking me to reopen the train robbery case."

"No, I'm not asking you to reopen the case, at least not yet."

He lumbered to his feet and turned to face her. "Oh no, you don't. We've had this discussion one too many times. The Ghost has been caught, the money was spent, and that's the end of that."

Victoria leaned back on her elbows to look up into his face. "Casting aside the flaws in your theory, namely that the gentleman who confessed to being the Ghost is a known liar and braggart and the fact that no evidence to prove the money has been spent exists, I will let you have your opinion for now." She held up a hand to stop his protest. "I am merely asking you to use your connections to do a background check on someone."

"Who?"

"Will Bowen."

"For what purpose?" He scowled and crossed his arms over his chest. "As if I didn't know."

"As I told you in the restaurant, this is strictly Pinkerton business." She adjusted the feather on her hat and made him wait a moment more before stating her reasons. "I have reason to believe Mr. Bowen's expertise could be of some use on a case I am investigating."

"I'll bet."

Victoria rose and turned to head for the solace of the apartment she shared with Moment. How dare the ruffian question her motives?

Certainly she *did* enjoy Will Bowen's company, and he *was* a refreshing change from the usual caliber of man to be found in the American West, present company included. Still, did he honestly think her unable to separate Pinkerton business from affairs of the heart?

Somehow Mr. Drummond reached the top of the stairs before her and blocked the door. "How about you and I talk turkey, Miss Vicky?"

Victoria held tight to the rail and stared up at her adversary. What had she been thinking when she considered actually kissing the man?

"What an interesting way you have with the Queen's English, Mr. Drummond. Would you please elaborate? I'm afraid I am unfamiliar with the term 'talk turkey.' " She pasted on a smile. "In Britain our turkeys are quite silent."

He took a step toward her and she stood her ground. She was, after all, a Pinkerton.

"Forget the Queen's English," he said. "You're asking me to use my sources to check out your gentleman friend. I fail to see how that can be called business." He paused. "Looks like it would come more under the heading of pleasure than business. But what do I know about the situation? Could be you and old Will are thinking of becoming the next crime-fighting couple."

Victoria let the accusation hang between them before

taking a deep breath and asking God for a bit more patience. "I have reason to believe that Mr. Bowen could be instrumental in determining what happened to the missing money. All I need is the assurance that he is who he claims to be so that I can feel safe in revealing my identity as a Pinkerton to him."

"I knew it!" He slammed his fist against the rail, and Victoria felt the wooden structure jump beneath her feet. "I told you that case is closed. Forget it! I will not play match-maker between a citified banker and a lady Pinkerton who wants to hang up her pistol and take on a husband."

With that, he stormed past her, shaking the stairs with every step. Victoria waited until he reached the ground to speak. While she longed to bite back with a harsh rebuttal of his ridiculous claim, she decided to present a composed façade. Only she would know what raged just beneath the surface of her smile.

"Oh, Mr. Drummond," she said in her sweetest voice. "I believe you've forgotten something."

He froze. "What?"

"You seem to have forgotten that you pledged to owe me a favor for saving your life." She watched with pleasure as he pivoted on his heel to face her. "I'm collecting that favor."

"And to think I almost kissed that man," she whispered as she watched him storm away.

Chapter 5

"To think I almost kissed that woman."

Gus rounded the corner, nearly knocking a farmer off the sidewalk. As he helped the man collect his bags, he let his mind wander to the pretty Pinkerton.

One thought of Miss Vicky and he got mad all over again. What was it about that lady that got his goat every time he tried to have a civil conversation with her? Worse, what was it about her that drew him like a moth to a flame?

Even covered in straw and horse manure, she looked prettier than any woman he'd ever met up with. The truth be known, he'd been as nervous as a long-tailed cat in a room full of rocking chairs ever since the first time he caught sight of her.

He'd gone to the Lord with his troubles, but the Man Upstairs seemed to be taking great delight in his predicament. He'd even mentioned in a letter home that a particular Englishwoman had been plaguing him. His dear Scottish mother's response: "Marry her then."

Marry her? The thought of spending the rest of his born

days in close proximity to the feisty female set his liver on edge. Since Victoria Barrett-Ames had arrived in Windmere Falls, he'd not had a moment's peace.

Gus tipped his hat to the farmer and continued toward the telegraph office. The worst of it all was that he ended up doing exactly what he'd decided he wouldn't do—meddling into a lead that might reopen a closed case.

No, she couldn't really want information on the banker for the reasons she claimed. The pretty Pinkerton had her fancy feathered cap set for the Bowen fellow, and there was nothing he could do about it.

Not that he would want to stop her. They were quite a pair, the both of them, and he wished them all the happiness in the world. The sooner he got this over with, the better. He did owe the woman a debt, and Gus Drummond always paid his debts.

He reached for the latch on the telegraph office's door, still grumbling inwardly at his predicament. In his haste, he nearly ran down Will Bowen coming out of the telegraph office. He stood back to let the banker pass and muttered a greeting. To his surprise, Bowen shook his hand and greeted him like an old friend.

"Pressing business, Mr. Drummond?"

"Matter of life and death." He took note of the folded paper in the banker's vest pocket, out of place with the perfection of his fancy suit and shiny shoes.

Bowen pushed the paper deeper into his pocket and clapped a hand on Gus's shoulder. "Ah, well, I won't keep you then, my friend. Take care."

While Gus had made casual acquaintance with the fellow, he hadn't seen fit to spend much time with him. About the only good thing he could say in regard to Will Bowen was that he had backed a posse of men when the worst of the robberies were taking place. At the time, he figured it had to do with Bowen's concerns that some of his money might get stolen in one of the robberies. Now he wondered if maybe he really was a good guy.

Miss Vicky sure seemed to think so.

"Oh, Mr. Drummond?"

Gus turned to see that Will had followed him back into the telegraph office. "Yes?"

The banker smiled. "I understand you and Miss Barrett-Ames were involved in a bit of excitement at the livery stable this morning."

News travels fast. "That's right," Gus said.

"I'd like to thank you for protecting Victoria. She's such a fragile creature and very precious to me." He paused and leaned close. "Actually, I'm of a mind to make her my wife someday soon, so you can see what a dear cost it would have been had she been injured or worse. I wonder if there is anything I could offer you as a reward for your valor."

Gus nearly slugged him. Instead, he turned him down flat and headed for the telegrapher before he could change his mind. Reward money held no interest for him, but landing his fist on the city boy's nose sure did.

So much for giving his penchant for irritation to God. But then it seemed his live sacrifices climbed off the altar regularly—another thing to work on.

Guess You and I will be talking about that later, Lord.

That evening what he and the Lord ended up discussing was another subject entirely, or maybe it was a related one. Ever since he sat on those cold steps with the prissy Englishwoman, he'd denied one thing—the feeling that the Lord had put them together for a reason.

Trouble was, he hadn't been able to decide whether that reason was crime fighting or courting. He decided to do neither until God spoke a bit plainer.

Late Saturday afternoon, Victoria surveyed the magnificent sweep of snow-covered mountains from her perch atop Paint, her favorite of all Will's horses. "The day is absolutely gorgeous."

Will rode to a stop beside her and smiled. "I'm glad you like it. I ordered it just for you."

They'd ridden a few times before, but never had Victoria been so nervous about being alone with Will. She attributed her uneasiness to the anticipation of waiting for confirmation from Mr. Drummond, but she knew a part of it was that she really liked spending time with the banker.

Their common backgrounds and shared love of horses gave them plenty to talk about, but today her side of the conversation had been limited to the occasional comment about the weather and the price of yard goods at the mercantile. Mostly Victoria felt content to enjoy the ride and the company in silence. Thankfully he seemed to agree.

"Race you to the river." He spurred his horse into a gallop

and headed for the valley and the ribbon of blue-green in the distance.

Victoria followed, trailing Will until the very last when she managed to pull ahead. At the river, he climbed off his horse and helped Victoria to the ground, lingering to hold her hand a moment longer than necessary.

"I'd like to speak to you regarding a matter of some importance, Victoria."

"Oh?" Her gaze met his. He looked much too serious for such a lovely day. Had he discovered her secret?

"I've made no secret of my feelings for you," he said. "But I'm not certain you understand the depth of my affection for you."

Victoria swallowed hard and tried to think of a diversion. As much as she cared for Will Bowen, a Pinkerton couldn't allow herself to fall in love while working on a case. It just wasn't done.

True enough, Ruth, Sydney, and Moment had found love while crime fighting, but this was different. Her friends had all managed to actually solve the crimes they investigated. She alone remained as the Pinkerton who had not earned her title.

"Will, really, must we talk about such things?"

The banker lifted her hand to his lips. "I had hoped you shared my feelings. Did I speak too soon, Victoria?"

She took a deep breath and let it out slowly. "Perhaps."

"I see." He released her fingers and turned to reach for Paint's reins. "Then we should agree to discuss this at a later date. Shall we return these horses to the stable?"

"Of course."

She knew she'd hurt him, and the knowledge stung. If only she hadn't pledged her allegiance to fight crime for the Pinkerton Agency. That vow precluded any others she might want to make.

Then there was the pesky matter of Gus Drummond.

For some strange reason, memories of her near miss with kissing him on the back stairs of the mercantile had stayed with her far longer than she deemed appropriate. Strange, considering she thought the Scotsman irritating at best.

Gus thought on the situation until his thinker got tired and he had to quit. In short order, Miss Vicky had crawled under his skin but good, and the Lord seemed to take great delight in pointing that out regularly.

Just yesterday he had been a man with a purpose— namely to take up the cause of justice as a Pinkerton and to settle someday in a nice quiet place, devoid of chattering females, to spend the last of his days before Jesus called him home. And then came Miss Vicky. Overnight his plan and his peace shattered.

Actually, if he were to admit the truth, the prissy Pinkerton hadn't achieved the feat quite so fast. No, somewhere between her arrival and this morning she'd become. . . what?

He shoved back from the clutter on his makeshift desk and stood to pace the tiny hotel room he'd called home for far too long. That's it—he must have cabin fever.

Leaning against the sill of the big window that faced the

mountains, Gus let his mind roam free. While his body stood in Windmere Falls, his thoughts headed for Denver and the little patch of heaven just west of town where the mountains met the flat plain. He saw the patch of ground he'd staked out for clearing last time he'd visited, and he imagined the little cabin he would build beside the brook that babbled slow in the winter and ran fast in the spring.

He made two more loops around the room and then reached for his gun belt. Rather than pace like a caged tiger, he decided to do his thinking in a larger and more convenient place—God's great outdoors.

Loping toward the rocky outcrop that was his favorite thinking spot, he gave thanks for the beauty of the day but soon found himself thinking of the beauty of Victoria Barrett-Ames instead. "She just ruins everything," he muttered as he reached the rocky point and dismounted.

"Who?" a voice said out of nowhere.

Gus went for his gun and nearly blew the feather off Miss Vicky's bright red hat. Where in the world did the woman buy her clothes? Surely no one in Windmere Falls could supply the outfits she wore.

And yet there she sat, curled up just as comfortable as you please in his thinking spot—his very own place of solitude. In her lap was a small sketchbook, in her hand, a pencil. He squinted to see that she'd drawn a passable sketch of the valley and the river beyond.

"Did I frighten you?" She closed the book and stuck the pencil behind her ear.

Gus holstered his pistol and forced his breathing to slow

to normal. "Miss Vicky, you frighten me on a regular basis."

She looked pleased. Funny, how he liked that look on her.

"Would you care to join me?" She patted the spot beside her. "It's such a lovely view. I've been coming here quite often since I discovered it."

Rather than comment on how long *he* had enjoyed this view, he settled beside her and stretched his legs out in front of him. The sun bore down almost warm, but the clouds off in the distance warned of impending snow.

"I didn't know you could draw."

He lifted the sketchbook out of her lap and opened it before she could protest. Unlike the sketch of the valley, which was still in its beginning stages, the other drawings in the book were fully formed and excellent in quality. He flipped past a picture of a crumbling castle, a scene that put him in mind of the cliffs at Dover, and a detailed drawing of the Statue of Liberty.

"Give me that." She took a halfhearted swipe at the book and missed.

"These are really good," Gus said. "I didn't know you were a Pinkerton and an artist."

Something between pleased and perturbed decorated her face. "There are many things you don't know about me, Mr. Drummond."

"Is that a fact?" He grinned. "Tell me something I don't know about you, and I might consider giving your book back."

She screwed her lips into a pout that nearly caused him to hand the book—and his heart—over immediately. Thankfully, she looked away.

"All right. I love horses." She looked at him expectantly.

"Nope, I figured that one out a long time ago. Try again."

"I'm hopelessly in love with eye-catching dresses and matching hats."

Again Gus shook his head. "You're going to have to do better than that, Miss Vicky."

"My grandmother called me that."

Something in the way she spoke the words melted his heart. "Oh?"

"Yes" came out soft as a whisper. "I miss her terribly. She taught me to ride and to paint. Drawing came about as a necessity when I found I preferred to sketch rather than work in oils."

"Nope, that's real sweet but not exactly what I was looking for." He weighed the open book in his hand. "For something this special, I'm going to need a real juicy secret."

"Is this how you interrogate all your suspects?"

"Just the hard cases."

The lady Pinkerton giggled. "Very well then. If you must know, my grandmother had a deep dark secret that I've never told another soul."

"Let's hear it." He pointed his finger at her. "And it better be good."

"Oh, it is." She leaned closer, and he could smell the soft scent of vanilla. "Before Grammy married Grandpa, she longed for a bit of adventure, so she left home and hearth and followed her dream."

He feigned boredom with an exaggerated yawn. "And?"

"And she joined the circus. As an aerialist, no less."

"You're joking."

"I assure you I'm quite serious." She gave him a direct look. "Now, I've shared my deep dark family secret. Please give the book back."

Gus shook his head and opened the book to the place where he'd stopped before. "I was expecting something a bit more adventurous. I mean, an aerialist isn't quite a lion tamer or a bearded—"

He turned the page and froze. Staring back at him from the white sheet of paper was a precise likeness of himself. From his crooked nose to the scar just beneath his right eye, she'd captured him in exacting detail. He allowed his gaze to drift from the art to the artist. Finally he allowed her to snatch the book back.

And then he kissed her.

Chapter 6

Threading his fingers together to form a pillow for his head, Gus Drummond shifted away from Victoria and leaned back against the rocky outcrop. "Now *that* was a kiss," he said with a satisfied sigh.

"Indeed."

Victoria clutched the sketchbook to her chest and measured her breathing, all the while listening to her pulse galloping. Yes, that *was* indeed quite a kiss. It was a kiss that made her long for many more kisses, a kiss that could spark a lifetime of more kisses. A kiss that had far exceeded her wildest dream of what the perfect kiss would be.

It seemed as if the Lord had given her a little taste of heaven on earth and called it a kiss. And yet the whole situation was most unsuitable.

Mr. Drummond was a fellow Pinkerton and a man who could irritate her with great ease. They had absolutely nothing in common, and merely being in the same room generally caused one or both of them trouble. He was everything she did not seek in a lifetime partner and was a

329

Scotsman to boot. What would her father, the loyal Englishman, say?

And what of her heavenly Father? Surely He did not mean for her to be yoked to a man like Gus Drummond.

Even if the Lord did bring him to mind regularly when she prayed for guidance regarding her future, the thought of actually having feelings for the man seemed preposterous. No, she must put a stop to this at once.

And yet, when she thought of that kiss. . .

Out of the corner of her eye, she saw that the object of her thoughts had tipped his hat low over his brow and closed his eyes. She braved a closer look and frowned. Could the brute be taking a nap?

How dare he kiss her soundly and then fall into a doze while she fretted? Victoria's ire began to rise. Did he think so little of their kiss that he could fall into a stupor upon its completion?

Well, she certainly did not have to stand for this sort of treatment. She crept off the rock and headed for her horse as quietly as possible. If the cad wanted to kiss and snore, he could do it without an audience.

"Farewell, Sleeping Beauty," she said under her breath as she headed for her horse.

Gus peeked at the retreating form of the pretty Pinkerton, cursing himself for a fool. He shouldn't have kissed her. And yet the power of that one kiss shook him to his boots.

He wanted to tell her so, wanted to stop her and convince her to marry up with him on the spot like his mother and the Lord had suggested months ago, but something inside him froze. So rather than make today the best day of his life, he let Miss Vicky ride away without saying a word.

Someday he would make it up to her; someday he would gather the courage to tell her just what she'd come to mean to him. Someday, if God gave him another chance, he'd be ready and he'd do right by her.

Right now he had enough trouble just sitting still and listening to the Lord shame him for a fool.

"You're just mad because Gus Drummond kissed you and then fell asleep. It doesn't help that he hasn't been around to court you properly for the last two days." Moment shook her head. "I'm sure he will make amends when he returns from Denver. Why don't you wait until then to do something you might be sorry for later?"

"You're my dearest friend, Moment, but I wish I hadn't told you a word of what happened between that irritating man and me."

The bell sounded as the door opened. Moment gave Victoria one last look of incredulity before calling out a greeting to the pastor's wife. While Moment went to wait on Mrs. Griffin, Victoria began to sort through the facts of the train robberies yet again, putting any personal thoughts of Gus Drummond as far out of reach as she could manage.

As the door closed behind Mrs. Griffin, Victoria reached the same conclusion as before. In her estimation, a large amount of stolen money was hidden and waiting for someone to find it.

When she shared her opinion with Moment a few minutes later, she met with the same resistance she'd encountered before. Given the fact that Moment was up to her sunbonnet in wedding plans, Victoria set about handling the situation alone.

If only she didn't have to wait for Mr. Drummond's results before she firmed up her plans. Prudence told her to delay, but a nagging suspicion that the more time that passed, the less likely the loot would be found forced her to a quick decision. She must take Will into her confidence.

"Moment, dear, would you mind terribly if I ran a quick errand?"

"Of course," she called.

Lord, if this is the wrong thing to do, please stop me.

A few minutes later, she'd donned her coat and slipped past the tellers in the bank to deposit herself in the chair across the wide desk from Will Bowen. Before proper greetings could be exchanged, a clerk appeared at the door and beckoned to Will, leaving Victoria alone in the office.

The wood-paneled space reminded her of her father's study. Her gaze flitted across the desk, carved of walnut and adorned with two neat stacks of papers and an ornate silver inkwell in the shape of a horse's head.

In a straight line to one side of the inkwell, three matching silver pens glittered in the afternoon sun. Directly behind the massive chair, a pair of polo mallets hung above a painting of a string of ponies.

Victoria smiled. How could a man who loved horses as much as Will Bowen possibly be deemed untrustworthy?

"Please forgive me, Victoria." He swept past her to take his seat at the desk and offer a warm smile. "To what do I owe the pleasure of your company today?"

As usual, his grooming was impeccable, his manners divine. She couldn't help but contrast him with the pesky Pinkerton. "Actually, I would like to discuss a matter of some importance."

"It wouldn't have anything to do with what you *didn't* want to discuss a few days ago, would it?" He gave her a hopeful look. "If so, I would declare it an answer to prayer."

Her heart sank. Someday soon she would have to confront the problem of Will's feelings toward her. Until the Lord told her otherwise, she could merely be his friend.

"I'm sorry, Will," she said slowly, "but, no, it wouldn't."

His smile faded a notch and then broadened once more. "Of course."

Victoria shifted in her chair and went over the words one last time before determining to speak them aloud. "You see, when last we spoke regarding my work at the mercantile, I was not at liberty to tell you that—"

"There you are!" Gus Drummond strode into the office like he owned the place and snatched Victoria up by the elbow. "I'm sorry, Bowen, but I'm going to have to borrow your companion for a moment. I'm sure you won't mind. Pinkerton business, you see."

"I'm afraid I'm going to have to protest, Mr. Drummond."

He whirled around to stare down at Victoria. "It's *Pinkerton* business, Ma'am, and right important."

Will rose and placed his palms on the desk. His gaze

went from Victoria to Drummond and then back to Victoria. "Perhaps you should go with him, my dear. I'm sure he merely wants information." He turned his attention to Mr. Drummond. "Am I correct?"

"You are correct," he said. "I'm merely after information. So if you'll excuse us, Bowen." He gave Victoria's elbow a firm tug. "Shall we, *my dear?*"

With that he led her out of the office and onto the sidewalk, ignoring her silent protests to the contrary. He covered the distance between the bank and the mercantile in record time, leaving Victoria to scurry to keep up.

"Morning, Miss Alexander," he called as he barged through the mercantile's front doors.

Moment called a greeting as she appeared from the back storeroom. "Is this your errand?" she asked, sizing up first Victoria and then Mr. Drummond with a smile. "Welcome back, Mr. Drummond."

"No, this is *not* my errand."

"It's grand to be back, Miss Alexander. Now would you excuse us?" he asked. "Your friend and I need to have a little talk."

"I just made a fresh pot of coffee." Moment smiled. "Help yourself."

He released his grip on Victoria and cast a glance at Moment over his shoulder. "If you weren't getting hitched to Brady Miller, I'd marry up with you myself. You make the best coffee this man's ever tasted."

Her friend practically blushed pink at Mr. Drummond's statement. Yes, Moment's coffee was excellent, but really.

The best he'd ever tasted? Worth marrying over? Well, that was taking it to the extreme.

Honestly, how difficult could it be to make a cup of coffee? Perhaps she should learn.

Victoria shed her coat and trailed the Pinkerton up the stairs and into the kitchen of the tiny living space she shared with Moment. His presence in the room seemed to shrink it to minuscule proportions. She thought of the last time they'd been together in such close proximity, and heat rose in her neck.

She certainly would not be kissing him this time. That would absolutely *not* happen. Besides, he couldn't possibly be interested in a woman whose coffee-making skills were nonexistent and whose kiss left him in need of a nap.

Why do I care?

Because you love him.

Victoria quickly discarded the ridiculous thought and pressed past the Pinkerton to lift two china teacups off the shelf. While he poured the coffee, she set out sugar and milk. Finally, they settled across from each other at the little table.

"What do you think you're doing?" he asked as he dumped spoonfuls of sugar into his cup. "Did you tell him you're a Pink?"

His stare bore hard on her, making her want to spill the contents of her soul in answer to any question he might ask. The effect was disconcerting, to say the least. No wonder he was considered such a good lawman.

Victoria stirred a bit of milk into her coffee and took a

sip. It scalded her tongue, and she bit back a cry as she settled the cup onto the saucer with a shaky hand.

"Not yet," she said when she recovered, "but I was about to."

Drummond slammed his fist on the table, and the cups rattled in their saucers. "Have you lost your mind? Do you know what it means to give away your identity as a Pinkerton?"

"Everything all right up there?" Moment called from downstairs.

"Everything's fine," they said in unison.

"Yes, I know what it means," Victoria said slowly. "It means I'm taking Will Bowen into my confidence, but I have a good reason."

He snorted. "I'll bet."

She ignored the ruffian's indelicate behavior. "I believe he has information that would make this a worthwhile risk."

"You do?" Again the sarcasm was evident.

"Yes." She toyed with her spoon and then glanced up at him. "What better person to help find a large amount of missing money than a banker, especially a banker with connections in Denver and New York?"

Mr. Drummond seemed to consider her words for a moment. Perhaps the man did not possess the extreme amount of stubbornness she believed. While he looked away, deep in thought, she studied him.

What was it about being near to Gus Drummond that befuddled her so? Why hadn't she noticed the width of his shoulders, the self-assured bearing, and the sparkle in his eyes before?

And then there was the way he spoke of the Lord as if He were a dear friend. How reassuring it would be to be loved and cared for by someone so capable, so close to the Lord. Yes, this gruff lawman did hold a certain appeal.

What am I thinking? This is insanity. No, this is love.

Without warning, he swung his gaze back in her direction and caught her staring. The collision rattled her, and she nearly dropped her cup. Thankfully, he seemed completely ignorant as to the direction of her thoughts.

"Let's say I do agree the money's still out there somewhere." He held his hand up. "Just for argument's sake, that is."

"All right."

"Then I'd have to say you might be on to something." When she opened her mouth to agree, he held his hand up once more. "However, that doesn't tell me *why* you think this Bowen fellow is so trustworthy."

"Because. . ."

She struggled to find the right answer. Mentioning his near-proposal was certainly out of the question, as was his connection to her brother. Until she could sort out her tangle of feelings for him, the less Gus Drummond knew about her, the better.

"I see." He pushed back from the table, eyes narrowed. "So there's no particular reason you want to tell me about?"

She averted her gaze. "None that I would like to share at the moment."

"You two in love?"

The question startled her. "Why do you ask?"

"Because in my line of work, I only know two reasons why a woman would trust a man with something that could mean her life. One of them is if he's a blood relative, and the other's if she's in love with him." He paused. "You're not kin to the banker, are you?"

She shook her head.

"That's what I was afraid of."

Moment's light step on the stairs kept Victoria from commenting. It did not, however, keep her from thinking.

"Did I miss anything important?" Moment asked as she stepped into the kitchen.

"No," they said in unison.

Mr. Drummond glared at Victoria and then offered Moment a much kinder look. "Your friend here is about to give away her identity to a civilian."

The look on Moment's face cast away any hopes of support Victoria might have had. "You can't be serious, Victoria."

"Oh, she's serious, all right." He rose from his chair. "Serious about pretending to catch a crook while she's busy catching a banker."

The comment stung, but Victoria could find no retort. She looked to Moment for help and found none forthcoming. Rather, her friend seemed to pity her, or at least the expression on her face conveyed that feeling.

Mr. Drummond paused to collect a piece of folded paper from his pocket and toss it toward her. It landed on the table inches from her teacup. The paper unfolded slightly to reveal a telegram.

"You'll be glad to know your banker checks out clean as

a whistle. I hope the two of you will be very happy together."

"Honestly, you sound as if I'm looking to marry the man."

Out of the corner of her eye, she saw Moment suppress a smile as she turned to make a discreet exit. Drummond, however, stood his ground and seemed less than amused.

"Well, aren't you?"

To continue this conversation from a seated position put her at a disadvantage. Standing, she realized she still possessed a disadvantage, and it had nothing to do with height.

She knew without a doubt that she loved this impossible, irritating scoundrel, and yet he bore her nothing but ill temper. She couldn't make coffee, couldn't solve a crime to save her life, and her kisses sent him into a deep slumber. To make matters worse, she would be returning to Chicago forthwith while he would reside in Denver.

With so many factors weighing against them, why would the Lord possibly want her to have feelings for Gus Drummond? And yet the knowledge that He did had enveloped her prayers even before their ill-fated kiss. She'd merely been too stubborn to acknowledge the fact.

She and God would be discussing this promptly. But first she must rid herself of the Pinkerton's presence.

"Thank you for the information, Mr. Drummond." She settled back down in her chair and pretended to busy herself by stirring her coffee. "I'll be sure to keep you informed as to the status of my investigation."

"You do that, Miss Vicky," he said as he stormed out. "Just don't expect me to come to the wedding."

"Who said you were invited?" she called.

"I didn't want to come anyway," came the answer from the bottom of the stairs. A moment later, the front door bell jingled, and he was gone.

Moment reappeared in the doorway, her smile broad. "It doesn't take a Pinkerton agent to see that Gus Drummond's in love with you."

"Do you think so?"

Her best friend nodded. "I know so."

Victoria allowed the spoon to fall from her fingers. "Moment," she said as she regarded her friend helplessly, "how did you know Brady was the one?"

Chapter 7

Long after Gus had gone and Moment had returned to her bookkeeping duties downstairs, Victoria sat at the table staring at the folded papers. Her conversation with Moment gave her the unfortunate reassurance that she was indeed in love with Gus Drummond. Worse, she realized her prayers led her to believe God blessed the union and planned for them to be together.

What she didn't know was how He intended to bring His plans to completion. According to Moment, Victoria's only recourse was to wait and see what He would do. No amount of action on her part, Moment had urged, would bring about God's perfect plan for Victoria's life.

The thought filled her with dread, disgust, and excitement all at the same time. She'd determined to make her own way in the world, and now this.

"Lord, can't You at least tell me what I can do while I wait? Surely there is something worthwhile I can accomplish here in Windmere Falls."

Quietness filled her spirit as the answer settled around

her like the softly falling snow outside. *Do nothing.*

Frustrated, she walked to the basin and rinsed the cups, taking care not to chip the delicate china as she dried each one and put it away. She thought of Mr. Drummond's big fingers wrapped around the fragile cup and smiled.

The Scotsman was nothing like what she'd expected God to give her in a man. But how like God to do the unexpected and have it turn out so much better than she could imagine.

Now if he could just get to work on Gus Drummond in a timely manner.

Outside, the snow had begun to fall in earnest, and a few inches of powder decorated the sill. The occasional snowflake bounced against the glass and slid to its doom in the gathering pile below.

The sky held nothing but gray, and if not for the snow, she could have been standing in her ancestral home in England looking out at the January sky over London. By nightfall, a blanket of white would cover all of Windmere Falls.

Despite the warmth of the little kitchen, Victoria shuddered. Would spring ever come?

An idea took form. God told her she must wait on Him, but He didn't tell her she must wait alone. The least she could do was continue with her plan to find the last undiscovered link in the train robbery case—that of the missing money—while the Lord took care of more important matters.

Surely He wouldn't mind if she took that small responsibility on herself. After all, He *was* terribly busy changing Gus Drummond into a fitting husband for her and could hardly be bothered with a few last details of a crime that seemed so easy to solve.

And He *had* given her the ability to solve crimes. Wouldn't it be a disgrace not to act on that ability? She tucked the telegram into her reticule and reached for her coat, secure in the knowledge that her endeavors were for the glory of the Lord and the cause of justice.

This time when she walked to the bank, she made certain no one detected her presence. Rather than enter by the front doors, she slipped in the unlocked employee entrance at the back. Announcing herself with a note delivered by a skeptical but willing teller, she awaited Will Bowen at a pre-arranged spot adjacent to the church.

While she bided her time, well hidden from the prying eyes of Gus Drummond or anyone else who might happen by, she prayed for God to bless her plan. With His help, she would have the answer to the riddle of the Ghost and his hidden treasure before week's end. With that feat accomplished, Victoria could wait and see how God would do His part.

She flicked an errant snowflake from the sleeve of her coat and frowned. Now if Will would just arrive before she froze to death.

"Victoria, I came as soon as I could."

She looked up to see Will approaching and held a finger to her lips. He nodded and crossed the distance between them in silence.

Before she spoke, she guided him out of sight of the street and into the small stable at the rear of the church. The earthy scents of the little barn contrasted sharply with those outside, but it was warm and private.

Besides, her purpose for being here would be short-lived. In the future they could arrange for a more suitable meeting place, one that included fewer aromas and more security.

A mule protested loudly as the stable door swung shut on creaking hinges. Will seemed positively appalled at the place where his polished shoes now stood. Ever the gentleman, she thought. He said nothing of his plight but rather focused his attention on Victoria.

"I'll be brief, Will," she said as she cast about for the words. "This is a matter of the utmost importance. Before I begin, I must have your word as a gentleman that you will reveal nothing of what I tell you."

Confusion marred his handsome features, but a smile touched his lips. "Of course, Victoria, but I must say this situation is highly irregular."

"I understand your confusion. Let me explain. I am not who you think me to be." She shook her head. "Actually, I am who you think I am, but I'm also more than a mere shop girl."

"I know that, my dear. You are much more than a mere shop girl. You're a woman of exquisite tastes and breeding. Do you think I would allow you into my heart...," he paused to broaden his smile, "...and into my stable if I thought otherwise? Why, my stable hands thought I'd lost my mind when I told them Miss Victoria Barrett-Ames was to be given complete access to all the horses at her very whim."

"I do appreciate what you've said, Will, and allowing me

the enjoyment of your horses has meant more than you'll ever know."

He took a step forward and reached for her fingers. "Not nearly the enjoyment I've received in knowing I've met someone who shares my enthusiasm."

"Yes, well, I don't think I'm making myself clear."

Victoria snatched her hand away. There could be no misunderstanding her purpose in what she would tell Will. From now on, their relationship would be strictly business, and it would be her job to make him understand this.

But first she had to make him understand who she was and why she now lived temporarily in Windmere Falls, Colorado.

"What I mean to say, Will, is that I am acting the part of a shop girl in order to fulfill my current assignment. You see, back in Chicago, I do not officially hold a secretarial position. I felt free in telling my family this because that constituted the bulk of my work for the past three years, and thus it is not a lie." She paused. "Besides, I knew Father and Charles would fetch me home if they knew the whole truth."

Will sagged against the wall and blinked hard. "What are you saying, Victoria? Are you involved in something illegal? If so, you have my complete assurance I will assist you in extricating yourself from the situation. You are very dear to me, and I couldn't bear to think of you in some kind of danger."

"No, Will, but thank you. Actually, quite the opposite is true."

"Oh?"

She locked gazes with him. "I am a Pinkerton agent. I was sent over from the Chicago office in response to a call for help from Gus Drummond." His blank stare gave her hope, so she pressed on. "I would like to enlist your help in ascertaining whether certain large deposits have been made in Colorado banks over recent months."

"Really?"

"Yes. It is my belief that the money from the train robberies is hidden rather than lost, and the man who calls himself the Ghost is still at large."

His chuckle surprised her—then it infuriated her. When it continued well beyond the point of propriety, she stormed toward the door.

Will called to her, and she ignored him. His laughter was soon joined by the braying of the mule whose home they had invaded.

Blast after blast of cold air slammed against her face and stung her eyes as she strode toward the street. Anger bit against her heels with every step, followed by remorse. Tears threatened. Why had she gone outside God's directive to wait on Him?

At least Will hadn't believed her when she stated she was a Pinkerton. The situation could be worse.

"So you did it. You told him."

Victoria whirled around to see Gus Drummond leaning against the side of the church. Gathering the remnants of her pride, she gave the lawman a wide berth and turned toward the mercantile. The last thing she needed right now was to hear the cocky Pinkerton's indictment of her impetuous behavior. She already felt enough remorse for the both of them.

The sound of boots pounding against wooden sidewalks echoed behind her. When she picked up her pace, he matched it. As the mercantile came into view, she practically raced through the heavy snowfall toward the glow of the upstairs lights.

At the last moment, he stepped in front of her and blocked her way. With the snow coming down in near-blizzard proportions, the streets were deserted. She and Gus Drummond were the only two fools still about on this bleak January afternoon.

"Go away," she said as she attempted and failed to move past him.

His eyes flashed anger. "What did Bowen say?"

Drawing herself up to her full height, she regarded him impassively. "If it makes you feel better, he didn't believe me." With that, she left him standing ankle deep in snow on the sidewalk.

The weather kept Victoria and the other citizens of Windmere Falls indoors for four days and effectively halted all commerce. Even the trains ceased their arrivals until the safety of the bridges in the outlying areas could be determined.

During that time, Victoria busied herself with two things, prayer and helping Moment to sew her wedding dress. Often she did both at once.

Knotting thread and stitching lace seemed to go together quite nicely with prayer, at least once she got past her inadequacies in the sewing department. Moment had patience in teaching her how to sew, just as God had patience in teaching her how to wait.

How thankful she felt that Ruth and Sydney had been chosen to work as seamstresses on this assignment rather than she and Moment. While she had no doubt her dear friend could hem and repair with the best of them, she knew no one would be fooled if she attempted to pass herself off as a professional in this area.

At the end of the fourth day, she'd nearly perfected her sewing technique. The waiting, however, would be much more difficult to master, for she ached to do something—anything.

However, when the sun shone bright on the morning of the fifth day, melting the snow so rapidly that it ran in rivers down the streets, Victoria almost felt disappointment. Life began to pick up its pace, and the next morning little was left to show of the snows save the mess it made of the unpaved streets.

Will visited the mercantile twice, but both times Victoria fled to her room. When she saw him picking his way across the street toward her for the third time that day, she knew she could avoid him no longer. Rather than race upstairs, she stood at the window and raised her hand in greeting. He returned the gesture and added a smile.

"You look lovely, Victoria," he said when he'd removed enough mud from his shoes to step inside. Taking her hand, he touched it to his lips. "Actually, I thought you might be avoiding me."

She looked away, toying with the ivory ribbons on a plum-colored bonnet. "I suppose I have," she admitted. "I felt a bit uncomfortable, as you can imagine."

"Understandable, considering the uncouth manner in which I behaved." He leaned against the doorframe and regarded her openly. "Honestly, I had no idea you would say what you said. Will you forgive me for my beastly behavior?"

"Of course."

Victoria tried and failed to read the emotions crossing his face. Dare she think he might believe she worked for the Pinkertons? And if he did, what did he think of the fact?

Will pulled a gold watch from his vest pocket and checked the time. "I'm afraid I must go, my dear. I've a train to catch."

He nodded toward the stairs. Victoria turned to see that Moment had joined them.

"Wonderful to see you again, Miss Alexander," he said. "I come bearing bad news regarding your wedding."

Moment looked alarmed. "Oh?"

"Pressing business in New York will keep me away from Windmere Falls for a few weeks."

He swung his gaze to Victoria. "It's my father. He's finally decided to retire, and he demands I come at once to assist with the arrangements."

"I see," Victoria said.

"We will miss you terribly," Moment added. "Even if you are an awful cad."

"Would you like me better if I brought you and Brady something wonderful from New York?"

Moment laughed and waved away the question as she busied herself at the cash register.

Will kissed Victoria's hand one last time and made his exit. Relief flooding her, Victoria sank onto the nearest stool and expelled a sigh while Moment merely smiled and headed back upstairs.

At least she would not have to keep up the game of hiding from Will Bowen. Now if Gus Drummond would stop hiding from her.

Chapter 8

The Pinkerton continued to make his presence scarce, even as January slipped into February. Victoria watched him ease into the back pew at church on Sunday, then noticed he'd already disappeared by the time she made her way out the doors afterward.

He no longer took his meals in the restaurant nor strolled the streets of Windmere Falls. Only the fact that his horse still remained stabled at the livery kept Victoria hopeful that Gus Drummond did indeed still reside there.

The morning before Moment's wedding, she awoke with a strange yearning in her bones. Stretching to climb out of her narrow bed served to make her want to fall right back in and pull the covers over her head. Contemplating which frock and hat to don made her wish she had the option of putting on her riding clothes instead.

Part of the trouble, she knew, was the impending nuptials. While she felt nothing but happiness for Moment and Brady, she did admit to a bit of jealousy that her best friend had found a partner for life so easily. She still believed the

Lord had something in store for her and Mr. Drummond, but without the big Scotsman's cooperation, how would He ever manage to accomplish it?

Then there was the matter of the missing robbery money. She'd prayed and pondered and still couldn't account for the theory that the money was not out there somewhere waiting to be found. Jackson Griffin's claims of being the Ghost also fell flat. To believe the man's confession would be to discount the fact he would have had to be in two places at once.

How could he pull off the robberies and hide the money, all the time going unseen by the others in the gang? In addition, he could produce neither the white duster coat nor the flour sack mask to back up his claim.

It made no sense. At times she wondered if perhaps her initial instinct that Mr. Drummond might be involved might actually be true. After all, he was the loudest critic of her theory.

And what of Gus Drummond? Since her time in Windmere Falls would end in a few days, had she misunderstood the Lord's leading? Perhaps she was destined to return to her Pinkerton duties in Chicago rather than contemplate a life with the Scotsman.

With these concerns weighing heavily on her, Victoria decided to seek solace in the one place where she knew she could find it—astride a horse. She ventured downstairs to clear her plans with Moment and found her friend deep in conversation with Brady Miller.

Nose to nose over the plans for an addition to Mr.

Miller's cabin, neither looked up as Victoria made her way across the mercantile to peer out the front window. "Lovely day, isn't it?" she called, noting with glee that the couple jumped at the sound of her voice.

"Well, good morning, Miss Victoria," Mr. Miller said. "Pleasure to see you today."

Victoria turned and smiled. Love was indeed a wonderful thing to behold, unless the Lord was making you wait on your turn at it.

"Oh, Mr. Miller, you're not looking at anyone but Moment these days," she said.

He looped arms with Moment and offered her a chaste peck on the cheek. "She's right," he said.

Moment patted her fiancé's hand and then turned to face Victoria. "You look a bit pensive this morning, Victoria. Something wrong?"

She shrugged. "We're not busy. Do you think I might take the morning and go for a ride? I promise to return in time for lunch, and then the afternoon is yours."

Ten minutes later, she released the latch on the gate at the edge of Will's property and began the short walk to the stables. The air felt crisp, with just enough bite to require a light wrap. Victoria snuggled against the soft knitted shawl, one of the few relics of her English past. Even on this sunny Colorado afternoon, the scent of England still awaited in the folds of soft wool around her shoulders.

The ground wore the first tentative shoots of what would be grass and flowers by March. Trees still bore their bare branches, but closer inspection revealed tiny buds of green awaiting the spring.

The beauty of the landscape was tempered only by the question of whether Victoria would be there to see it upon full bloom. Only the Lord knew the answer, and today she decided she would leave the knowledge with Him.

To ride and forget that question and all the others was her goal. What a privilege to have the finest equine stock in Colorado from which to choose.

Victoria released the latch on the stable door and stepped inside. The earthy scent of hay and well-groomed horses wrapped her in familiar comfort as she waited for her eyes to adjust to the dimmer light.

At the far end of the stables a half-door filtered sunlight across two dozen magnificent thoroughbreds. Rather than call for help from one of the stable hands, she strolled toward the tack room. Generous to a fault, Will had secured all the items necessary for a lady to ride.

Today, however, Victoria decided to be bold. Bypassing the sidesaddle she generally chose, she headed for the one Will preferred. Heavier than she expected, the saddle slipped out of her grasp and plunged to the stable floor, knocking down a barrel and a stack of blankets as it fell.

She tried and failed to right the barrel and ended up dragging the saddle mere inches before tiring. Out of the corner of her eye, she saw a figure pass by the small, high window.

"Perhaps I shouldn't attempt this myself," she said as she stepped over the saddle and headed toward the window. If she climbed on the side of the trunk that sat beneath it, she could look out the window and beckon to whomever stood outside.

A patch of white nearly hidden by the overturned barrel caught her attention, and she stopped to reach for it. Rather than the cloth she expected, a bleached feed sack emerged— a feed sack with eye holes cut into it.

The Ghost's mask.

Her pulse began to gallop as the importance of her discovery dawned. A rattling noise alerted her to the opening of the stable doors.

Rather than be caught inside the stable without backup, Victoria elected to seek an exit and return to fight another day—or at least with another Pinkerton in tow. To that end, she climbed atop the trunk and pressed against the tiny window. It refused to budge.

The horses stirred. Someone definitely had walked into the barn, but whom? Will wasn't due back for another week, possibly longer. Could it be that the Ghost had used Will's absence as an opportunity to hide the evidence?

Perhaps the vile creature even intended to set Will up.

Hay crunched outside the tack room door, and Victoria discarded her theories in favor of finding a place to hide. The barrel might have worked had it not been upended by her own incompetence.

The only place left was the trunk. She raised the lid and prepared to climb inside, only to find it full of tack, saddle blankets, and a single white duster coat.

"Victoria?"

She whirled around to greet Will, losing her footing

when her riding boots tangled with one of the saddle's stirrups. Plunging forward, she reached for Will and caught his hands. The mask fell, but thankfully she did not.

"Oh, Will, I'm so glad you're here," she said when he caught her elbow and righted her. "You're not going to believe what I found."

"Good work, Pinkerton."

"You believe me."

"I always did." His fingers tightened around her elbow as he led her away from the tack room and into the stable. "Perhaps you and I should take this evidence to the sheriff."

"Good idea. We'll need to stop and let Mr. Drummond know." She began to contemplate just how she would bear the news to the stubborn Pinkerton. Several different scenarios began to take form, none of which she intended to carry out.

No, better to take the evidence to the sheriff than send word to Drummond that it rested there. Any further investigation could be done by Drummond and whomever the agency sent to take her place.

Funny how she felt a certain peace in knowing she'd been right, and yet she would not be staying around to finish the job. Suddenly there was no great urge to *do something*. It was as if God had chosen this very inopportune moment to work His miracle on her. Dare she hope He had worked a miracle on Mr. Drummond too?

Without warning, Will took a sharp turn to whirl her around and face him. "This is as far as you go, my dear. I'd hoped it wouldn't come to this, but you're just too persistent."

"What are you talking about?"

"The Ghost." His tone was mocking, cold, and the expression on his face matched it. "How clever of you to deduce it was me."

"But I—"

"No matter. The funds will never be found. After all, what safer place for money of any kind than in a bank?"

"A bank?" She shook her head. "You mean you had the train robbery money in your bank all along?"

He laughed as he thrust her against the wall and then pushed her into an empty stable. She fell backward, landing with a thud in a thin layer of hay. Her head cracked against the hard-packed dirt beneath the hay. The room began to spin.

The last thing she saw before the room went black was Will Bowen standing over her with a gun. The last thing she heard was the sound of the gun as it fired.

"Victoria."

The voice teased at her ears and pulled at a memory. A fog thicker than any she'd seen in London settled around her and weighed her down.

"Victoria. It's all right. Bowen's never going to hurt you again. After the doc patches him up, the sheriff's got a warm bed for him down at the jail. We've already got men at the bank auditing the vault. By next week, the banker'll be sleeping at the penitentiary."

Again the voice, gruff yet tender, pleading but firm. This time she knew it to be Gus Drummond's. She tried to answer, searched in vain to formulate a response. She felt herself being lifted off the ground, possibly being cradled in someone's arms.

Was this how the Lord carried one home? If so, it felt fine.

"Victoria, wake up."

She tried to open her eyes. Failing that, she began to pray. *I'm waiting on You, Lord.*

"Sleeping Beauty, if you don't wake up, I'm never going to get the chance, and the Lord's going to be right irritated with me."

Then came the kiss.

Slowly, Victoria's vision returned and the image of Gus Drummond swam before her. "No more irritated than I, Gus Drummond."

He cradled her to his chest and held her there. "I'm a fool and I know it. I hid from you all this time because I was a plain coward. I didn't know how to tell you I love you."

Even though her head throbbed, she managed to focus long enough to capture his gaze. "Are you telling me that now, Mr. Drummond?"

"I am, and call me Gus." He smiled at her. "I'm not afraid to add that I want to marry up with you. Will you take this Pinkerton to be your wedded husband, Miss Vicky?"

Chapter 9

Will you take these Pinkertons to be your wedded husbands?"

Moment and Victoria responded with an "I do." A short while later, they walked down the aisle with their Pinkerton husbands to the strains of Mabel Hawkins playing the wedding march. Outside on the lawn, the guests gathered to offer their congratulations to the two newlywed couples.

Gus tore himself away from his new bride long enough to take Moment and Brady aside. "I'm right thankful you didn't mind sharing your day with us, Mr. and Mrs. Miller."

"Pleased to accommodate the last-minute arrangements," Brady said.

Gus cast a glance over his shoulder at his bride, who was engrossed in conversation with the pastor's wife. "I feel real bad I didn't believe her about the missing money. I'm a Pink. I should have seen something was wrong."

Moment touched Gus's hand. "None of us believed her. Who would have thought Victoria would be the one to solve the most complicated of all the crimes?"

The object of their conversation strolled toward them, the feather from her blue wedding hat dancing in the soft breeze. "What am I missing?" she asked as she linked arms with her husband.

Ruth and Sydney and their husbands joined the circle of friends.

"Not a thing as far as I can see," Gus answered. "And I intend to make sure I don't miss anything either. Now how about you and me say our good-byes and head for the honeymoon? I've got another mystery for you to solve."

"Oh, really? And what might that be?"

"How many kisses we can share in this lifetime." He scooped her into his arms and winked. "Here's the first clue."

And then he kissed her.

KATHLEEN Y'BARBO

Kathleen is an award-winning novelist and sixth-generation Texan. After completing a degree in marketing at Texas A&M University, she focused on raising four children and turned to writing. She is a member of American Christian Romance Writers, Romance Writers of America, and the Houston Writer's Guild. She also lectures on the craft of writing at the elementary and secondary levels.

A Letter to Our Readers

Dear Readers:

In order that we might better contribute to your reading enjoyment, we would appreciate your taking a few minutes to respond to the following questions. When completed, please return to the following: Fiction Editor, Barbour Publishing, Inc., P.O. Box 719, Uhrichsville, OH 44683.

1. Did you enjoy reading *To Catch a Thief?*
   ❏ Very much—I would like to see more books like this.
   ❏ Moderately—I would have enjoyed it more if _____
   _____
   _____

2. What influenced your decision to purchase this book?
   (Check those that apply.)
   ❏ Cover   ❏ Back cover copy   ❏ Title   ❏ Price
   ❏ Friends   ❏ Publicity   ❏ Other

3. Which story was your favorite?
   ❏ *Tangled Threads*   ❏ *Skirted Clues*
   ❏ *Rescuing Sydney*   ❏ *Victorious*

4. Please check your age range:
   ❏ Under 18   ❏ 18–24   ❏ 25–34
   ❏ 35–45   ❏ 46–55   ❏ Over 55

5. How many hours per week do you read? _____

Name _____

Occupation _____

Address _____

City _____ State _____ Zip _____

E-mail _____

If you enjoyed

To Catch a Thief

then read:

Wildflower Brides

Four Romances Blossom Along the Oregon Trail

The Wedding Wagon by Cathy Marie Hake
A Bride for the Preacher by Sally Laity
Murder or Matrimony by Pamela Kaye Tracy
Bride in the Valley by Andrea Boeshaar

Available wherever books are sold.
Or order from:
Barbour Publishing, Inc.
P.O. Box 721
Uhrichsville, Ohio 44683
www.barbourbooks.com

You may order by mail for $6.97, and add $2.00 to your order for shipping.
Prices subject to change without notice.

If you enjoyed

To Catch a Thief

then read:

Church in the Wildwood

A Church Stands as a Landmark of Love for Four Generations

Leap of Faith by Pamela Griffin
Shirley, Goodness, and Mercy by Kristy Dykes
Only a Name by Debby Mayne
Cornerstone by Paige Winship Dooly

Available wherever books are sold.

Or order from:
Barbour Publishing, Inc.
P.O. Box 721
Uhrichsville, Ohio 44683
www.barbourbooks.com

You may order by mail for $6.97, and add $2.00 to your order for shipping.
Prices subject to change without notice.